D0440899

Praise for *The Monk Downstairs*

"This gentle, luminous love story shimmers with warmth, honesty, and self-deprecating humor. The finale does not disappoint, as these two intelligent and engaging characters ultimately succeed in their quests for love."

—*Booklist*

"In Rebecca, Farrington has created one of the more palpable female leads in contemporary fiction, witty and wise but still vulnerable. . . . And in *The Monk Downstairs* Farrington has written a relationship novel that is so sensitive and accurate it just may steal your heart."

—*Body & Soul* magazine

". . . funny, touching . . . Laced with elements of spiritualism but never veering far from reality, this intelligent story immerses readers in the action and endears us to the two likeable main characters."

—*Book Page*

"*The Monk Downstairs* is a quiet bit of wisdom, an exploration of emotional and philosophical space that doesn't even exist for us unless we agree to accept, once again, that certain underlying questions are answered."

—*Books & Culture*

"In *The Monk Downstairs,* Tim Farrington creates a world one is not only happy to read about, but to dwell in, to savor, to learn from and laugh in. Open it up and prepare to be delighted."

—Lorna Landvik, author of

Patty Jane's House of Curl and

Welcome to the Great Mysterious

"Farrington writes startlingly well; there are sentences to marvel at on every page. "

—*Book Street USA*

"keep[s] you turning the pages until the end."

—*San Francsico Chronicle*

". . . gracefully funny, heartwarming novel."

—*Seattle Times*

". . . funny, appealing romance . . . breezes pleasantly along to a satisfying conclusion."

—*Boston Herald*

THE

MONK
DOWNSTAIRS

THE

MONK

DOWNSTAIRS

Tim Farrington

HarperSanFrancisco
A Division of HarperCollinsPublishers

HarperCollins books may be purchased for educational, business, or sales promotional use. For information please write: Special Markets Department, HarperCollins Publishers, Inc., 10 East 53rd Street, New York, NY 10022.

HarperCollins Web site: http://www.harpercollins.com

HarperCollins®, ☙®, and HarperSanFrancisco™ are trademarks of HarperCollins Publishers, Inc.

FIRST HARPERCOLLINS PAPERBACK EDITION PUBLISHED IN 2003

Designed by Jessica Shatan

Library of Congress Cataloging-in-Publication Data

Farrington, Tim.
    The monk downstairs / Tim Farrington.— 1st ed.
        p. cm.
    ISBN 0–06–251785–6 (cloth : alk. paper)
        I. Title.
PS3556.A775 M66 2002
813'.54—dc21   2001051541

03 04 05 06 07 QM 10 9 8 7 6 5 4 3 2 1

in loving memory of my mother,

BEVERLY ANNE JOHNSON FARRINGTON

November 25, 1937–December 24, 1997

And Jesus answered, and said unto her, "Martha, Martha, thou art careful and troubled about many things: But one thing is necessary: and Mary hath chosen that good part, which shall not be taken away from her."

Luke 10:39–42

THE

MONK

DOWNSTAIRS

PART I

*Let us face the fact that the monastic vocation
tends to present itself to the modern world
as a problem and as a scandal.*

THOMAS MERTON

Chapter One

Rebecca finally finished painting the in-law apartment on a Friday night, and on Saturday morning she rented it to some poor guy who had just left a monastery. The ad had not even appeared in the papers yet, but she had tucked a tiny Apt. for Rent sign in the front window and he just wandered by and rang the bell. His name was Michael Christopher.

He was a lanky man in his early forties, a little Lincolnesque, with rounded shoulders and a long, sad face muffled by a beard in need of trimming. His hands were too big for his arms and his feet were too big for his legs. His hair was cropped close, the merest new dark stubble on a skull that had obviously been kept shorn until recently. The in-law apartment's ceiling was low and he kept his head ducked a little, whether from fear of smacking it or out of some deeper humility, Rebecca could not tell. It was her impression that he was in no danger if he wanted to straighten up, so maybe the hunch was meekness. He wore plain black trousers, rather rumpled, a shirt that had once been white but had yellowed remarkably, a black jacket with the shoulder seam split, and some white, high-top Converse sneakers from the era before athletic shoes made statements. After twenty years of living a monk's life, he could fit all his other possessions into a comically small black satchel. It looked like a doctor's bag.

"Why did you leave the monastery?" she asked him.

He shrugged. "I had a fight with my abbot. Among other things."

"A fight?"

He smiled, a little wearily. "To put it in layman's terms."

Rebecca laughed. "Well, that's not very Christian, is it?"

"It's sort of a long story." Christopher hesitated. "I was fed up with that place anyway, to tell you the truth. I had prayed myself into a hole."

The evidence of hotheadedness, along with his frankness, was strangely reassuring. She liked his smile and his unguarded brown eyes. He had no credit history at all, of course. He didn't even have a driver's license. He had a check, some kind of severance pay—did contemplatives get severance pay?—that he hadn't been able to get cashed. He had no job as yet. As far as she could determine he had no prospects, no plan, and no résumé. But there was something about him that she liked a lot, a gloomy depth. And there was the appeal of the quixotic. He had devoted his adult life to the contemplation of God. *That* was his résumé. He had done what she had always intended to do with her own life and flung it into the maw of Meaning in one grand, futile gesture, and he had nothing to show for it but the clothes on his back. He'd been sleeping in the park and he hadn't eaten in three days, but he seemed unperturbed by that. It was all very New Testament.

The apartment showed fast. A bathroom, a minute, stoveless kitchen with a half-fridge on one counter and a hot plate on the other, and the single real room in the place, an 8 x 15 box carpeted in a brown that had not seemed so dishearteningly the color of mud in the samples. The walls, at least, were a fresh cream. Rebecca was proud of her paint job.

The room's lone window opened into the barren backyard. Christopher went right to the glass and stood looking out at the weedy waste. Rebecca could feel his melancholy. It was not much of a prospect.

"I keep meaning to put in a garden back there," she said. "Or something. But there's never any time, it seems. And when there's time, I just want to recover."

"I'd be glad to do some work back there myself. It's a nice space."

"Ah, well—" Rebecca murmured, flustered, assuming he was angling to reduce the rent through work exchange. "If I could afford a *gardener* . . . "

His look was genuinely uncomprehending; it had not occurred to him to charge her. Well, that was very New Testament too, of course. But mortgages were Old Testament, and hers was about to balloon. She had been hoping to rent the apartment to a quiet spinster with an obvious income, not a down-and-out man of God.

As they stood there, she clearly heard his stomach growl. Their eyes met. His look was apologetic, with a trace of dry amusement; he had lovely warm brown eyes. Rebecca took him upstairs, gave him a bowl of Cheerios, and introduced him to her daughter. At six years old, Mary Martha was an infallible detector of bullshit. Christopher was immediately easy with the child in an unflamboyant way. So many adults just turned up the volume, as if a kid couldn't hear. But Christopher got quietly attentive, like a shy child himself. The two of them sat at the kitchen table with their twin bowls of cereal and studied the back of the box together. Mary Martha soon was chattering away, and when she invited Christopher to see her unicorns, Rebecca took it as a sign and let him have the apartment.

She was tempted to renege the next day. The deluge of applicants responding to the newspaper ad included a number of solid citizens. But by then she had cashed his monastery check for him and accepted first and last in cash, and he was settled in. And Rebecca had to admit that Christopher's delight in the in-law apartment was charming. She'd never seen a man so grateful for a shower, a hot plate, and a half-fridge.

To Br. James Donovan
c/o Our Lady of Bethany Monastery
Mendocino County, CA

Dear Brother James,

Thank you for your letter, and for your very touching concern. I have indeed "settled nicely" into a situation here in the city, as you hoped. The details you request are not that important. Suffice it to say that I am content. (I must ask, incidentally, that you not address me any longer as "Brother Jerome." I am Michael Christopher now. Again . . . The name seems strangely like an alias after twenty years. But that is all the more reason to insist on using it. My identity itself has become a kind of hair shirt.)

Forgive me if I say that I am not sure what purpose would be served by "continuing our conversation in faith," as you put it. You are young, and eager, and were struck upon your arrival at Our Lady of Bethany by something in me that you took for depth. I was a seasoned monk, you thought, with an inner life rich in God. You took me for a model of sorts, and I confess that I was flattered. But surely my "depth" has revealed itself by this time as a side effect of less appealing qualities; the "richness" of my inner life is a complexity more riddled with doubt than illumined by faith.

It is true that our conversations in the past were delightful. I cherished the gift of your friendship from the moment you came to Our Lady of Bethany. Your fresh eye, your intelligence, and the purity of your commitment to the contemplative life were a joy to me, and sparked a renewal of my spirit. But paradoxically enough, it was in trying to convey to you something of my own love for the contemplative life that I came to realize how desperately little I had to show for twenty years of prayer. It became a kind of torment to me, to see your innocent eagerness. I realized that something in me was saying, was fairly shouting, Go back! Go back to the world! It is not too late for you to avoid becoming what I have become.

And what have I become? You ask what prayer is for me now. I used to have so many lovely answers. Prayer is communion, adoration, praise; it is the practice of the presence of God. Prayer is abiding in love. I had a catalogue of ready definitions through the whole of my novitiate, all substantial and high sounding, an impressive array. But all that holy busyness seems like a kind of sand-castle building to me now, and the zeal of my answers is a heap of soggy kelp left by the tide. There is a prayer that is simply seeing through yourself, seeing your own nothingness, the emptiness impervious to self-assertion. A prayer that is the end of the rope. A helplessness, fathomless and terrifying. No matter how holy or well meaning you were when you started out, no matter how many fine experiences you had along the way, by the time you reach the point of this prayer, you want only to get out of it.

And God? God is that which will not let you out of it.

Do you see my point? I am a ruined man. Your kindness at this point only pains me, and forces a fresh consciousness of my failure. Certainly there is nothing to be gained by your "following my secular career," as you so cheerfully put it. I anticipate no secular career. More than ever, I am certain that I am in God's hands, that my life is paper to His fire. If I am sometimes inclined to feel now, with Jeremiah, He hath led me, and brought me into darkness, but not into light, *that has more to do with my own temptation to bitterness than with your religious vocation. My seemingly endless squabbles with Abbot Hackley and with the creeping staleness of monastic routine are ancient history: It is with my bitterness and my sense of failure that I must struggle now; it is to this that God has led me. That cannot possibly be edifying to you; and certainly I would prefer to endure my humiliations in private.*

Forgive me if I have put this too harshly. But believe me when I say that I'm doing you a favor. I am at best a cautionary tale; I am some shattered glass and metal rimmed with flares on the road to God. Drive on quietly, Brother James, and don't look back.

Yours in Christ (as you say),
  Michael Christopher

The Friday after Rebecca rented the in-law apartment to Michael Christopher, Bob Schofield proposed. Rebecca was startled but not truly surprised. She had seen his delusion building for months, but she had been ignoring it, hoping it would go away. Bob was earnest beyond her comprehension, impervious to her slights and neglects, as uninsultable as a tank. He simply took every nonrefusal on her part, every concession to see a movie or let him buy her a meal or a drink, and worked it patiently into the scheme of their Relationship, as he had called it from the start. She knew that he was serious. She had been to his apartment, she had seen the shelf of books devoted to Relationship. The project had a paint-by-numbers quality to it, but there was no denying the way Bob laid the color on. Apparently Rebecca's utter lack of enthusiasm was not a problem for him.

She had held out hopes, in the beginning, for a harmless friendship. For companionship, a simple muffling of the loneliness of single motherhood. She had even toyed, early in the relationship, with the unnerving inkling that she might . . . not come to love Bob, but perhaps in time to resign herself to him. That such a resignation might be the lost key to her deferred adulthood, some yet-unprayed penance for her misspent youth. Maybe grown-up-ness hinged upon the exhaustion of passion into affectionate benignity. Maybe that was how they did it.

Bob had taken her and Mary Martha to his church one Sunday during this unnerving phase. Despite his bright pop notions of Relationship, he was an Episcopalian, which seemed to Rebecca at once admirably substantial and safely dilute, a sort of Catholicism Lite, without the high guilt content and devotional ferocity of the Church of her childhood. The mass, which Bob called a service, echoed with eerie near precision the liturgy she had grown up on, and she couldn't help chiming in from time to time from struck chords of memory, only to find herself a word or two off in the Anglican version or praying on when everyone else had ceased or ceasing while the rest of the congregation prayed on. She knelt instinctively at the consecration, out of old Catholic reflex, and Mary Martha, who had never been in a church before, knelt unhesitatingly beside her. Everyone else had remained standing. Perhaps it was the touching faith of Mary Martha following her example against the grain; or perhaps it was simply some deep-seated orneriness or a residual bit of Catholic team spirit, a contempt for the humanistic Protestants' unwillingness to bend their knees; or maybe it was just the sharpness of the emptiness that the posture brought home, the piercing sense of kneeling before a mystery too alien by now for proper worship. In any case, Rebecca remained on her knees, stubbornly, even defiantly, and rose only for the Our Father, which she treated as concluded after "and deliver us from evil," leaving the Episcopalians to finish out the longer Protestant version on their own and to say "Ah-men."

The awkwardness culminated at communion. Bob insisted to the verge of public embarrassment that Rebecca accompany him up the aisle. He seemed to think it would be crucially good for her. She followed him up and knelt resignedly beside him at the polished cherrywood rail, feeling blatant, a fraud, and half anticipating some sudden blaring of an alarm sensitive to the presence of religious impostors. The priest approached and held up the Host, saying, "The Body of Christ—" and Rebecca said "Ay-men," conscious of her Catholic accent, and stuck out her tongue to receive the wafer, according to the training of her childhood.

"—the bread of heaven," the priest concluded, with a mild note of having been preempted. He wavered, host in hand, apparently baffled by her protruding tongue. There was an awkward pause. Beside her, Bob was miming broadly with cupped hands, and after a bad moment Rebecca recovered and shaped her own hands likewise to receive the blessed wafer. The priest dropped one in Bob's palm too and hurried on, clearly eager for smoother exchanges.

Bob consumed his bit of bread with a suitably reverent air. Following his example, Rebecca moved to eat her own Host, but she caught herself with the wafer halfway to her mouth, overcome by a sudden intimation of sacrilege. How could she possibly just pop the Body of Christ into her mouth like an hors d'oeuvre at a church picnic, after all these years, these literal decades of laxity, if not actual sin? She hadn't even prayed, "Lord, I am not worthy to receive You . . ." These blithe Episcopalians left that out.

A deacon was approaching with a chalice, stooping to give the woman beside Rebecca a sip of the wine, intoning, "The Blood of Christ, the cup of salvation—" Before he could move on to her, Rebecca rose abruptly, charged with a violent certainty that she was not ready, not ready at all for the cup of salvation, for the blood of the Lamb.

Bob gave her a startled glance, then actually reached for her arm. Apparently he believed that she was simply unclear on the procedure. Rebecca dodged him easily and fled, shouldering through the muddle of approaching communicants. She hurried down the central aisle, out the door at the back of the church, and into the parking lot, where she finally came to an uncertain halt. She couldn't remember what Bob's car looked like. There were so many silvery luxury cars in the crowded lot that it looked like a Mercedes auto fair.

She was still clutching the communion wafer in her hand. It felt weirdly hot against her palm, a point of fire like a needle or a nail. A stigmata of ambivalence, she thought ruefully. The spring morning was warm and incongruously beautiful; somehow the usual San Francisco fog would have suited her better. She was remembering the day she had ceased to believe in a God who could punish her. She had been sixteen, capable at last of driving to church herself, and she had talked her mother into letting her take the family's second car, a dumpy Ford Pinto, the model that was later determined to be an explosion waiting to happen because of the placement of the gas tank. Instead of going to mass, though, she had bought two Krispy Kreme jelly doughnuts and a large coffee and driven out to the beach. She'd eaten the doughnuts as a condemned inmate might eat his last meal, fairly sure that the Lord would strike her down for bailing so calculatedly on church.

But nothing had happened, an awesome nothing. She had finished the doughnuts and licked her fingers and sipped her coffee. The waves had broken on the gray New Jersey sand and the gulls had careened and shreed. It had just been a lovely sunny day like this one. She'd felt, somehow, that God had let her down. The least He could have done was shown some interest in her sacrilege. A rear-ender, maybe, the Pinto smacked from behind by the hand of a vengeful Lord, square on the misplaced gas tank. A fireball. That'll teach you to skip mass. Nothing fatal; an attention grabber merely. She could have emerged from the purgative flames scorched but chastened, seared into unassailable belief.

Mary Martha popped out of the church now with her tiny legs pumping hard, squinting in the sunlight, containing tears. Spotting Rebecca, she started toward her at once, already beginning to cry. Bob, a step behind her, was struggling comically to hide his embarrassment and chagrin, to arrange his face in a way that facilitated Relationship.

The communion wafer had turned to a lump of soggy bread in Rebecca's clenched hand. But she didn't know what to do with it. You couldn't just toss the body of Christ aside in a parking lot for the pigeons to eat. As Mary Martha and Bob strode toward her, forcing the issue, she licked her palm surreptitiously and swallowed, and the bread stuck in her throat.

In the car on the way home, listening to Mary Martha sniffle, Rebecca began to cry too, to her own dismay. Bob, disconcerted, stammered for a while and finally stopped, a little desperately, at Dairy Queen, where he bought all three of them vanilla ice cream cones with colored sprinkles. It was so sweet and touching that Rebecca was afraid for a while that she might have to marry him, that it was a message from God after all, the perfect humiliation. But she'd come back to her senses soon enough. Bob had kept the Dairy Queen receipt. She didn't even ask him why. It didn't really matter. She couldn't live with a man who'd found an accounting niche for ice cream cone expenses.

It wasn't that Bob was unattractive. There were those who thought him quite good-looking, with every wiry black hair in place and trusting brown waif's eyes. He was undeniably a nice guy. He was smart, and he could be witty. But his chin was weak, and he had a wispy softness of manner, a breathiness. He would have made a great gay friend, Rebecca had often thought. She treated him, indeed, as she might have treated a gay friend, with a frank, easy camaraderie, as one of the girls. But Bob was straight enough, in his programmatic way. He lingered at the end of their outings, which he insisted on calling dates, allowing the awkward pause at the doorstep to grow ponderous, waiting with painful obviousness for a goodnight kiss. Rebecca had taken to kissing him on the cheek just to deflate the moment's significance, but recently Bob had begun to try to meet her lips. Their neck dynamics had gotten as intricate as those of fighting cocks. There had been lip contact. How he could possibly have found any of this grist for the mill of Relationship was beyond her. Bob had no pride. Combined with his fundamental obtuseness, this actually made him a little dangerous. Things should never have gone this far.

He pulled out the ring at a lovely, ridiculously expensive Italian restaurant in North Beach. On cue, a violin player and a waitress laden with lilies approached the table. Bob got down on one knee. Everyone in the restaurant was watching indulgently, waiting to applaud. It was not possible to explain to them that the drama was entirely Bob's. Rebecca knew that she had never done anything more encouraging than to shrug off his more flagrant hints: not a single yes had crossed her lips. It had seemed pointless to hurt his feelings.

She was thinking of Rory now, inevitably. Rory with his gift for ad lib, who had proposed on the N-Judah train on a Tuesday afternoon. He hadn't even had a ring—he'd rummaged through his pockets for a token of their enduring love and given her a guitar pick.

"Say you will make me the happiest man alive," Bob said from the floor at her feet, his wishful thinking writ large and public. Rebecca looked at him and all she could think was how tiresome it was, and how sad.

"We'll talk about it later," she said. "Okay?"

Emboldened by the sympathetic crowd, perhaps, he held his ground. "I need an answer now, darling."

He had begun to call her "darling" on their third outing, right after the fiasco at the church; she had fought the endearment off until their seventh date. Bob was the only one counting, of course. Rebecca leaned closer and lowered her voice so that only he could hear.

"Get back in your goddamned chair, Bob, right this minute. I am not going to marry you."

His face fell, but he obeyed. He was good that way, of course; it was his strength. The other patrons applauded uncertainly. The clueless violinist began to play something screechy and romantic. The wine waiter arrived on cue with champagne.

"May I be the first to offer my most sincere congratulations," he said, laying on the fake Italian accent.

In Bob's Lexus on the way home, Rebecca lit a cigarette. She allowed herself five Marlboro Lights a day and thought of them as little suicides. There was also a certain amount of frank hostility in the act. Bob had a horror of his car smelling of smoke. She ran the electric window down and let the cold night air blast in.

"I'm sorry," Bob said.

"So am I, Bob."

"I really thought—"

"I know you did. It's my fault as much as yours. I should have been ruder, sooner."

"Oh, I think you've been rude enough, often enough. I just haven't wanted to believe it."

Rebecca glanced at him appreciatively. She had always wondered if he even noticed. The car radio was leaking something stupefying and symphonic at an anesthetizing volume. Bob had it set to a classical station, as always. He kept the ambiance as orthodox as a dentist's waiting room. Sometimes he would make jaunty little conductor's motions with his free hand as he drove. Rebecca took the last drag off her cigarette, the breath most laden with carcinogens, and flipped the butt out the window. Holding the smoke in her lungs, she felt a moment's compassion for both of them.

Let me just stay here, she thought. Let me not have to go back into the fray. Let me not have to be unkind.

"I love you, is the thing," Bob said. "Call me an incurable romantic, but I have to believe in that."

Rebecca let her breath out. The night tore the smoke away. She pressed the button and the window hummed up. She had one cigarette left in her daily allotment of small deaths, and she was determined not to spend it here.

"It's a movie, Bob. Don't you see? It's just a movie, and you've miscast the lead. I like you. I admire your . . . spunk. Your grit, your uncrushable goodwill. I'm not even looking for more than that at this point in my life."

"Of course you are. Everyone is."

"No. I had the romantic thing with my first husband, thank you very much. I'm thirty-eight years old, and I've got a daughter learning to read and a job I don't quite like. I've got a mortgage. I'm making my middle-aged peace with network television. Tomorrow is another day I've got to get through. If you could just behave yourself, we could have the occasional movie or meal together and I would feel that much less like a troll and a drudge. But I don't need the violin music, Bob. I don't want it. I find it sort of pathetic, really."

Bob took this in a silence that had a touch of sulk in it.

"So we're back to junior high school," he said at last. "You 'just want to be friends.' I have a great personality. It's nothing personal. It's you, not me."

"I would love it if we could do this without regressing completely. But if junior high school works for you—"

"What works for *you?* What can I do differently? I'm willing to change, Rebecca. I'm willing to grow. I'll do anything."

He would, she knew. Rebecca sighed. "If you got any better, Bob, I would die from guilt. Just take me home."

They did not speak for the rest of the drive back to the Sunset. Bob pulled up in front of her house on 38th Avenue and put the car in neutral. Pointedly, he did not turn the engine off, and he made no move to get out. Rebecca found that she was grateful for his pique. It made things so much easier.

"Well, goodnight," she offered, playing on the inadequacy

of it, hoping to share at least the camaraderie of fiasco. But Bob just hunched his shoulders.

"Goodnight," he replied curtly, as obvious as a child. He had both hands on the steering wheel and he would not meet her eyes. He wanted another round of drama; he wanted at least the dignity of a scene. Rebecca shrugged and opened the car door herself, feeling cruel. She got out, closing the door carefully, not wanting to feed his sense of melodrama by slamming it, and walked up the steps to her front door. At least there would be no neck dance tonight, no avoiding or succumbing to deluded kisses.

Bob's tires gave a petulant yelp as he pulled away. Rebecca shook her head, wondering if there would ever be anyone in her life again who slipped between the cartoon predictabilities and the emptiness. She knew she had been trying to fake a friendship as hard as Bob had been trying to fake a romance.

Inside, she paid the baby-sitter and sent her home, then went to check on Mary Martha. Her daughter was sleeping soundly. Rebecca resisted the urge to go sit by her bed and gaze at her perfect face. It was enough just to hear her contented breathing. In the darkness, a throng of stuffed animals softened every surface of the bedroom. Mary Martha's unicorn phase went on and on. Sometimes, watching her at play, seeing the look of absorption on her face as she put her magic animals through their paces, Rebecca would feel a tender ferocity rising in herself, a readiness to battle the world. All she really wanted was to protect her daughter's joy in unicorns. It was like loving soap bubbles, she knew, treasuring that innocence. Yet nothing else in her life right now moved her in the least. She often thought that must be a little pathetic; surely she should have found a larger cause by this time. But the larger causes of her youth had bled away. Her sense of the Big

Picture had fractured and decayed. She loved her daughter, the blessing of a good book, a glass of wine after the day's wave of vanity had passed.

And the occasional cigarette. Was that shallow? Then she was shallow, it seemed. Rebecca closed the bedroom door and slipped down the hallway, moving with the instinctive wariness she still caught herself in now. Five years after the divorce, the house remained dangerous in unforeseeable ways, like a children's playground riddled with unexploded mines from a previous war. Little bits of Rory surfaced, devastatingly: a bookmark halfway through the collected short stories of Flannery O'Connor, a twenty-dollar bill tucked under the silverware tray for a rainy day, birthday cards he'd bought and never sent. Evidence of promises not kept and promises abandoned.

She passed through the kitchen to the back porch. The abalone shell on the top step was filled with butts; she kept meaning to empty it. She sat down, tugged her coat around her, and lit the day's last Marlboro. Above her, the stars themselves seemed weary in a sky bleached thin by the city's lights. The dark backyard at the bottom of the stairs communicated neglect. She was really going to have to drag herself out of bed some Saturday and hack back some weeds, at least.

The phone rang inside, and that deep, crazy part of her rose to the sound at once, like a trout to a dry fly. As if it still might be Rory, as if it all might have been a mistake. As if the death of a marriage through a thousand small cuts of violation and neglect could still be healed by the Band-Aid of a single communication.

But it was Bob, of course. She listened to his voice on the message machine, apologizing already. Apparently he had had time to get home and research the problem in his library of

Relationship. He had failed to give her her space, he said. He had not been sensitive to her needs. He had "pushed the river."

It went on for a while; he had worked out the lines of a solution too, in excruciating detail. Rebecca stopped listening and took a deep drag on the cigarette. In four good puffs, maybe five, she knew, she would stub the butt into the shell and her life would seem very small and sad to her again. It was the evil magic of nicotine that buoyed this little moment of peace. But it was lovely, nonetheless, to sit quietly, fingering the guitar pick that hung from a silver chain around her neck and listening to the untrimmed bushes rustle in the breeze that blew in from the sea.

Chapter Two

On Saturday morning Rebecca woke from a dream that she had swallowed a diamond. The stone was so large that the doctors were sure that it would kill her. Certainly it was indigestible. On the other hand, someone said, it was a very valuable gem. And it wasn't like it was lost. They knew exactly where it was.

"Fat lotta good *that* does me," Rebecca had said, and woke. The dream had been so vivid that she could still feel a lump in her bowels, a sensation that only slowly dissipated. She wondered briefly whether her body was trying to tell her that she had cancer. That was all she needed now, a horrible, lingering death to fit into her schedule.

The bedroom was bright; she'd slept even later than usual. Normally by this time Mary Martha would have trooped in two or three times with urgencies real and imagined. Her daughter suffered Rebecca's weekend sloth, Rebecca knew. She felt bad about it herself. She was constantly making vows to pop up early and seize the day. But the week just seemed to blast every good intention into rubble. Come Saturday morning, she was the same old featureless heap in the bed.

Rebecca roused herself, drew her threadbare terry cloth robe about her, and padded down the hall toward the bathroom, expecting her daughter to bound up at any moment. But there was no sign of Mary Martha. The TV in the living room was silent and her daughter's bedroom was empty except for the usual unicorn tableau and a scatter of books. Rebecca hurried back up the hall to the kitchen, which was also deserted.

"Mary Martha?" she called, hearing the panic-quaver in her voice.

There was no answer. She was trying to decide whether to begin screaming right there in the kitchen or to run screaming out into the street when she noticed that the back door was ajar. Rebecca went to the window and looked down into the yard, and there was Mary Martha, sitting on the bottom step in the sunlight, talking with Michael Christopher, who was on his hands and knees pulling up weeds.

With relief came anger for the scare, but the two of them made such a sweet scene that Rebecca didn't have the heart to break it up. She could not make out their words from where she stood, but she could hear the clear, eager music of Mary Martha's chatter and the respectful baritone of Christopher's replies. The discussion appeared to be lively. Her new tenant had kept a low profile since moving in. If he went out during the day, he went out after she left for work. As far as Rebecca knew, he was down there praying, or drinking, whatever ex-monks did. But he seemed normal enough now in jeans and a T-shirt. His hair was growing in a little, and the escaped-convict stubble he'd sported upon his arrival had given way to a softer fuzz. She noted that he had shaved, revealing a sensual mouth and a determined jaw. His face seemed surprisingly vulnerable without the beard. With the downy blur of the new hair and his awkward neck, he looked like a freshly hatched gosling.

While she was standing there, the phone rang. Probably Bob again, Rebecca thought, and let the machine get it. But it was her mother. Rebecca picked up.

"Screening, are we?" Phoebe noted, amused. At seventy-two, she had one of those wonderful brisk old-lady voices like rung crystal, and something of the freedom to take the world lightly that Rebecca longed for.

"Bob proposed last night. I'm expecting some aftershocks."

"Ah. Which one is Bob, now?"

"The Thai food." Bob had insisted on taking them— Phoebe, Rebecca, and Mary Martha—out for dinner on the previous Mother's Day to some place in the Marina. "His girls," he had called them, at least three times. He had almost broken his back opening doors and pulling out chairs, but the conversation had lagged. The main thing Rebecca could recall from the outing was Mary Martha's delight in the peanut sauce and Bob's insistence on a broad view of social evolution into the twenty-first century, which had filled the intellectual void like Styrofoam packing pellets. Phoebe, at the end of the evening, had merely remarked, devastatingly, "He seems nice enough." From someone as capable of intricate analysis as her mother, Rebecca thought, it amounted to a dismissal.

"Ah, of course," Phoebe said now. "Mr. Megatrends 2000."

"It was a debacle, I'm afraid. He made quite a production of it."

Phoebe was briskly unsympathetic. "Well, you could see it coming. I hope you weren't too hard on him."

"I was as nice as I could possibly be, under the circumstances."

"Oh dear."

Rebecca laughed. "I suppose you think I should have taken him up on it."

"And become Mrs. Megatrends?" her mother asked dryly. "Yes, that's an appealing prospect."

"He's reading something else by now, I'm sure."

"Don't give it another thought, Rebecca. There's no need to settle for mediocrity."

"I wasn't even tempted," Rebecca declared. But she knew that she had been. Not by Bob as he was, but by Bob as he might have been with just a little tweaking here and there and some mysterious infusion of chemistry. A New and Improved Bob. From such wishful thinking it was one short step to trying to do the tweaking yourself and betting the ranch on the mysterious infusion. She had come soberingly close to a ruinous compromise over these past months. If Bob had not so characteristically blundered with his comic opera proposal; if he had made his offer in private, with a touch of humility and a dignified appeal to the longing for companionship, to the sharing of loads; if he had come on with a little humor and frankness about diminishing prospects and caught her on one of those days when the laundry and shopping hadn't gotten done and there had been no one to pick up Mary Martha at day care and the car's transmission was making a funny new noise . . . Well, who knew? It was easy for Phoebe, who had snagged the love of her life in classic fashion, to counsel holding out for excellence. Phoebe had married Rebecca's father at nineteen and kept his house for forty-two years in perfectly contented devotion. When John Martin had died of a heart attack on the NJT 5:10 out of Penn Station one night on the way home from his office, some ten years ago, Phoebe had been shattered. She had languished for several years, keeping to herself—rattling around the old place, as she said, drinking too much and doing melancholy watercolors. Then, some five years previously, she had moved to California, ostensibly to be near her daughter. She had bought a small house near Stinson Beach and begun to show a surprising zest for widowhood. She was always bopping off to some Shakespeare Festival or orchid show; she worked part-time at a funky little art gallery in town, and she had a hip, even occasionally edgy, set of new friends, painters and writers and Bolinas secessionists.

The sound of Mary Martha's laughter rose from the back-yard. She sounded almost giddy. Rebecca edged over to the coffee machine to get a pot of French roast started.

"So how's the hermit?" Phoebe asked, mercifully changing the subject. Rebecca had told her mother about her new tenant, and, predictably, Phoebe was delighted with the notion of a monk downstairs.

"He appears to be coming out of his shell a bit. He's out in the backyard right now doing battle with the weeds. Mary Martha likes him a lot."

"Ask him if he does baptisms."

Rebecca laughed. "Why? Are you pregnant?"

"Not me, Sherilou just had a kid. She wants to have some kind of ceremony, a touch of spirituality. Though if you ask me, she'd be better off having some kind of father around. But it's too late for that, alas."

Sherilou was one of Phoebe's projects, a thirtyish poetess living on food stamps and prone to rants. The two of them spent a lot of time at Phoebe's kitchen table eating Oreo cookies and dissecting the work of Adrienne Rich.

"I doubt that Mr. Christopher is doing any freelance sacramental work," Rebecca said. "I get the impression he left the monastery on an awkward note."

"Just a few words in the proper spirit is all we're looking for. A soupçon of ritual. It's not like Sherilou is looking to renounce Satan and his works or anything. It's a fragmented culture. We don't need the whole nine yards."

"I'm sure the man just wants to be left alone, Mother."

"Of course, of course." Phoebe paused. Rebecca could picture her mother, spry and lean in charcoal gray Nordstrom slacks and running shoes, her silver hair cut short, looking out her kitchen window at the Pacific Ocean, one foot thumping like a rabbit's, her mind already on to something else.

Sure enough, Phoebe said, "I should get going. We've got an opening today and I promised Jack I'd help set up."

"Of course. Love you."

"Love you too, darling. Are you going to get up here this weekend?"

"We can't; Rory's got Mary Martha. Theoretically." Rebecca glanced at the clock. It was almost eleven. Her ex-husband, a professional surfer, kept vampire hours and seldom showed up before noon for his every-other-week bit of fatherly quality time. More often than not, he took Mary Martha straight to Ocean Beach and left her on the sand all day with his current girlfriend and a bag of potato chips while he tried to coax a ride out of the chop. But Mary Martha adored him. "Maybe next weekend?"

"I suppose that will have to do. Kiss Mary Martha for me and tell her Grandma loves her."

"I will."

"And ask the monk about the baptism. I think the fact that's he's a renegade will appeal to Sherilou."

"He's not a renegade, Mom. He's a sad man having one helluva midlife crisis."

"All the more reason to get him involved in something meaningful. I've really got to run. Kiss-kiss."

"Kiss-kiss." Rebecca smiled as she hung up. The coffee was ready. She poured herself a cup and went to the back window again. Christopher was on his knees again, wrestling with a deeply rooted weed. He had cleared about three square feet of ground by now. The dark earth looked fresh and raw against the burned yellow skin of the rest of the yard. Mary Martha was sitting contentedly on the bottom step in her pajamas, watching him with perfect absorption, offering the occasional comment or advice.

On an impulse, Rebecca opened the window.

"Hey, there, Don Quixote, how about a cup of coffee before you finish off that windmill?" she called down.

Christopher glanced up, startled and even a little alarmed, apparently unprepared for conversation with a grown-up. "Oh! Hello!"

"Good morning. Would you like some coffee?" she repeated.

"Coffee?" Christopher echoed, as if the word were new to him.

Rebecca laughed. "Didn't they have coffee in the monastery?"

"They had the world's worst coffee, actually," Christopher conceded. "Gallons of it."

"Well, I make the world's best, if I do say so myself."

"I wouldn't want to trouble you."

"It's no trouble at all. It's already made."

Christopher hesitated, clearly seeking a way to gracefully refuse. He looked so much like a deer in the headlights that Rebecca felt a moment's compassion for him. All the poor man wanted was to be left alone.

"I hope Mary Martha's not bothering you," she said.

"*Mom!*" Mary Martha exclaimed indignantly. "I'm not *bothering* him!"

"Not at all," Christopher affirmed.

"Okay." Rebecca paused. "Well, you let me know if you change your mind about that coffee."

"I will," he assured her, with obvious relief, and turned back to his weeding. Rebecca watched for a moment more, then shrugged and closed the window. There were worse things, after all, than a reticent tenant bent on cleaning up the yard. The last guy who'd lived downstairs had played the drums.

Dear Brother James,

It is common courtesy to thank you for your most recent letter, yet I continue to feel you are misguided in your zeal for communication. You seem gripped by an ambition to save my soul. But I assure you such a hope is in vain. The word monk *comes from the Late Greek* monakhos, *"solitary," and ultimately from* monos: *"alone." The first monks were men who went into the Egyptian desert to be alone with God. That dangerous solitude is still at the heart of the monastic vocation. (If I can still speak of a monastic vocation, in my own case. Perhaps I am called to a simpler ruin.) All monastery walls, in principle at least, are the borders of a wasteland, and every monk is a man who lives alone. But what we learn in the monastery, eventually, is that the walls are false, a convenience and a lie. There are no borders to the wasteland. The desert is everywhere; it is that which we call the world. And every man is a man alone.*

You fear that in leaving Our Lady of Bethany I have somehow pronounced the life I led there—and thus, by implication, the life you lead there—"irrelevant." You may find my real sense of the issue more disheartening still: I believe it is a mistake even to ask whether the monastic vocation is relevant. It is no more relevant now than it ever was. The truths of the desert are useless truths. A man alone is a useless thing. And it is a useless thing to speak of God.

It is to such lucid uselessness, I still believe, that I am called. But I may well be perverse. We expect God's presence to be thunderous, spectacular, monumental; but it is our need that is so large. The real presence slips past our demands for spectacle. It slips past our despair. Not just like a child—sometimes it is a child. She walks down the blistered steps to where you kneel and says the simplest things. She is entertained by butterflies. She has opinions about unicorns. She does not seem to care that you are ruined and lost. She does not even seem to notice. Find an earthworm in the neglected loam and she will make you feel for a moment that your life has not been wasted. Name a flower and she will make you feel that you have begun to learn to speak.

May your own path lead you, dear Brother James, to whatever degree of relevance you desire.

Yours in Christ,
Michael Christopher

Mary Martha came trooping in from the backyard just before noon, pink with sun and a little manic. Mike had had to go to work, she announced. He had gotten a job at McDonald's. This sounded suspiciously like a six-year-old's fantasy career to Rebecca, or some kind of miscommunication—perhaps Christopher had said McDonnell Douglas, or Macintosh, though what an ex-monk might do at either corporation was beyond her. Still, whatever the factual basis of the rumor, it was good to hear that Christopher had found work.

She hustled Mary Martha into the bathtub and out and had her daughter dressed in jeans and sneakers, with her overnight bag packed with a change of clothes and a traveling contingent of unicorns, by 12:30. Rory didn't show up until just after 1:00, which was not bad, all things considered. Any appointment was an approximation with her ex.

Rory bounced in wearing his wet-suit bottoms and a T-shirt that said *Maui Legends,* trailing sand and smelling of marijuana smoke. He had promised Rebecca after endless battles not to get stoned in front of Mary Martha, and according to his strict constructionist reading he abided by the rule, taking his last hit in his car out front before he came in to pick her up. Rebecca hesitated, wondering as always whether to call him on it. The spirit of the law, she felt, was not to *be* stoned in front of Mary Martha. But it was a hard thing to fight about with their daughter right there and Rory already toked into imperturbability and acting hipper-than-thou. And she just didn't have the energy to fight it anymore. Maybe that was what your life became, eventually: a series of stalemates you had fought to the point of exhaustion.

"Flying high, are we?" she said impotently, hating herself.

"Always," Rory smiled. He met her eye and almost, but not quite, winked, riding the edge of her irritation like a tricky wave before he ducked away to give Mary Martha a hug. He didn't quite have rock-star good looks, though he acted like he did and usually pulled it off. He was actually a little funny looking in a lopsided Irish way, with an off-center grin and a face like an amiable fisherman's, bright blue eyes, and an air of perpetual, puppylike alertness. He had a tough, square body, thick through the chest and bandy-legged. He'd kept his waistline, burning endless calories in the cold Pacific, but there were distinct threads of silver in his long, dishwater-blond hair, which Rory had worn pulled back into the same monotonous strand for twenty years. He was going to do the gray ponytail thing. He was going to play forever.

"Mike said I could plant some flowers," Mary Martha told him.

"Wow, flowers, wonderful!" Rory exclaimed, readily enough. "Who's Mike?"

"Our new tenant downstairs," Rebecca said. "I finally got the in-law apartment in shape."

"He's a *monk,*" Mary Martha announced.

"Wow, a monk, no kidding. Does he wear a robe and sandals?"

She giggled. "No, silly."

"Does he keep you up all night with his incessant chanting?"

"No!"

"He's very nice," Rebecca said, before things got out of hand. "Very ordinary. Just a guy. Makes his own coffee, keeps to himself."

"I suppose it was inevitable you would end up with an ascetic, on the rebound from me."

"I'm not on the rebound from you, Rory. And all I did was rent an apartment to the man."

"Of course," he said, maddeningly. He bent to Mary Martha again. "Are you ready to go, Number One?"

"Yes."

"There's an eight-foot break down by Half Moon Bay, I hear. Are you up for that?"

"Yes!"

"Make it so, then. Warp speed."

"Aye, aye, Captain!"

"She's already had her lunch," Rebecca said. "There's a snack in the bag, for later in the afternoon. And some sunscreen."

"Okay," Rory said, clearly humoring her. He picked up Mary Martha's bag and took her hand, and they walked together toward the front door. Rebecca followed and watched them down the front steps to Rory's ancient Rambler station wagon, with his long board in the rack on top and his boogie board in the back.

Seeing her daughter off with Rory, she always had the sense of sending her out to sea in a paper boat. Rory would bring Mary Martha back on Sunday evening, and she would have had nothing to eat in the meantime but 7-Eleven food, plastic-wrapped tacos, Fritos, and Mountain Dew. Her nails would be painted some weird shade of industrial green by Rory's current girlfriend. She would be sunburned if the weather had been good and chilled to the bone if the fog had come in. She would have done nothing in his apartment in the Haight but watch *Star Trek* reruns. Rebecca knew these things not just from debriefing Mary Martha—who found nothing particularly wrong with the time she spent with her father—but because she had lived this way herself with Rory for years. They had cherished a few artistic aspirations and a vague, drug-fueled sense of mission. But the dreams they'd had had come to nothing.

It wasn't that Rory was stupid, though he liked to pretend he was. He was widely read in literature and philosophy; he was at home with Hesse and Camus and could ramble on about Buddhism and the Tao. He was perhaps too at home with Alan Watts. But essentially Rory lived for that clean moment when the wave lifted him free of everything but the Zen of balance. He called that freedom, and he had built his life around it. It seemed like enough to him, and it had seemed like enough to Rebecca for what, in retrospect, was an embarrassingly long time. If she hadn't had Mary Martha, she thought, she might still have been sitting there on the tailgate of the woody, doing her futile little watercolors and drinking Budweiser out of cans, oohing and aahing every time someone found a wave to work offshore. She might have been painting her nails industrial green and living in the eternal moment from joint to joint. Waiting for Rory to grow up.

Rebecca realized that she was fingering the guitar pick that hung over her heart. She let go of it self-consciously, irritated with herself. She was really going to have to put the damned thing in a drawer someday. At the curb, Mary Martha waved from the passenger seat as Rory turned the key and the balky ignition labored.

"Seat belt!" Rebecca hollered. Mary Martha nodded and obeyed. The Rambler's engine caught at last. Rory put the car in gear and gave Rebecca a jaunty, slightly condescending wave, which Mary Martha echoed. Watching them drive off together, side by side, Rebecca had to admit to herself that the two were unmistakably father and daughter. Mary Martha had Rory's eyes, his coloring, and his grin; she had his nose and something of his bandit leprechaun's twinkle. But that was something Rebecca usually tried not to notice too much, because really, if you dwelled on it, it could break your heart.

The prospect of a free afternoon was almost daunting. She'd brought her current project home from the office on Friday, intending to dutifully ruin her weekend with it, but in the unaccustomed silence that settled over the house after Mary Martha's departure, Rebecca could not bring herself to plunge right into the work. Maybe it was seeing Rory, still flaunting his freedom from the trappings of responsibility; she knew how appalled he would be by her spending a Saturday afternoon yoked to her computer, in the service of a paycheck. In a way, she even appreciated his sturdy sense of spontaneity. Say what you might about her ex-husband, he had always given her the courage to play. She wondered sometimes now whether she had lost that courage without him.

At the far side of the kitchen—beyond the counter she kept meaning to clear off, the one cluttered with a broken toaster, a 1992 Makaha Surfing Festival Souvenir Cutting Board that Rory had given her, which could not be used because the paint flaked off, and a misshapen Play-Doh pot full of wooden spoons, made by Mary Martha at the age of three—the door to the garage was ajar. Mary Martha was learning to take out the trash, but she had not yet mastered doorknobs and locks. Rebecca moved to close the door, then on a second thought opened it and descended the stairs into the garage. Sometimes Mary Martha put the garbage in the wrong can too. Michael Christopher did not look to be a man who would generate much trash, but Rebecca liked to keep things as separate as she could.

In the dim light, the garage was crowded with debris, useless utensils and objects of dubious sentimental value, broken bicycles and broken rakes, the paddles to a lost canoe, and boxes whose contents had long since passed into obscurity. One of Rory's old surfboards lay askew against the near wall, mottled with dings he had never bothered to repair. The square space that Rebecca had cleared in the back corner for Michael Christopher to use for storage was the only empty spot in the whole garage. The previous tenant had filled that space almost to the ceiling with amplifiers, bongo drums, and boxes of old LPs, but Christopher had put nothing there and the austere expanse of bare concrete seemed vaguely like a reproach.

Mary Martha had managed to drop the garbage into the right can but had failed to replace the lid. Rebecca secured the plastic top and started toward the stairs but paused near the middle of the garage, where an old easel with a sheet thrown over it jutted from the jumble of shadows. In the poor light it looked vaguely like a tombstone.

The dream had been that they would live off their art: she would paint her Turneresque seascapes and Caspar David Friedrich skies and sell them to tourists, while Rory surfed professionally; they would wander the earth together, skipping lightly along the border between the ocean and the sand, stopping at the occasional flea market or boardwalk show to unload a canvas or two and hitting all the big surfing events. The plan had even worked for a while. She'd acquired a glib knack for sunsets and sailboats, and her work had sold well, while Rory in his prime could count on enough prize money to keep them in beer and sandwiches and gasoline. But in the end, the hustling had worn them down. As Rebecca's work had grown subtler and more structural, less Turner and more Cézanne, she'd found herself resisting and finally abandoning those Jonathan Livingston seagulls scything against an azure sky and the neat white sails beneath the Golden Gate, which the tourists loved so much; while Rory in the long run had had little patience for the discipline of competition. And so there had been restaurant work, and janitorial work, and some dealing on

Rory's part. There had been brushes with landlords and the law. By the time Rebecca had gotten pregnant with Mary Martha, the dream of living free, brave artists' lives had been muddied by the simpler scramble for survival, and with her daughter's birth the easel had been relegated permanently to the garage.

The string to the overhead bulb had frayed away years before. Rebecca dragged a three-legged chair beneath the light, clambered onto it, and reached precariously to click the light on. Safely back on the ground, she slipped the sheet off the easel, exposing the work in progress there. In the watery sixty-watt light, a sea of dream-pure aquamarine threw a perfect wave against a forested shore. Beyond the breakers, a figure showed—not quite a surfer, not quite a merman—a figure lost in the glare at the edge of myth. On the shore, a woman dwarfed by the sea and trees and sky walked alone.

More canvases were stacked nearby and still more strewn haphazardly through the garage's disorder like the half-burned tinder of a fire kicked apart in breaking camp: paintings barely begun or nearly finished, paintings botched and abandoned or painted over, with the occasional near success thrown in to keep deluded hope alive. All cold and gray with time now, the dead ash of her once-bright art.

Rebecca found the sunlight in the painting on the easel holding her eye, even in the bad light; she'd caught something there, a knifing fire, slicing the sky and sea. She was half tempted to dig her palette and oils out of the detritus and see what she could make of that brilliant hint. But that way lay only frustration, she knew. She didn't have time to paint the bathroom these days, much less finesse some ephemeral effect she'd glimpsed on water years ago. She threw the sheet back over the canvas and turned toward the stairs.

In the end, as she had known she would, she spent the afternoon on the computer, trying to make a lightbulb sing and dance. The graphics company she worked for had started landing corporate accounts in recent years, including this PR bit for PG&E. Relatively huge amounts of money were at stake, and suddenly deadlines mattered. There was even talk at work of "changing the dress code." There had never been a dress code before. For years, the company's founder, Jeff Burgess, had prided himself on running a hip little operation staffed by artists who did impeccable idealistic things like pro bono work for the women's shelter and witty homages to the Grateful Dead. Utopian Images had been aiming for a world of beauty and a three-day workweek. But Jeff had two kids and a house on Potrero Hill now, and everybody was working weekends.

The lightbulb was supposed to be some kind of animated hybrid of Woody Guthrie and Fred Astaire, "but hip," according to the brief Rebecca had been given by Jeff. Some genius at PG&E was shooting for the moon. Utopian Images drew a particular sort of corporate type, people who no longer took LSD but wanted to remember that they had. Apparently a lightbulb singing "This Land Is Your Land" and gliding from the redwood forest to the Gulf Stream waters in a tuxedo at the behest of a monopoly kept the flame of vision burning.

The problem now was technical. The new animation program they were using was the latest thing, and Rebecca hadn't figured it out yet. She struggled with it into the evening, adrift in that special, almost psychotic frustration that came with computers. She couldn't figure out how to turn off the sound either, and the chipmunk-voiced version of "This Land Is Your Land" played every time she tried to run an image sequence. She tried calling Jeff, to beg for some kind of tech support, but he wasn't home or wasn't answering. No doubt he was out somewhere enjoying his life.

At last she gave up, saved everything, including the spiteful little sequence of the lightbulb guy tumbling off a Humpty-Dumpty–like wall, and took a long bath to try to get back in her body. The sun was just going down when she got out of the tub. Rebecca put on some old sweatpants and a thermal underwear shirt, feeling the luxuriousness of sloppy comfort. She poured herself a glass of red wine, took her cigarettes out to the back porch, and sat down on the top step. She had taken only one smoke break all afternoon, smoking two cigarettes then, so she figured she had three to burn. She lit the first and breathed in, still trying to slow down, still trying to get that chipmunk song out of her head.

The sun across the rooftops was half a hand above the Pacific, bright and brisk in a colorless sky. There wasn't a scrap of fog or a cloud to be seen; it had been one of those rare August days when San Francisco seemed to have a summer.

Below her and to her right, the door from the garage opened tentatively, and Michael Christopher stuck his head out. Even in the shadow, his stoop was distinctive, the shoulders rounded as if against rain, the curve of his skull still barely blurred with his new secular hair. He was wearing something that looked like prison garb or a clown suit. Rebecca realized that it was a McDonald's uniform. So Mary Martha had gotten it right after all. She hardly knew whether to be amused or sympathetic.

"I couldn't help but smell the smoke," Christopher said apologetically.

"Oh, I'm sorry! Is it disturbing you?"

He hesitated, apparently diffident, and Rebecca felt a stir of panic at the thought of losing her back porch reveries. But

Christopher said, "Actually, I was hoping you had one to spare."

Rebecca laughed in relief. It was reassuring somehow to know that he had a vice compelling enough to overcome his moroseness. Christopher took her laughter for assent and started up the stairs. She picked up her whole operation, seashell, cigarettes, lighter, and wine, and met him halfway, instinctively protecting her haven at the top of the stairs. They settled on the fourth step from the bottom. She offered him the pack, banging one cigarette expertly into prominence, and Christopher slipped the Marlboro free and lit it. In the lighter's flare she noticed again how young he looked without his beard. Or maybe it was just the McDonald's uniform that made him seem like a teenager now.

"I wouldn't have thought a monk would smoke," Rebecca ventured.

"You'd be amazed. Some of the old-timers were like chimneys. The younger ones, not so much."

Her own cigarette was down to the filter. Rebecca stubbed it into the abalone shell and took another. Christopher reached for the lighter, gallantly enough, and she bent over the flame.

"I wanted to thank you for taking a shot at the yard," she said. "And for putting up with Mary Martha all morning."

"Hardly 'putting up with.' She's wonderful."

"Don't be afraid to draw your lines with her. She needs that."

"Don't we all," he murmured. She glanced at him dubiously, not quite sure what he meant. Christopher noticed and smiled. "Having just spent almost twenty years so very much inside the lines myself, is all I was getting at. I've been feeling my linelessness, a bit."

"God, twenty years. I've never done anything in my life for twenty years."

"I was no marvel of stability. Sometimes it seems to me that all I really did was keep my costume on and attend the events. But it does set up a certain tension."

"And now you've got a different costume."

He smiled ruefully. She had been speaking metaphorically; she hadn't meant the McDonald's uniform, but there was no way around it once the words were out of her mouth. Rebecca laughed. "Oops. Sorry."

"It's okay. I was lucky to find work at all. There's a big hole in my résumé."

She met his eyes briefly. In the twilight, he was, ever so slightly, amused by his own plight. She found herself liking him better for it: this forty-something man reduced to flipping hamburgers for minimum wage, keeping his sense of humor. There was a kind of nobility in it.

"Why *did* you leave?" she asked.

Christopher shrugged and attended to his cigarette. "It's a long story."

"Yes, so you said."

A silence followed. Christopher smoked his cigarette down to the filter and lit another off the butt. Rebecca sat quietly, feeling helpless as the pause grew awkward, and then painful.

"You said you had a fight with your abbot," she offered at last, tossing it into the silence like a life ring.

"My abbot was a jerk," Christopher conceded. "But that had nothing to do with it, ultimately."

The blanket denial rang a little false, the first such note she'd heard from him. But who was she to judge? She'd built her life on issues half resolved at best. Rebecca hesitated, then offered, "I suppose it's a little like a marriage breaking up."

"I suppose it is," he said glumly. "Apparently, I've got irrec-oncilable differences with God."

She thought that this might be a joke but didn't dare smile. They sat in silence again for a moment.

"After I broke up with Rory I couldn't stop hating either him or myself, for years," Rebecca said at last. "Like someone has to fail, for love to fail. Even now . . ." She shook her head. "Jesus, deep waters. Don't get me started. I see your point. I promise, I won't ask again."

"No, I—I like it, that you asked."

He meant it, perhaps too intensely. It seemed dangerously intimate. Certainly it was more than she had bargained for, making small talk with the new tenant. Rebecca realized that Christopher reminded her of a boy she had known in high school, Fulmar Donaldson. Fulmar had been a gloomy, taci-turn presence at the back of her English class during her ju-nior year. He was a skittish, prematurely philosophical kid suffering under the burden of the ordinary, who always ate lunch alone at the top of the bleachers on the far side of the football field, immersed in *The Fountainhead* or *Franny and Zooey*. One day after class, without any previous indication of interest, he had edged up to her in the hallway and asked her to a school dance. Rebecca, startled, had accepted, out of some mix of compassion and curiosity, letting herself in for a long, strained night. Fulmar danced like someone surprised by his own body. His conversation had been intermittent at best, veering from an overheated silence to Kafka, whom he appar-ently felt to be relevant to the scene in the gym. During the slow dance, to Cat Stevens's "Wild World," Rebecca had felt him trembling. It was like holding a wounded animal. The col-ored lights flashed on the gym walls, the music blared, the other couples danced around them in varying degrees of happiness and self-consciousness, and Fulmar simply floundered, beyond self-consciousness, nearly paralyzed. But he kept trying, nobly, to be her date, according to his vague understanding of the role. It had been a kind of heroism on his part, Rebecca had realized, to ask her to the dance at all: a sweet futility, a kamikaze charge into a realm in which he was not really fit to function, tilting at some windmill hope of relationship.

Finally, to end his suffering, she had taken matters into her own hands. She bought them two Cokes from the machine in the gym lobby and led him outside, around the dark track and up the steps of the dark bleachers to the top row. Beneath the stars, away from the music and the crowd, on his home turf, as it were, Fulmar had calmed down. They talked about movies and books and integrity. Fulmar had been very big on integrity. Clearly, he felt his own to be embattled. He thought like he danced, flailing rather more than was necessary and not accomplishing much. But he was genuine, and passionate. He had also been big on truth.

He had driven her home in his father's Pontiac and walked her to the front door. Before the pall of expectations could stymie him again, Rebecca had taken his face in her two hands and kissed him. Fulmar had been startled, but not unhappily so. She could still remember the way he had become simple for a moment, the way his lips had softened. Any kiss was an adventure, at that point in her life, and Rebecca's own heart had been pounding in her chest. She lay awake half the night, wondering what it meant. It was going to be hard to explain to her friends what she saw in Fulmar Donaldson. It would be a kind of martyrdom. But on Monday at school, Fulmar wouldn't meet her eyes. She had known, even then, that he was just afraid. But knowing that changed nothing. He had gone back inside the cloud of himself. And she had found that she was relieved.

Christopher seemed to sense her misgiving and instantly drew back. They sat for a moment in silence, their faces turned to the last glow of the vanished sun. At the base of the stairs, the ragged patch of dirt that Christopher had reclaimed that morning from the weeds was deep in shadow. It still looked oddly like damage, Rebecca thought. It looked, somehow, like a mistake.

She started to reach for her wine, then stopped herself, feeling that it would be rude to drink in front of him without offering him a glass, but not wanting to offer him a glass, not wanting to go any deeper, not wanting the responsibility of that.

Christopher, abruptly, stubbed his half-smoked cigarette out and stood up.

"I should go," he said, seeming genuinely pained, and fled before she could object. Rebecca watched him disappear through the garage door and thought that perhaps she had gotten spoiled, dating men like Bob, who couldn't take a hint. There was something very appealing in Christopher's hair-trigger sensitivity to thoughts she hadn't even voiced. But she felt no urge to run after him and apologize for what was after all a relatively subliminal rudeness. All she'd done, really, was draw a little line.

The fog came in overnight. Rebecca spent the morning in bed with the Sunday paper and a mug of coffee, warm and contented, savoring the contrast with the cool gloom outside. She let the answering machine handle two calls from Bob and three hang-ups, probably also Bob. He sounded peevish, perhaps justifiably so. But she had no desire to talk to him. The marriage proposal had hardened something in her, Rebecca realized. She had scared herself, letting it go that far with Bob. What she really needed, clearly, was a deeper self-sufficiency. Not picking up the phone for his plaintive ramblings seemed more cruel than self-sufficient, but it was a start.

She had a late breakfast and got to work on the computer, feeling noble and committed to a calm professionalism when she turned it on but squandering the long morning's measure of serenity almost instantly. The program was as balky, convoluted, and maddening as ever, and the job was idiotic. When the machine crashed for the second time, taking two hours' futile labor with it, Rebecca simply turned it off and fled to the back steps, where she smoked three of the day's five cigarettes one after the other, feeling herself careening irresponsibly toward lung cancer, toward leaving Mary Martha motherless.

She lit a fourth cigarette off the butt of the third. At the bottom of the stairs, the hacked-out corner of dirt that Christopher had weeded the day before seemed naively optimistic beneath the low gray sky. He had left his trowel beside the back door, Rebecca noted, as if to have it handy to his return, but he had not been out today. Probably she had scared him off and forever discouraged whatever feeble energy for improvement he had had.

On an impulse, she descended the stairs. Avoiding the blank stare of the in-law apartment's window, she picked up the trowel and went out into the yard. She put her cigarette between her lips and knelt at the edge of the fresh dirt. Feeling a little ridiculous, she worked a weed loose and tossed it onto the pile that Christopher had left nearby. The effect on the sea of weeds was negligible. The small yard seemed vast from this perspective. Rebecca stubbed the cigarette out and attacked another weed.

She worked for almost two hours without feeling that she had made much progress, breaking two nails in the process, but she went inside to shower feeling cheerful. Perhaps she was a peasant at heart, Rebecca thought. A simple soul, craving simple labor: see weed, pull weed. There had been no sign of Christopher, but it gave her some pleasure to know that he would discover the little beachhead of cleared ground mysteriously enlarged, as if by elves. She felt absurdly proud of that few square feet of churned new dirt.

Mary Martha came home that night trailing sand from every pocket, ensconced in the combination of elation and smug reserve that she often had when Rory dropped her off. Rebecca suspected that Rory was allowing Mary Martha some slightly outrageous liberty and having her promise not to tell. It was infuriating, but there was nothing Rebecca could see to do about it.

She gave Mary Martha her bath and made her dinner, which she just picked at. Rory, invariably, won the Sunday food battle. There was no competing with microwave burritos and nachos. Afterward, they curled up in front of the TV and watched *Star Trek: Voyager.* The show seemed much longer than an hour, but Rebecca had found that if she could just endure the space adventures it was a great way to reestablish some rapport.

"Daddy has seen flying saucers," Martha Mary confided at the first commercial. "He sees them over the ocean all the time."

"How about that," Rebecca said, which probably wasn't the best way to deal with such a complex claim. But it seemed preferable to her gut response, which was that Mary Martha's father was a drug-addled flake. And Rebecca knew she was vulnerable on this ground of belief. Rory, at least, had faith in UFOs. What sort of spiritual sustenance was *she* offering her daughter? What cosmic certainties? The tepid Catholicism of her own childhood was more like a lingering headache than a source of strength. She had picked for years at the smorgasbord of Californian spirituality and come away hungry. She felt her frustrated need for ardor as a burden and her longing for depth as a kind of dull pain. Sometimes, to be sure, smoking the last cigarette of the day, looking up at the stars, she would feel for a moment that life was bearable. But that wasn't much to offer a child's soul: *Someday, sweetheart, with enough wine and nicotine, you too will be glad just to have survived another day. You may even, briefly, be content.* It wasn't enough for anyone, really. But it was what she had.

The gallant crew of the starship *Voyager* lived to fight another day. The credits rolled and the teasers came on: next week's battle would be tougher still. Rebecca put Mary Martha to bed and read to her for a while from *The House at Pooh Corner*. Her daughter settled in and listened raptly, as she always did, with no indication that further intergalactic intrigue was required, and something in Rebecca began to relax. Every other Sunday, Mary Martha came home half a stranger. Rebecca could feel the strain of having to compete with the glamorous sea and a sky full of aliens and the menu at the 7-Eleven for her daughter's trust. But there always came that moment when the real world of her intimacy with Mary Martha reasserted itself, when the warmth and the familiar closeness overcame the jangle. She didn't have to sing and dance, dazzle with special effects, or communicate with distant stars. All she had to do was keep the home fire burning and wait it out. All she had to do was love.

Her daughter's eyes closed, and her breathing turned regular and slow. Rebecca sat quietly by the bedside, in no hurry to go anywhere. No, she would not give in to that jangling world without a fight. She had something to offer too. She had the best thing.

PART II

But often, in the world's most crowded streets,
But often, in the din of strife,
There rises an unspeakable desire
After the knowledge of our buried life. . . .

MATTHEW ARNOLD, "The Buried Life"

Chapter Three

The offices of Utopian Images were located five blocks south of Market Street, on Stillman, near Bryant, in a half-converted warehouse under the freeway, on an alley that never saw sunlight. Rebecca stepped off the 45 bus on Monday morning just after 8:30, nursing a massive cup of Starbucks' coffee, clad in her usual black tights and black skirt, sneakers, and a baggy black sweater, the casual attire still allowed the artists at Utopian Images. She felt the usual Monday sense of the week ahead as a dead weight to be lifted. It embarrassed her, to be so much a creature of the usual. She had vowed, when she was young, to never hate Mondays.

"Is Jeff here yet?" she asked the company's receptionist, Moira Donnell, who was busy with a magazine and a bagel.

Moira, with her mouth full, just shook her head and kept reading *Marie Claire*. Staffing the front desk, she was the best-dressed employee in the place by far, a chestnut-haired, green-eyed young woman of twenty-five or so, almost beautiful in a determined, much-attended-to way, and seldom less than impressive. Today she wore a navy blue suit that deftly minimized a slight tendency to heft. Moira regularly gained and lost the same ten pounds, like the moon. A second bagel in the bag on the desk suggested that the current waxing phase had not yet peaked.

"Could you tell him when he does get in that I need to see him?" Rebecca said. "Like—desperately?"

Moira swallowed heroically. "Sure."

The magazine's cover promised 288 Cool Summer Looks, 4 Weeks to a Beach-Ready Body, and a Get-What-You-Want Guide to Sex, Love, and Money. Rebecca tried to recall the last time she had felt that her body was Beach-Ready or even within four hopeful weeks of being so. Like her attitude toward Mondays, it seemed like a kind of moral defeat that she still cared.

"How was your weekend?" she asked.

Moira brightened. "Super! Yours?"

"Super," Rebecca echoed dryly, and they laughed. The contrast between Moira's supposedly glamorous life and Rebecca's mundane one was a running joke between them. Not that Rebecca would have traded places for a moment. Moira had way too much suffering ahead of her, following that glossy Get-What-You-Want Guide. But there was something touching about the younger woman's faith.

Moira turned back to her breakfast. Rebecca went on, past the drooping fern and up the steps to the suite of offices. Most of them were still empty at this hour, but Bonnie Carlisle was at her console with her door ajar, and Rebecca paused to stick her head in.

"Boo," she said.

"I hate EasyDraw," Bonnie said without turning around.

Rebecca laughed. "Me too."

Bonnie spun her chair. She was a solid woman Rebecca's age, with intelligent blue eyes, sand-colored hair, and a dry, languid wit. Her face always seemed a little mournful to Rebecca, like a sad clown's; there was an air of weary wisdom about Bonnie. But she had a magnificent laugh. She was Rebecca's best friend at Utopian Images.

"I'm going to grab Jeff as soon as he comes in and demand help," Rebecca said.

"Not if I grab him first."

"It's crazy. I spent half my weekend tearing my hair out."

"Only half?"

They considered Bonnie's computer monitor glumly. After a moment, the screen saver kicked in with a series of images from Georgia O'Keeffe. Bonnie reached for her coffee mug, a giant plastic thing that said *49ers* on the side.

"Other than that, Mrs. Lincoln, how was your weekend?" she asked.

Rebecca shrugged and leaned back on the edge of the desk. "Quiet. Rory had Mary Martha. You?"

"The highlight was taking Bruiser for a walk on Ocean Beach." Bruiser was Bonnie's German shepherd—her "longtime companion," as she liked to joke. "He almost caught a seagull."

"I think those seagulls are just toying with Bruiser, frankly."

"This one seemed genuinely scared."

Rebecca smiled. This was the moment to tell Bonnie that Bob had proposed and have a big girls' laugh over the ridiculous details, but Rebecca found that she didn't want to. Bonnie had been insisting for weeks that Bob would do exactly what he had done, though she hadn't foreseen the violin. What was even more awkward was that Bonnie had made it plain that she felt that Rebecca could do worse; she had been rooting, subtly, for a compromise, for what she called realism. To treat

Bob's proposal too scornfully or casually was oddly a sort of backhanded slap at Bonnie herself.

On the other hand, it was even stranger not to tell her. Rebecca said, "Bob asked me to marry him, Friday night."

"You're *kidding.*"

"Oh, he was serious, all right."

Bonnie, seeing which way the wind was blowing, regathered herself to be supportive of the refusal. "Ah, you heartbreaker, you."

"You are entitled to *one* I-told-you-so."

"Well, I did."

"That counts."

"You weren't even tempted? Not even a little?"

"Not tempted. The whole thing was a triumph of wishful thinking."

"I still don't see what's so wrong with the guy, frankly."

"Nothing. He's beyond reproach. I'm just not in the market."

"Yeah, right."

"It's true. I just can't *date* anymore, I can't *have a relationship.* It's all so dramatic and overwrought. I'd rather stay home in my flannel pajamas and watch TV. I'd rather read a good book. I'd rather—oh, hell, I don't know. I'd rather pull weeds."

Bonnie laughed. "Of course, I forgot what a passionate gardener you are."

"I was out in the yard for several hours yesterday, I'll have you know."

"And what about sex?"

"I didn't think it would be appropriate, what with the neighbors and all."

"I mean, forever. I mean, for the rest of your life."

Rebecca shrugged. "My new tenant has been celibate for

something like twenty years, and he seems happy enough. Well, actually, he seems miserable. But it seems like such a peaceful misery."

"The monk?"

"He's working at McDonald's now, very serenely."

"Yeah, he sounds like a great role model for the transition into spinsterhood."

"The point is, Bob is all very well. Men are all very well. Rory, God bless him, was all very well. But I'd rather have friendship. I'd rather have frankness and freedom and belly laughs, and not this perpetual tiptoeing around, this constant, demeaning, junior high school concern for the state of the Relationship. It's *tiresome*, isn't it? I mean, is there a single man on the planet that you can *talk* to?"

"Well, when you put it *that* way," Bonnie laughed. "But why stack the deck?"

"I'd join a monastery myself, I swear, if it wasn't for Mary Martha. . . . And if I had a better relationship with God, I suppose."

"Yeah, well, I think you're bluffing."

"Aren't you happy, with Bruiser?"

"I love Bruiser dearly, Becca. I have a great life, and I'm very grateful. But let's not fool ourselves. I'm an aging single woman with a dog, making the best of things."

"And I'm an aging single mom."

"Turning down marriage proposals left and right."

"Just left, so far." They laughed. "So you think I blew it, huh? I should have grabbed Prince Charming-Enough?"

"Oh, jeez, Rebecca. Nobody's holding out for the fairy tale thing anymore. Except maybe you."

Rebecca blinked, stung. "Hey, I'm as thoroughly disillusioned as the next gal."

Bonnie shrugged stolidly. They sat for a moment without speaking, watching the O'Keeffe flowers succeed one another on the computer screen, labial lilies and voluptuous lilies and lilies like a maw.

"Oh, what the hell," Bonnie said at last, relenting. "He's just a guy. There's no sense getting too worked up about it."

"Exactly," Rebecca said, relieved.

"I ate an entire box of See's chocolates this weekend. One after the other, like a machine."

"I exceeded my cigarette limit both days. And I didn't do the laundry."

Bonnie nudged her mouse, and the screen saver dissolved into EasyDraw. "And now it's Monday," she said. "Can you believe this shit?"

Jeff Burgess came in just after ten o'clock, bristling and peremptory. He was spending a lot more time lately wining and dining corporate clients, and he tended to make up for being around the office less by acting more urgent while he was there. Rebecca could remember a time when marijuana, poverty, and an overlay of sixties' idealism had made Jeff seem like a very mellow man, but as his responsibilities had accumulated over the years, his latent perfectionism had emerged. He was constantly trying to muffle the tendency, catching himself in midflare and saying, "Well, it's no big deal, of course," but all this had really accomplished was that among the employees of Utopian Images, "no big deal" was now a joking synonym for anything of enormous importance.

Rebecca tried to flag him down on his first pass through the commons, but Jeff waved her off furiously and hurried on to some more pressing crisis. She retreated to her office and waited. Twenty minutes later he charged by again, and this time she was able to get him to stop.

"I can give you thirty seconds," Jeff said from the doorway. He looked like a kid who had been forced to dress up for a wedding, with his thinning brown hair still slopping over his collar, baggy gray pants and black leather shoes with tassels, a button-down white shirt, and a swirling yellow Jerry Garcia tie. Rebecca supposed that the tie was supposed to make some kind of statement. Cultivating his defiant little incongruities, Jeff thought he had pulled off a higher integration of hipness and capitalism, but basically he was just a corporate wannabe on the rise now, in need of a haircut and a shave. He was a nice guy who had tried to change the world and failed.

"This animation program is hopeless," Rebecca said. "I can't get it to do anything except make stick figures and play 'This Land Is Your Land.'"

"It's supposed to be the hot new thing."

"I think I might do better with the old thing."

Jeff sighed. "Let's see what you've got so far." He let go of the doorjamb, which he had been clutching as if to keep himself from flying off to other, more crucial, business, and crossed to her desk. Rebecca ran the lightbulb man sequences she had, to the maddening helium-voiced chorus.

Jeff winced. "Is that really the sound track we decided on?"

"You wanted 'incongruity.'"

"And what's that he's wearing?"

"A tuxedo." Jeff looked blank. "Fred Astaire. You and Marty Perlman at PG&E were ecstatic over the concept. Cross-generational appeal."

Jeff considered the herky-jerky animation unhappily. "I don't think you've got it yet. The lightbulb dancing—it's a lark, see? You want a very smooth feeling."

"I had it in the sketches. I just can't make the machine keep that quality."

"Perlman's gonna shit when he sees this."

"Well, I don't think we should *show* him this."

"He's going to have to see something by next Monday. They still haven't fully committed to this project, you know."

Rebecca could smell Jeff's fear, sweaty and metallic through the pall of his cologne. It was the wrong cologne too: he smelled like somebody trying to smell like somebody else. She had slept with Jeff for a month and a half some five years ago, not long after her divorce, about a year before he had married one of the other artists. Everyone in the company had been sleeping with everyone else at that point. Close to Jeff now, immersed in his alien scent, feeling how pathetically near he was to panic, Rebecca tried to remember that intimacy and could come up with nothing. Not even regret. It had happened and it was gone. All she felt was a weary, almost unwilling compassion.

She said, "I think that if I work like an absolute maniac, I could probably have thirty seconds or so of good dancing for you by Monday."

"It's not that big a deal, of course," Jeff said, too relieved by half. "But thirty seconds would be great."

R ebecca turned her computer off and worked through the afternoon with a pencil and paper, as she often did when she got stuck on a project. This was so pleasurable that it felt like cheating, as if she were back in her sixth-grade social studies class, sneaking sketches into her notebook while she was supposed to be reading about tariffs.

There were actually some interesting qualities emerging in the sketches, some relative subtleties. Absurd as the concept was, Rebecca felt that she had a good sense of the lightbulb man's longing for grace in motion. It was largely unrealized, which was the character's comedy and his pathos. He was shaped like a lightbulb, after all. He was a cartoon, at the mercy of bad music, in the service of a corporation. And yet he longed to dance.

This had happened to her before, on projects equally silly. Once you crammed yourself inside the premise and stopped fighting it, the small joys of craft took over. On the train ride home, she found herself humming cheerfully. Mary Martha had had a good day at day care too, and the two of them walked home together hand in hand, discussing animals and objects that began with the letter P. The answering machine light was flashing when they got home, but not even another plaintive message from Bob could shake Rebecca's good mood. He had come around, he assured her. He was prepared to be her friend.

She stood by the kitchen window, listening with half her attention. The evening was balmy; the sun was still up, on a glorious summer day. She could see at once that Michael Christopher had been at work again in the backyard below. The cleared ground now covered almost a quarter of the yard in a spreading arc. It was almost too weird, this anonymous, invisible labor. The familiar tangle of weeds and dead shrubs had been a symbol to Rebecca of the mediocrity and inertia in her life for so long that she had come to take a kind of comfort in it. It was the devil she knew. She had believed it would take some heroic moral effort on her part to change the situation, some energy of will that it never seemed possible to sustain. Now the change was happening almost in spite of her. But did transformation count if you didn't do it yourself? Was this un-foreseen renewal a kind of grace, calling for a grateful acquiescence, or just another abdication on her part?

Bob ceased at last to ramble on. The upshot seemed to be that he would be anything she wanted him to be, which was just plain sad. Rebecca erased the message and put a tray of frozen fish sticks in the oven for dinner, to Mary Martha's delight. There was the usual discussion over vegetables, and a compromise amount of peas was apportioned. Afterward they settled into the love seat in the living room and watched *The Little Mermaid* for perhaps the fiftieth time. The phone rang about halfway through the movie, and Rebecca let the machine get it but ran out to the kitchen to pick it up when she heard her mother's voice.

"So, it's all set for Saturday," Phoebe said.

"What's all set?"

"The baptism. Sherilou is thrilled with the idea. I told her we could have the ceremony at the beach near my place. Dress is casual, of course, though if the spirit moves you, anything goes. I thought we could just do some kind of picnic barbecue potluck and make an afternoon of it."

"This may not be the best weekend for me. I've got a tough job with a Monday deadline."

"Oh, really, Becca. I don't think you want to let your work interfere *too* much with your spiritual life."

"This is Sherilou's spiritual life, I think."

"Still and all . . . "

Rebecca laughed. She had never quite understood what her mother meant when she said "Still and all," but it had carried a certain unanswerable weight since her childhood. "Oh, we could probably get up there for the afternoon. Mary Martha loves that beach."

"Of course she does. And I'm sure Brother What's-His-Name will enjoy it."

"What?"

"Your friend the monk. I'm sure it will do him good to get out."

"Oh, Mother, tell me you didn't."

"'Didn't'?" Phoebe said, with that superb, slightly oblivious aplomb that seemed to carry her through everything.

"Didn't base this whole thing on some wishful notion of Mr. Christopher's participation."

"Well, Sherilou was delighted, of course, at the idea." There was a pause. "You mean you haven't discussed it with him yet?"

"I certainly haven't!"

"I distinctly remember you saying you were going to talk to him about it."

"I distinctly remember telling you, 'No way.'"

"Well, this is a little awkward. But not to worry. There's still plenty of time."

"Plenty of time to do what?"

"Why, to talk to the man, of course. I'm sure that once you explain the situation to him, a single mother who has wandered beyond the confines of institutional religion, an innocent child without a sacramental structure, and so forth—"

"I have no intention of explaining the situation to him."

"It's a small thing, Rebecca. Give it a chance. He's perfectly capable of saying no."

"He certainly is. The man won't even drink coffee, Mother."

"Well, obviously, one can't twist a person's arm over something like this. Either the spirit moves, or it doesn't."

Rebecca considered this glumly, sensing that she had been flanked. "I'm afraid the whole thing sounds pretty flaky, Mom."

"Tell him, Better flaky meaning than no meaning at all," Phoebe said cheerfully.

Rebecca wasn't so sure of this, but her mother had based a sort of second career on the premise since coming to California. "I really feel like I've had enough awkward conversations with the guy already."

"Well, maybe I'll tell him myself, then."

"He's not a social person, Mom. He's some kind of recovering hermit. I think he's actually misanthropic."

"He just needs to get out more, I'm sure."

There was no talking to Phoebe once her mind was made up; they hung up soon after that, having made no further progress. Rebecca stood for a long moment in the kitchen, conscious, as she often was now, of the silence beneath her feet, the deep, almost palpable quiet in which Christopher lived. She knew that the only thing standing between her and acute embarrassment at this moment was whether Michael Christopher's new number was listed, because Phoebe was no doubt already dialing information.

Sure enough, a moment later she heard a phone ring downstairs. Steps thudded, and she heard Christopher's muted murmur through the floorboards. The ensuing conversation went on for quite a while. Rebecca was unable to make out anything in particular, but the long silences at Christopher's end seemed plain enough. Phoebe was making her usual relentless case. But several times Christopher's warm laughter surprised Rebecca. She felt absurdly grateful for her tenant's good humor. It seemed like a miracle of compassion.

At last Christopher's indulgent murmur ceased. The usual silence, deepened now by the contrast of disruption, settled below the floorboards. A moment later, Rebecca caught a whiff of cigarette smoke, drifting up from the backyard.

Rebecca smiled, unexpectedly heartened. She often lit up herself, after a phone call with Phoebe. She slipped out to the back porch. In the deep shadow below, Christopher was sitting on the step in front of the open back door to the garage, a dark shape hunched around a spot of glowing orange. He started as she came out, as if about to flee.

"I couldn't help but smell the smoke," Rebecca said, to calm him down.

Christopher relaxed a little and laughed sheepishly. "I do owe you one, I suppose."

"Well, I've come to collect." She came down the steps, conscious suddenly that she was wearing her baggiest sweatpants, that she was barefoot, her hair awry. It made for an odd relationship, having someone live beneath you. Inevitably, certain formalities were dispensed with.

Christopher held the pack out and she took a cigarette. He smoked the old-fashioned Marlboro Reds, just like the boys in junior high. She took a nervous drag and almost coughed at the harsher smoke, and that too was just like junior high. The doorway from the garage was too narrow for them to sit side by side, so they stood awkwardly for a moment, unsure what to do with themselves. Christopher's hair, just starting to be long enough to seem fuzzy, was damp from a recent shower, and he was dressed in clean, faded jeans and a T-shirt. No doubt he had just gotten off work, but Rebecca decided not to ask him how the job was going. It might seem too much like rubbing something in.

"I just had the most remarkable conversation with your mother," Christopher said.

She glanced at him appreciatively. How nice to have a man cut to the chase. "I was afraid of that. What can I say, except that I'm sorry? She means well—"

"Oh, it's all right. Really. She's an extraordinary person."

"What a kind way to put it."

"No, really. Very brave. Very . . . *loving*. Very real." Christopher bent to stub his cigarette out on the concrete, then straightened, still holding the butt, with nowhere to put it. Their eyes met briefly and they smiled at the silliness of the dilemma.

"There's an abalone shell on the steps over there that I use as an ashtray," Rebecca said.

"Thanks." He crossed the patio and dropped the butt in. She trailed him desultorily, realizing that she was praying: *Dear God, let me not be embarrassed. Let me find a graceful way through this.*

Christopher turned around. He seemed a little startled to find her so close.

"Again, all I can say is that I'm sorry. From the bottom of my heart. My mother is a force of nature. She gets an idea into her head and—"

"She made an interesting case for noninstitutional baptism. She actually cited scripture."

"She was on the debate team at Catholic U, and she has no fear and no shame. She could make an interesting case for the baptism of iguanas."

Christopher laughed. It transformed his usually saturnine face, and Rebecca found herself smiling at him.

"Well, I liked her," he said. "She reminded me a little of Abbot Hackley."

"I thought Abbot Hackley was a jerk."

Christopher blinked. But he recovered and said, "Well, he is. But he's a very well meaning jerk. You have to admire that. He always felt I should be more active in the world."

Something in the way he said "the world" irritated Rebecca. It was a note verging on disdain, rife with subliminal superiority.

She asked, a little aggressively, "Is there really an alternative?"

Christopher glanced at her, brought up short. "To what?"

"To being active in 'the world.'"

"I hope so," he said, so fervently that she felt disarmed.

They were quiet for a long moment, a gap that Rebecca recognized by now as characteristic. Conversations with Christopher had an unnerving way of running aground on invisible issues. On God stuff. It was so easy to forget he was a monk, until the talk crapped out like this. And then it was hard to remember he was anything else. In a way, he was like Rory, given to disappearing into his element: as Rory paddled out to sea when things got tough, Christopher fell into an impregnable silence.

At last she said briskly, by way of moving on, "Well, I hope Mom didn't make it *too* terribly hard to say no."

Christopher looked sheepish. "Actually, she made it impossible. I promised to show up." He laughed at her horrified look. "It's okay, I'm sure they'll give me the day off work."

"You're much too kind. I couldn't possibly let you spend your Saturday at some weird ceremony with a whacked-out old woman, her flaky friends, and her old maid daughter—"

"Hardly an old maid," Christopher demurred.

Something heartfelt in his tone unexpectedly thrilled her. Rebecca met his eyes, not quite sure what to say. She had not thought of him as a sexual being until this moment. It was a little unnerving.

"It's still too much to ask of any man's good nature," she persisted. "A long afternoon of unadulterated neopagan nonsense. I mean, let's face it, it's *the world.*"

"I was told there would be hot dogs."

Rebecca laughed, surprised by how pleased she was at such distinct male energy. A monk with a hint of a come-on and a sense of humor. It was definitely going to take some getting used to.

Just then the back door opened above them, and Mary Martha appeared in her Little Mermaid pajamas.

"The movie's over, Mom."

"Hit rewind, and I'll be up in a minute," Rebecca said.

"You shouldn't be smoking so much, it's bad for you."

Rebecca glanced at Christopher, who smiled and shrugged sympathetically. She stubbed her cigarette out.

"Hi, Mike," Mary Martha called flirtatiously.

"Hello, Mary Martha."

She flushed with pleasure, turned, and ran back inside.

"Well, I guess I'll see you Saturday, then," Rebecca said, a little resignedly, to let him know the ordeal would not be her responsibility.

"Saturday it is," Christopher agreed, his tone of almost weightless camaraderie getting it just right.

Chapter Four

Dear Brother James,

I see that my worst fears have been realized and that you have taken me on as some kind of project. I have nothing whatsoever to contribute to the sort of dialogue you suggest on "the relevance of prayer." It seems that I cannot say this plainly enough. My prayer life has run aground. I am lost, disheartened, demoralized—my "sense of God's loving and enlivening presence," as you put it, is shot to shit. This is a torment to me, but it is not a motivation to well-behaved and high-minded exchange. Perhaps you mistake me for one of those very nice people who attend your weekend retreats.

I am afraid you also misunderstood my remarks on the "irrelevance" of the monastic life. No doubt I erred, exulting in the paradox. It is true, as you say, that the world needs men who do not need the world. I set out to be one of those men myself; unfortunately, I have arrived instead at an abyss of self-contempt.

As for my "despair," which you would so love to tame . . . God knows, the beast is present. I am not good company. I am bitter, lonely, and gaining weight. As the hair grows in on a skull shaved close for all these years, I find that I am balding. There is a certain kind of cookie at the corner store that I apparently cannot resist. Perhaps I will become an alcoholic; perhaps I will buy a television set and collapse into the American dream. I read police procedural thrillers on my breaks at work as avidly as I once read Brother Lawrence on The Practice of the Presence of God, and as ever I smoke too much. My mind is a stretch of barren country and swirling dust; my heart has shriveled to the size of a dried pea. But this is all my private comedy. The emptiness of prayer is deeper than mere despair. Preparing us for a love we cannot conceive, God takes our lesser notions of love from us one by one.

Have you really never seen it, Brother James, somewhere in the grim efficiency of your industrial meditation? Have you never once seen all your goodness turn to dust? I tell you that until you do, all your prayer is worse than useless. It is gears of greed, grinding. Love is not fuel for the usual machinery.

Let us speak simply, if we can, man to man. I don't give a damn for your well-meaning efforts to prop my faith. I trust this failure that God has brought upon me more deeply than any comforting truth you can offer. I do not know what can come of such a thorough wreckage as I seem to myself to have made of the life I meant to offer humbly to God. Clearly, I was not humble enough. We don't hear much of the danger of prayer, but it is the deepest sea and I believe there are many who are lost in it. Count me among the lost, Brother James; if your prayer has really borne such fruits of mercy as you are willing to proclaim, for God's sake, spare me the pain of further admonitions.

Yours in Christ (as you insist),
  Michael Christopher

Saturday dawned unpromisingly, a low sky yielding grudging light. Rebecca woke early and lay in bed with the quilt pulled up to her chin, rooting like a child for the fog to go away. She was surprised by her own anticipation of the afternoon on the beach. It wasn't like her to be so eager. She realized that she was thinking of Michael Christopher. She was picturing the two of them on Stinson Beach. They had slipped away from the crowd with a blanket and some wine. The afternoon air was warm and quiet, and they were laughing and talking easily. There was no hurry to get anywhere in particular. They were just glad to be together. They found a perfect spot, nestled in the soft hollow of a dune, and Christopher spread the blanket with a gentle flourish. They settled on it side by side, close and comfortable, and the wine was already open, and the crystal glasses caught the sun just right and glittered like the sunlight on the sea.

"I've been so lonely," Rebecca pictured herself telling him, and in her mind Christopher didn't get edgy or weird or pompous; he didn't try to bluster through the pain and the waste or explain it all away or promise that everything would be different now. He just met her gaze with his delicious brown eyes and said, "I've been lonely too." She could tell by the intimate angle of his body that he was going to kiss her soon, but there was time for that. There was time for everything. It was going to be late afternoon forever, and everything they said and did from now on was going to be simple and gentle and true.

Rebecca caught herself and shook her head self-consciously. Such schoolgirl fantasies were unnerving; she hadn't let herself run on like this in years. Aside from the sheer adolescent ridiculousness of it, the guy was a *monk*. There was nowhere to go, with Michael Christopher; he was already Involved. With

God, albeit, and unrequitedly it seemed, but that in its way was worst of all. An ex-wife or a twenty-three-year-old lover at least had the virtue of reality, of the usual fallibilities; but there was no competing with an unconsummated relationship to the immaterial Ground of Being. God would never wake with morning breath and a fresh zit on her nose, her knee jammed into the small of Christopher's back, on the day after a stupid fight; God would never forget to restock the Cheerios or miss the red sock in the load of white laundry. The Lord did not clog the toilet or burn toast or wail while calculating her income tax. Most tellingly of all, perhaps, God had no encumbering daughter, no looming mother, and no ex-husband; God was not damaged goods, surrounded by damaged baggage. God was love, whatever the hell that meant. God made all things new.

And she was only getting older. Even assuming Christopher had room in his life for someone besides God, there was the sticking point of belief. No doubt he'd want someone who could pray with a straight face. Rebecca closed her eyes and gave it a shot but came up blank. She thought she should probably start with at least a decent Act of Contrition, addressing the backlogged sins of several decades, but all she could remember of the prayer were the lyrics to the Madonna song, in that singsong parody beat.

Oh my God, I'm heartily sorry, for having offended Thee . . .

But she wasn't sorry, certainly not sorry enough, not by a long shot. She'd done the best she could. And who was God, really, to take offense, while all those Ethiopian children He'd made were sifting the dust for grains of wheat on the evening news, with ribs pricking through their skin like accusatory fingers?

Rebecca opened her eyes resignedly and blinked in the gray, secular Saturday light. The truth was, Christopher was only coming to the party because Phoebe had twisted his arm. She didn't have to settle the nature of the universe or her relationship with Divinity this morning, positioning herself for fantasy make-out sessions on the beach. All she had to do was get through another tricky day.

She delighted Mary Martha by making pancakes for breakfast. As she cooked, Rebecca hummed "Singing in the Rain." She'd stayed up late the night before watching old Gene Kelly movies, trying to glean some moves for the lightbulb man, and she was feeling a little silver-footed herself. She even did a quick soft-shoe for Mary Martha as she brought her pancakes.

"Do it again!" Mary Martha exclaimed. Rebecca obliged, shuffling in her bathrobe and her ragged pink slippers, ending with a flourish. It was almost crazy, how fine she was feeling, how much she was looking forward to the actual outing, her failures of religion notwithstanding.

She made potato salad and ham sandwiches, filled a cooler with root beer and Diet Coke, and threw in a few Bud Lights for herself and some Sam Adams in case Michael Christopher cared about decent beer. She hesitated over her wardrobe, leaning briefly toward some hot pink short-shorts that she had bought once on a drunken tear with Bonnie and never found occasion to wear. She still had the legs for it, Rebecca thought defiantly. But clearly that was the morning's inexplicable optimism talking. She settled on some navy blue shorts that showed enough thigh to make the point. She tied a lime green bikini top behind her neck—it was the beach, after all—then pulled a red Bee-Well Day Care sweatshirt over that in case she lost her nerve and decided to keep things matronly.

She frowned over her hair but finally kept it simple with a ponytail; she toyed with creams and powders and brushes before deciding at last that no amount of makeup was going to help in bright daylight on a beach. She spritzed a little cloud of Obsession to walk through, then ducked away from it at the last second. By the time the whole considered process was over, it was almost noon and she looked like exactly what she was, an unremarkable single mom in a sweatshirt, shorts, and sneakers. A woman defeated into ordinariness. She shook her head at herself in the mirror and went to fetch Mary Martha.

Outside, the fog had begun to burn off. The sky's blue seemed particularly crisp, almost startling, as it sometimes did after deep fog: a blue like the return of health after a long illness. It was going to be a gorgeous day after all. Rebecca began to load the food and drinks into the car, keeping one eye on the door to the in-law apartment. Sure enough, Michael Christopher emerged a moment later, blinking like an animal unused to daylight, dressed in his black I-just-left-a-monastery jacket and slacks. His feet were encased in some incongruously new dress shoes, lumpen brown leather things that looked like primitive orthopedic devices and clearly didn't fit him.

Mary Martha ran to greet him, and he stooped to give her a hug, then straightened and gave Rebecca a shy grin.

"*Nice* shoes," she smiled, feeling it was best to get it out in the open right away.

Christopher grimaced, acknowledging the footwear's grotesqueness. "They're a gift. Charity, I'm afraid."

"Oh?"

"A very nice woman who used to come up to the monastery for retreats. She just heard that I'd left and is showering me with kindness."

"How nice of her," Rebecca said, appalled by a little surge of jealousy.

"I'd much rather be ignored."

Rebecca realized that she was feeling a little shy with Christopher, as if he might somehow have gotten wind of her fantasies. It was as if something significant but undiscussed had happened between the two of them since the last time she had seen him, and she could feel herself a little out of sync.

"So, are you ready for this extravaganza?" she asked brightly.

"Hardly."

"That's the spirit. Into the valley of death rode the six hundred."

Christopher nodded unhappily.

"Where's your bathing suit?" Mary Martha demanded. "And your towel!"

"I don't think I'm going to be swimming," Christopher told her.

"You should at least bring some shorts! It's the *beach*."

"Leave him alone, Mary Martha," Rebecca said. And, to Christopher, apologetically, "Her father is a surfer, I'm afraid. She has very strict notions of proper beach culture."

"Ah, of course, her father," he echoed inconsequentially, seemingly flustered. The moment just seemed to get more awkward. "Well, maybe I *should* go get some—"

"No, no, don't let her bully you."

Still, Christopher wavered. Their eyes met, and she saw him briefly for what he was, a man desperately out of his element. His sense of normality was stunted. He was scared to death. Twenty years of ritual and renunciation had left him helpless, at the mercy of six-year-olds, unprepared to decide whether to bring a bathing suit to a beach party or not.

Rebecca touched his arm. "You'll be fine. It's not that big a deal."

He smiled gratefully. "To tell you the truth, I don't *have* a bathing suit."

Mary Martha looked appropriately shocked. Rebecca laughed and turned to finish loading the car.

They set out a few minutes later, north through the park and across the Golden Gate. The bay was crowded with white sails. Mary Martha chattered happily with Christopher, forestalling any question of keeping up a conversation. He sat half turned in the passenger seat, his long legs folded at a comical angle, replying gravely to her questions and observations, attentive without condescension. Every once in a while he would glance at Rebecca and give her a what-can-you-do? shrug and a smile, as if apologizing for the neglect of grown-up talk. He still seemed miserable, a man being gracious on his way to the gallows; but each time their eyes met, Rebecca felt a little thrill. There seemed to be a promise in those glances, a nod toward some future privacy.

They turned west and then north along the coast, climbed above the sea on Mt. Tamalpais's twisting roads, through stone and meadows of late-summer dun, and finally wound down the back side of the mountain, into the cluster of shops, shanties, and art galleries of Stinson Beach. Phoebe lived just north of town, a left turn onto a gravel road through some stunted pines and cypress, past a No Solicitors sign full of shotgun holes and several shacks in dubious repair. Phoebe's place at the end of the road was the class of the cul-de-sac, a neat cottage of weather-grayed redwood with cedar shingles, on a rise with nothing but ocean beyond it. The driveway and sandy front yard were already crowded with cars. Rebecca noted Bob Schofield's silver Lexus stand-ing out amid the VW vans and third-owner Toyotas like an Armani suit in a cowboy bar. He had phoned her at work on Friday afternoon to ask her out, "on a purely platonic basis," and she had been forced to concede that Phoebe was throw-ing a party, to which he had promptly invited himself. As soon as he had hung up, Rebecca had rushed off to beg Bonnie Carlisle to come to the party too, for moral support, but she didn't see Bonnie's sleek white Prizm anywhere now.

Rebecca's own battered Honda fit in nicely. She parked as far away from Bob's car as she could.

"Why are we doing this, again?" Christopher asked as she turned the engine off.

Rebecca laughed. "As far as I can tell, because my mother reminds you of your abbot."

"That's a pretty stupid reason, isn't it?"

"I'm pretty sure I told you that at the time."

Christopher sighed, conceding the point. They sat in the car for a long moment, with neither willing to make the first move, but at last Rebecca opened her door. It was strangely invigorating, she noted, to be arriving at a party with someone who wanted to be there even less than she did. She usually nailed down the grudging end of the social spectrum. She felt almost motherly toward Christopher in his dismay, as if she were shepherding a skittish adolescent.

Christopher unfolded his legs reluctantly and picked the cooler out of the trunk. Mary Martha promptly insisted on carrying the picnic basket, and she approached the house at Christopher's side, staggering self-consciously beneath her burden.

The front door was open; Bob Marley was wailing on Phoebe's expensive sound system. The living room was packed with people drinking wine out of Phoebe's finest stemware and eating perfect canapés off silver trays. Beyond the similar crowd on the back patio, a jazz quartet was setting up on the beach. Even for a beach party baptism, Rebecca thought, her mother's effortless sense of style prevailed.

Christopher paused near the fireplace. Rebecca noted with alarm that he was gazing up at the painting over the mantel, a sprawling vista of Point Reyes as seen from Mt. Vision. She'd painted it not long after she had first come to California, and she'd made the mistake of giving it to Phoebe, who now insisted on telling everyone who admired it that it was her daughter's work.

"Are you 'RM'?" Christopher asked, as she had known, somehow, he would.

Rebecca nodded grudgingly. It wasn't that she thought the painting was so bad. Her acrylic palette of those days seemed a little loud to her now, but she loved the green scimitar of the primeval peninsula, the incongruous softness of the land slicing into a yielding sea of silvery steel. She liked the sky's mirroring silver-blue and the hint at an echo of the hills in whispers of lavender cloud.

Christopher considered the painting quietly, then looked at her again. She felt his glance as a sudden heat in her belly, an almost palpable weight of new interest, visceral and shockingly intimate, as if he had slipped his hand inside her sweatshirt.

"You didn't tell me you painted," he said reproachfully.

Rebecca laughed, trying to minimize the disconcerting quality of the moment.

"I don't," she said; and, as he moved to object, she added hurriedly, "It's complicated. Now come on, let's go find my mother."

Christopher hesitated, clearly inclined to pursue the matter, but at last he shrugged in surrender and allowed her to lead him toward the kitchen.

Phoebe was at the wooden block table in the center of the room, with the sleeves of her sumptuous, pumpkin-colored silk blouse rolled up, skewering chunks of meat and vegetables for shish kebab and talking about Paris with a painter from Argentina.

"Rebecca!" she called. "Darling! So glad you made it! And Mary Martha, look at you, you beautiful little beetle, lugging that tremendous load!"

Mary Martha flushed with pleasure and allowed herself to be relieved of the basket and thoroughly kissed. Phoebe straightened and smiled at Christopher.

"And this must be our wayward monk. Should we call you Father Christopher? Oh, dear, that sounds a little Christmassy, doesn't it? Or is it 'Brother'?"

"*Mother*—" Rebecca began menacingly, but Christopher just smiled.

"You can call me Mike."

"Mike, it is. You can just put the cooler by the back door there, Mike. The ceremony should be starting in half an hour or so. It's a little complicated, but stay close and I'll give you the high sign when you're on. Think of it as a jam session of sorts, and you're the bass riff. I hope you've got your mojo working."

"Mother!"

"Don't fret, sweetie, it's just shoptalk."

"We used to do the same thing before mass," Christopher agreed, with a perfectly straight face. He liked her mother, Rebecca noted; he had already relaxed perceptibly. For some reason, Rebecca found this annoying. Perversely, she had liked him better awkward.

"Now come along, you must meet the guest of honor," Phoebe said. "Where has she gotten to? Ah, there she is. Sherilou! *Sherilooou!*"

Phoebe seized Christopher's arm and frankly hauled him along. Rebecca trailed in their wake, a little apprehensively. The star of the show was sitting on the stairs to the loft, receiving admirers with her baby on her knees. Sherilou wore a shapeless blue frock of unclear intent, part postnatal *schmata* and part Virgin Mary in Marin. She was a blowzy woman in her midthirties, with hair like a whisk broom, teeth in need of attention, and the air, somehow, of having just been wronged. The baby girl, her features a softened echo of Sherilou's blunt face, was swaddled in a cherubically white gown with a white lace collar.

"Sherilou, darling, our baptist has arrived!" Phoebe trilled, in that way only she could carry off.

Sherilou eyed Christopher dubiously. "So you're the priest?"

"Such as I am," he allowed, to Rebecca's surprise. She had gotten used to him wasting no opportunity to disavow his former status. But apparently this was not about his former status. There was a firmness in him that she had not seen before, a subtle dignity.

"I hope you're not going to get into a bunch of gloom and guilt and hellfire," Sherilou told Christopher. "I don't want this to turn into some kind of patriarchal head trip."

Christopher shrugged. "I thought I'd just wait and see how the spirit moves."

Sherilou examined this suspiciously, like a squirrel with an unfamiliar nut.

"I'm sure it will move just fine, Sherilou," Phoebe said hurriedly. "I had to practically break the poor man's arm to get him here, now don't scare him off."

"I see the water as a feminine element," Sherilou insisted.

No one seemed inclined to dispute this. As the silence grew awkward, Christopher bent closer to the baby, who promptly seized his finger. The two of them smiled at each other.

"She's gorgeous," Christopher said. "What's her name?"

"Hope," Sherilou conceded.

"Hope. How perfect." He would have straightened, but the little girl continued to clutch his finger and he stayed hunched over to accommodate her.

"The sweet sister of Faith and Charity," Phoebe chimed in, in her helpful, ecumenical way.

Sherilou smiled, pleased and proud and shy in spite of herself, and stroked the baby's soft, drab hair.

"The last thing out of Pandora's box," she said.

Phoebe dragged Christopher away not long afterward to continue briefing him on the ceremony. Rebecca looked around for Mary Martha and finally spotted her in the backyard beside Phoebe's exquisite little fish pond, feeding Cheetos to the carp. Her daughter seemed contented enough, as did the fish. Rebecca helped herself to a beer from an iced tubfull on the back porch and went to the railing. On the beach below, the jazz band had swung into action, and a number of barbecue grills had been fired up. People were milling around several picnic tables laden with hamburger buns and baked beans and fruit salads, pickles and condiments and three kinds of quiche, assembling meals on paper plates. Beyond all the activity, the ocean shone in the afternoon sun.

As she stood there contemplating the Pacific, Rebecca could see Bob Schofield making his way up from the beach like the posse in *Butch Cassidy and the Sundance Kid,* a puff of determined dust on the horizon, approaching relentlessly. She considered making a run for it, back into the house, then decided that now was as good a time as any to deal with him. Bob was inevitable, in his small way.

"Rebecca!" he exclaimed when he arrived at her side, winded and sweating.

"Hi, Bob."

"What a party, huh? Your mother is a wizard."

"She is that," Rebecca agreed.

"Can I get you a beer?"

She held her bottle up.

"Ah, of course." He moved to the cooler for a beer of his own, shuffling self-consciously in his ultrabaggy khaki shorts and untied Nikes. With his Tommy Hilfiger T-shirt, his swoosh cap turned backward, and his aviator shades, he was an advertiser's dream, a forty-year-old man trying to look eighteen on the basis of television commercials. He was even carrying a Frisbee, which may have been how he had tried to look like a teenager when he *was* eighteen.

"So—" Bob said broadly, giving her a smile as he opened his beer and raised the bottle in an informal toast.

His tone had a bit too much of *Alone at last, darling,* but there was no way to leave that beer of his just hanging in the air. Rebecca tapped the Heineken with her own Bud Light, with what she hoped was brisk cordiality. Out of the corner of her eye, she had spotted Michael Christopher coming their way, and it was her sense that the timing could not have been worse.

Sure enough, Christopher seemed flustered as he drew near. He hesitated a few steps away, obviously inclined to leave her to her intimacy with Bob.

"Oh, Mike—" she said quickly. It was the first time she had called him by name, and it felt strange and false, even presumptuous. "I don't think you've met my friend Bob Schofield. Bob, this is Michael Christopher."

Bob extended his hand in a hearty male manner, keeping his body aligned with Rebecca's, casually insisting on the two of them as a unit. "Mike. Nice to meet you."

Christopher nodded formally and allowed his hand to be pumped. He had the air of a man who had walked into the women's bathroom by mistake and wanted only to get out.

"Mike has just moved into the in-law apartment downstairs," Rebecca said, dismayed by how feeble the relationship sounded, when you put it like that. She was edging to her left, trying to get out of Bob's territorial aura.

"Ah, well!" Bob beamed. Shadowing her deftly, he had managed to corner her against the railing. "Congratulations."

"Thank you," Christopher said, for lack of anything else to say.

It was all so wrong. Rebecca considered just pouring her beer on Bob's head, but Christopher would probably take that as a lover's spat and dash off to give them a chance to reconcile. It was a sitcom, and she was trapped.

A conch sounded, sputteringly at first and then with more confidence. The tribe was gathering for the ceremony. As people began to stream down to the beach, Christopher said with obvious relief, "I'd better get to my station."

"Of course," Rebecca said, but he was already hobbling away in his ludicrous shoes.

"Nice guy," Bob said, meaning that he had perceived no threat. "But where did he get that *jacket?*"

"I think it's sort of cute," Rebecca said.

The baptismal crowd had assembled beside a broad, shallow stream that slipped out of the mountains and ran across the beach just north of Phoebe's cottage. As Rebecca and Bob arrived, everyone was joining hands at Phoebe's direction to form a large circle. Rebecca found Mary Martha and took her hand. There was no way to avoid Bob taking his place on her right. Across the circle, on the shore of the stream, Christopher stood flanked by Sherilou and Phoebe, looking somber and absorbed. His habitual hunch looked odd out of doors, as if the sky itself might be a little low.

When everyone had settled, a red-haired woman in a sleeveless black tunic invoked the spirits of the four directions and led them all in a chant. Then there was some kind of weaving dance that somehow wound everyone past everyone else, through the center of the circle and out again. At some point during the dance Sherilou's baby began to cry, but there was no stopping the giant snake once it was in motion, and the dance went on and on, with everyone chanting something about the goddess of the summer and the baby wailing herself hoarse.

Rebecca glanced down at the unhappy baby as she wound past Sherilou for the third time. Hope's face was bright red from screaming, and her cheek was smeared with two colors of lipstick from misguided kisses delivered along the way. But there was no relief in sight.

At last the circle straightened itself out again along the bank of the stream. Hope screamed on, to everyone's dismay. The mistress of the ceremony said something uplifting about love and joy and community, then nodded to Sherilou, who said something about the water being a feminine element. Then Sherilou turned and handed the baby to Christopher. And the baby stopped crying.

In the sudden, stunning silence, gooseflesh rose on Rebecca's arms. It was a miracle, she realized. This was what miracles felt like when they happened. She had suspected all along that it would take a miracle to pull this baptism off.

"As it is written in the book of Isaiah the prophet—" Christopher declared in a strong, simple tone. He had straightened, owning his full height for once with an actor's instinct. "The voice of one crying in the wilderness, *Prepare ye the way of the Lord, make straight in the desert a highway for our God.*"

"Amen," somebody said. A murmur of assent rippled through the crowd. Something had happened, and they all felt it. Some magic had kicked in.

"*Every valley shall be filled, and every mountain and hill shall be brought low. The crooked shall be made straight, and the rough ways made smooth; and all flesh shall see the salvation of God.*"

A mild breeze stirred the cypresses; Rebecca was conscious suddenly of the languid crush of the waves. A gull cruised overhead, brilliant white against the blue sky. Everything seemed to be moving in slow motion, in a deep, perfect hush.

Christopher eyed them all for a moment, then turned to the stream with the child in his arms and waded briskly in, which seemed to take everyone off guard. Phoebe, as the godmother, hesitated for a moment, thinking perhaps of her slacks, then followed cheerfully enough; and Sherilou promptly splashed in after her, wetting her heavy blue gown to midcalf.

As Christopher handed the baby to Phoebe, there was a general hesitation, a sense that this was not in the script; the circle wavered, then collapsed, and everyone moved to the bank of the stream and plunged in, laughing and exclaiming. Rebecca moved forward in the crush and hesitated on the bank, but Mary Martha jumped right in, squealing with delight. Beside her, Bob was vacillating, clearly concerned with his Nikes, which somehow made it easy. As he began to remove his shoes, Rebecca hopped into the water beside Mary Martha.

The hubbub gradually settled. Christopher, comfortable in the clear, cold stream, cupped a handful and poured it gently over the baby's forehead. "I baptize thee, Hope, in the name of the Father, and the Son, and the Holy Spirit."

"And the Mother!" Sherilou exclaimed.

Christopher hesitated for a beat, then echoed, agreeably enough, "And the Mother." He cupped another handful of water and let this wet the baby's cheek, taking the opportunity to rub away the lipstick there. A final rinse and dab and the lipstick was gone and the baby was beaming in Phoebe's arms. "Amen."

"Blessed be!" Sherilou declared.

"Blessed be," the crowd replied, and everyone broke into applause. Sherilou took the baby from Phoebe and led the boisterous exodus from the stream. Christopher and Phoebe clambered out last, grinning at each other like children who had gotten away with something. The band struck up a reggae version of "Forever Young," and as everyone headed for the food and drink, their shoes all squishing, the redheaded priestess hastily thanked the spirits of the four directions and dismissed them.

Amid the general hilarity, Rebecca found herself watching Christopher. Whatever spirit had seized him for the ceremony had departed; he was laughing and joking now, dumping water from his shoes like everyone else and accepting a Budweiser from Phoebe. He was stooping again, ridiculously, a six-foot-three-inch man trying to pass for five-eleven. But it was hard to shake the impression the baptism had made on her. She had never known a man who would stand up in public and say that all flesh would see the salvation of God.

In the scramble for food and drink that followed the baptismal ceremony, Rebecca tried her best to establish an independent orbit, but Bob proved unshakable. He took it upon himself to balance two plates deftly in the line for burgers; he supplied beer after beer and scuttled across hot sand at the hint of a need for sunscreen. His small talk was impeccable and unfaltering. From fifteen feet away, there seemed no happier couple on the beach. Rebecca noted glumly that Michael Christopher seemed to be taking the burlesque at face value and was scrupulously giving her space. He had removed his jacket and shoes by now, rolled up his trouser legs, and was kneeling at the water's edge with Mary Martha, absorbed in an ambitious sand castle project.

Bob had sallied forth in search of more refreshments. Rebecca realized that Phoebe had slipped up from behind and was squatting beside her chair. Following Rebecca's gaze, her mother smiled.

"He's good with her," Phoebe noted, nodding toward Christopher and Mary Martha.

"Thank God."

Phoebe laughed. "So fervent!" She sipped her wine and gave Rebecca a sly glance. "He's good with you too."

"Don't even go there, Mom."

"He's a keeper, is all I'm saying."

"Is that all you're saying?"

"Unless he goes back into the monastery, of course."

"Jesus, Mother."

Phoebe sighed in exaggerated patience. "If he'd just come out of a twenty-year marriage, I'd be wondering about his wife, Rebecca. That's all I'm saying. It's a factor."

"The man is my downstairs tenant, Mother. He's here today because *you* invited him. He's being polite. *I'm* being polite.

We're all being nauseatingly polite. And that's all there is to it. I don't care whether God grabs him back or not."

Phoebe looked amused, and Rebecca realized that she had already protested too much. There was no hiding, really, from her mother. But Phoebe shrugged obligingly and made a merciful zipping motion across her lips.

The two women sat for a moment in silence. The surf's dull surge made it impossible to hear, but Rebecca could see that Mary Martha was telling Christopher knock-knock jokes. Her daughter always messed up the punch lines, but it never seemed to affect the hilarity level.

"Knock-knock?"

"Who's there?"

"Banana."

"Banana who?"

"Banana you glad I didn't say 'orange'?"

"I should probably go down there and offer our guest some lunch," Phoebe said at last. "Get him off the old knock-knock hook, eh?"

"Give them a little while longer," Rebecca said. "Okay?"

Phoebe met her eyes. "Ah! Well, of course." She hesitated, then said, "He likes you, Becca."

"We'll see," Rebecca said carefully.

"I suppose we will," Phoebe said, seemingly content with that, and she rose and made her way toward the rest of the party.

Bonnie Carlisle showed up with her German shepherd half an hour later to find Rebecca glumly ensconced in the low beach chair Bob had provided, watching the volleyball game with two empty beer bottles and five dead cigarettes arrayed in an intricate pattern in the sand to her left, like a distress signal in Morse code. Bob had dashed off yet again in search of yet more sustenance. He appeared to believe that the afternoon was going well.

Bonnie, blithe in a floppy straw hat, huge pink plastic sunglasses, and a purple one-piece Victoria's Secret suit cut to maximize her cleavage and minimize her hips, settled into Bob's empty chair. She let Bruiser off his leash and watched with satisfaction as he bounded off in pursuit of the nearest shorebird, a savvy-looking gull that never let him get closer than fifty yards.

"You are *so* late," Rebecca told her.

"Oh? What did I miss?"

"A legitimate miracle during the baptism: the Quieting of the Child. Two miracles, I suppose, if you count all these Marin County pagans getting their feet wet."

Bonnie began smearing sunscreen onto her arms. "And Bob?"

"The Spirit seized him with the rest of us, but he stopped to take off his shoes."

"I meant, is he behaving himself?"

"He's *behaving,*" Rebecca said grimly.

"Oh, Becca, you're always so hard on the poor guy."

Bob reappeared just then, carrying two fresh beers. "Oh! Hello!"

"Hi there," Bonnie purred, giving him her best Scarlett O'Hara smile and smearing some sunscreen between her breasts.

"Bob, you remember Bonnie Carlisle," Rebecca said, noting that Bob was following the sunscreen action with interest. "You met her at my office; she's my best friend from work."

"Of course," Bob said. "Good to see you again, Bonnie."

"Did I take your chair?" Bonnie asked, stopping just short of fluttering her eyelashes.

"Not at all," he said gallantly.

"Actually, Bob, you can have this seat," Rebecca said, rising. "I was just going to check on Mary Martha."

"Oh!" he said, but she was already past him, one step, two steps, every step easier. It felt cruel, but it always felt cruel, not being in love with Bob. Rebecca didn't allow herself a glance back until she was almost at the water's edge. By then, Bob had resigned himself to the coup and given the second beer to Bonnie. Bruiser had returned, and Bonnie was making introductions. Bob looked uneasy with the German shepherd, who had discovered Bob's Frisbee and clearly wanted to play.

Christopher and Mary Martha were kneeling over the moat of their city, dredging wet sand and patting it into the wall, so absorbed in their work that they didn't sense Rebecca's approach. She stopped a few feet away, wishing she had a camera. Seeing the two of them together like this was almost too perfect; it was an inordinate pleasure, like chocolate in the morning. It was all the moments that should have been, and hadn't been. And so it hurt a little too.

Mary Martha noticed her first. "Mommy! Look at our castle!"

"It's beautiful, sweetheart."

"It's *amazing,*" Mary Martha asserted.

Rebecca laughed. The word was new for her daughter. She must have picked it up from Christopher. "It *is* amazing."

"The tide's coming in, but it hasn't been able to get over our walls!"

"Yet," Christopher added—gently enough, Rebecca noted appreciatively, tuning the six-year-old's hubris down a bit— and Mary Martha promptly echoed, "Yet."

"Well, when it does, maybe we should get you something to eat."

As if on cue, a wave broke five feet away and reached the castle in a sizzling rush, slopping over the walls and soaking Mary Martha and Christopher to the waist. As it receded, leaving the moat silted and the eroded ramparts topped with foam, Mary Martha's face puckered uncertainly; she wasn't sure whether to laugh or to cry.

"I think I have a fish in my pocket," Christopher muttered, surveying his soggy trousers sorrowfully. Mary Martha decided to take the setback well and giggled.

"I *told* you to wear shorts," she noted primly.

The three of them headed for the food tables, a little self-conscious of being a unit in motion together. Even Mary Martha seemed to feel the burden of appearances. She wasn't sure whose hand to hold and clung briefly to Christopher, then to Rebecca, like someone trying on hats in front of a mirror. She even tried holding both adults' hands at once, and for a few steps they moved as a clumsy six-legged creature, a mythical beast, an American family right out of a car commercial, before Mary Martha got antsy and ran ahead. Christopher and Rebecca exchanged a glance, acknowledging the awkwardness.

"She's not used to having so many grown-ups around," Rebecca suggested.

"Neither am I, to tell you the truth."

She laughed, touched by his note of helpless candor. She felt that she had offered him a way out, a chance to deny the situation's implied intimacy, and he had not taken it. But she didn't want to make too much of that.

Mary Martha was already applying ketchup to her hamburger when they arrived at the food tables. Christopher fell in beside her, loading up a hot dog with every condiment available and heaping potato salad and beans onto his paper plate. It was all very American. Rebecca, who had already eaten with Bob, contented herself with yet another beer.

Phoebe, holding court on a big blanket nearby, waved them over. Sherilou lounged beneath an umbrella, her gown open to the baby, breast-feeding languidly. Rebecca had looked forward to sitting next to Christopher, but Phoebe offered him the spot on her right, and Mary Martha insinuated herself instantly on his free side. Rebecca settled across the blanket, beside someone named Bart, who nodded affably.

Everyone had a good laugh over Christopher's soaked pants. The still-impressive ruins of the sand castle were pointed out by an insistent Mary Martha and duly marveled at by all the adults. Rebecca noted that her daughter had ketchup all over her face and a caffeinated cola in her hand; Mary Martha was so revved up by now from all the attention that there was no containing her, and it was just a matter of time before they had a scene. But there seemed to be no stopping the machine.

Phoebe and Christopher meanwhile chatted amiably about this and that, weaving a graceful thread of small talk: the pope's position on birth control, liberation theology, the badness of most Catholic music. Rebecca began to feel oppressed, trapped somehow by the impenetrable surface of niceness. She realized also that she was a little drunk. She'd had a beer before the ceremony and a couple more, enduring Bob; and with the beer in her hand her blood alcohol had reached near-maudlin levels. Like Mary Martha, she was close to getting out of hand.

"So what do you do?" Bart asked her. He was a beefy, pleasant man, a former market analyst turned to yoga, draped in some ill-advised lavender cotton pants and a matching smock.

"I'm a graphic artist."

"How fascinating."

Across the blanket, Mary Martha was tugging at Christopher's arm, disrupting his conversation with Phoebe, trying to get him to start a new sand castle with her.

"Mary Martha, let Mike hang out with the grown-ups for a while," Rebecca said.

"It's okay," Christopher said uselessly.

"It's *not* okay. It's rude and it's greedy, and she knows better. . . . Mary Martha, stop."

"I just want to build another sand castle!"

"I'll build a sand castle with you," Bart offered, with surprising gallantry.

"No! I want *Mike!*"

"Mary Martha, I think you need a time-out," Rebecca said.

"I *don't* need a time-out!" Mary Martha shrieked. "All I want to do is—"

Rebecca stood up and took her firmly by the hand. Mary Martha promptly started wailing in protest. Half-leading, half-dragging her daughter away from the blanket toward an unpopulated area, like a bomb defuser with live explosives, Rebecca could only be grateful for the way the sand and sea took the edge off Mary Martha's howls. She felt monstrous and public, everyone's bad mother nightmare come to life. The look of ill-concealed dismay on Christopher's face had pained her deeply. It was of course one of the main reasons she hadn't had a decent relationship with a man since leaving Rory; why she had been so pathetically pleased, at first, with Bob's unnatural forbearance. She was a package deal. She had fifty-three pounds of baggage, and sometimes her baggage screamed and threw a fit.

She steered her daughter toward a rocky prominence some hundred yards away. Mary Martha kept crying as long as she could, but without an audience her sobs began to lack conviction. By the time they had reached the rocks she had calmed down enough for Rebecca to pause and wipe the ketchup off her face. She lifted her daughter up onto a boulder and clambered up beside her. At their feet, the incoming tide hissed over surf-smoothed stones. Just beyond the breaking waves, Rebecca's eye was caught by what looked like another rock, but then the rock blinked at her.

"Look, Mary Martha, it's a seal."

Mary Martha, unwilling to relent too easily, gave a grudging glance, then gasped with pleasure. The seal peered back at them, sleek and cheeky.

At the edge of earshot to their right, the party went on. The volleyball net had been rolled up and people were dancing now, casting long, exotic shadows on the sandstone bluffs. A bonfire roared into life as the golden light started softening toward rose. Phoebe, Christopher, and company were still chatting on the blanket. The discussion seemed to have turned serious; Sherilou was gesturing earnestly with her free hand, making some fierce point, while the baby slept in her arms. Farther down the beach, Bob Schofield had surrendered to the inevitable and was playing Frisbee with Bonnie and Bruiser. As Rebecca watched, Bob flung the disc as far as he could. The dog loped after it. The Frisbee hung in the air, hauntingly, spinning in its own timeless moment. At the last possible second Bruiser leaped and snagged it. As he trotted back toward them, Bob and Bonnie exchanged a gleeful high five. Rebecca marveled. She'd never seen Bob laugh like that; but then, she'd never wanted to. It was too much of a commitment, having that much fun with someone.

Mary Martha snuffled and wiped her nose on her forearm. She seemed to have recovered from her tantrum. She waved to the seal, who barked at them obligingly.

"He said hello!" Mary Martha exclaimed. "Isn't that amazing?"

"It sure is," Rebecca said, resigning herself to life's small joys.

They started back to San Francisco as darkness fell, just as the party was starting to get its second wind. Phoebe, aglow with a successful production, did her best to persuade them to stay, but Rebecca would have none of it. The day's complications had had a purging effect; she was feeling the scorched lightness of surrender to her fate, and all she wanted to do was get her daughter home to bed, pass out herself, and wake tomorrow to the drudgery of trying to get the lightbulb man to dance. She wanted her tiny life to resume without illusion.

"You're welcome to stay," she told Christopher, as Phoebe persisted and he seemed to waver. "I'm sure it would be easy enough for you to catch a ride home to the city later."

"I'm as ready to go as you are," he assured her, in a clear appeal to their previous camaraderie in social reluctance, but she couldn't tell whether he meant it or whether he was just being polite. He had spent the day being indiscriminately kind to everyone, and now he was being kind to her. It made Rebecca feel unreal. If they had been married, she thought, they would have been on the verge of one of those air-clearing fights couples were prone to after parties. As it was, she just felt unreasonably ornery.

Mary Martha fell asleep in the backseat right away. Rebecca concentrated on driving. She had sobered by now and was glad she had. The coast highway's spectacular vistas shrank in the dark to the next fifty feet of yellow line and guardrail; the headlights splayed uselessly beyond the road's twists and turns, now blunted by the cliff face, now petering out in the black void over the sea. Christopher was silent as the car wound up and down, and Rebecca wondered briefly whether he was worried about her driving. It was the moment she had waited for all day, of course, and she didn't have a thing to say. But that was how it went. She felt silly by now to have built things up so much in her head.

"So did you enjoy the party?" she asked.

"To the point of exhaustion."

She laughed, startled and pleased. It was not a polite response.

"And you?" Christopher asked.

"Oh, I always try to enjoy myself at these things, and I always fail miserably. Then I hate myself for a while, for being so incapable of enjoying myself. Then, if I'm lucky, I resign myself to being me. Then I go home."

"Sounds like fun," he said, without a trace of sarcasm, and they both laughed. "It sounds like the religious life, actually."

"You really *did* seem like you were having fun. And you were very good at the ceremony."

Christopher sobered instantly. "Ah, well, the ceremony . . . "

"I thought it was very moving," Rebecca persisted.

He gave a cryptic grunt, his face turned to the black window. They reached a switchback, and the headlight beams groped through emptiness before swinging back to the comforting solidity of the road. She had a fleeting sense of his God out there somewhere, like the sea itself, invisible and dangerous, a vastness wrapped in darkness, just a long fall away.

At last he said, "I'm afraid it was a mistake for me to come at all."

"Oh, come on—"

"No, it's true. I was way too ready to believe that God had called me out of the desert to a new ministry—how's that for bloated ego? Suddenly I had something to *do,* something priestly. It made it easy for a moment to believe I hadn't wasted the last twenty years. As if somehow I could cash in my monastic experience for a nice new meaning, as if I'd gotten a good exchange rate, changing dollars into yen."

The afternoon was taking on unsuspected dimensions in retrospect. Rebecca drove for a moment in silence, not knowing what to say. Christopher brooded through the next three twists in the road, then sighed heavily into the window, fogging the glass in a ragged circle.

"God, maybe Hackley was right," he said.

"Your abbot?"

"He said when I left that I was running away from myself. That I didn't have the guts to stick it out."

"I don't think it's possible to run away from yourself. Monastery, in-law apartment, mansion on the hill—it's all pretty much the same, isn't it? I mean, it's basic bumper-sticker wisdom: 'Wherever you go, there you are.'" Christopher said nothing, unhappily. "Except Oakland, of course," Rebecca added, trying to get him to smile.

The joke went right past Christopher; he was too intent on his own thought-thread. He said earnestly, "The really funny thing is that Abbot Hackley would have loved this whole scene today. New sacraments for a scattered flock. Ad-libbing the gospel. He was always trying to get me to plunge into the world with my sleeves rolled up and do God's work."

"And that's a bad thing, somehow?"

He gave her a rueful glance. "For someone like Hackley, of course not. He was a dynamo, always had six balls in the air and a hula hoop spinning around his neck; he was the Lord's original busy bee. I mean, the man *thrived* on activity, he needed it. And he needed to be surrounded by it, he fed off the buzz. But for someone like me . . . "

His voice trailed off. Rebecca steered through a sharp switchback, cresting a rise and glimpsing the stars over the ocean before the headlights found the cliff face again and they started downward, angling into another fold in the hills.

"For someone like you—" she prompted.

Christopher shrugged, suddenly remote. "I just wasn't that kind of monk."

"What kind of monk *were* you?"

He drew a breath and hesitated, seemingly inclined to answer, then shook his head wearily and turned back to the window. In the backseat, Mary Martha snored softly and stirred in her sleep, then settled again. Rebecca waited, letting the silence sharpen. When she was sure that Christopher wasn't going to say anything else, she ventured, gently, "You're being too hard on yourself, Mike. It was a lovely baptism."

He snorted dismissively, without turning.

"It *was.*"

"It was theater. Feel-good stuff. And I was just a sideshow freak, the man neither here nor there."

"'All flesh shall see the salvation of God' is feel-good stuff?"

He turned from the window to face her with a sigh, as if resigning himself to painful articulation. "John the Baptist and Isaiah both had teeth in their message: *Repent, ye generation of vipers. The chaff will soon be sorted from the wheat.* A real baptism *begins* with that insistence on the need for repentance, with an acknowledgment of sin. But I didn't have the nerve to make a scene. I was too busy being Father Mike, everybody's harmless New Age priest."

"You're asking for too much. The thing had its own flaky loveliness. All anybody ever intended was to do something nice for Sherilou and the kid. Nobody really wanted more."

"I did," Christopher said. "But that was foolish. That's my *point.*"

She was reminded anew of Fulmar Donaldson, brooding in the high school bleachers after the fiasco of the dance: all that misspent intensity turned inward on the metaphysical. But she felt humble too. Christopher was not the only one who had choked most of the life out of an ordinary afternoon, longing for miracles.

They drove awhile in silence. The highway turned away from the sea and started up the switchbacked rise toward Mill Valley. She wanted to take his hand in the darkness. There was still time. She wanted to tell him that everybody was disappointed almost all the time, and not just about their failure to be prophets. But the truth was that on a road like this she needed both hands to drive and she hardly knew where to start, with all that God stuff of his.

"I suppose it's always a mistake to expect too much from a beach party," she offered at last, as they crested the ridge, hearing her mother in the facile, bright summation. Christopher grunted a sort of agreement that was worse than silence, and Rebecca wished she'd had the nerve to hold her tongue. But it seemed like a kind of fate, to miss the mark with him. They rolled down the mountain, back and forth through the black groves of eucalyptus, and soon enough there were streetlights, and houses on either side of the road, and the night seemed like a smaller thing.

PART III

I circle around God, around the primordial tower.
I've been circling for thousands of years
And I still don't know: am I a falcon,
a storm, or a great song?

RILKE, *Book of Hours*

Chapter Five

Dear Brother James,

I have to admire your truly oblivious courage, in persisting with your chipper letters. Have I not been sufficiently abusive?

You are determined to discuss the role of the monk in the modern world, the need for contemplation amid frantic secularity, the exemplary quality of a life of prayer, as we used to do so enjoyably. But you just don't get it. I'm no longer the ambitious student of the saints you knew at Our Lady of Bethany. I'm just another guy who's been busted up by life and is scrambling to cover the rent on a couple of shabby rooms. I work at McDonald's, Brother James. Four days a week I stand at the grill and cook Big Macs. My supervisor, who is twenty-two years old, seems happy enough with my work. My co-workers are all teenagers preoccupied with girls and drugs, and afraid of dying in a gang cross fire at school. They look at me as an oddity, though they are remarkably kind. I come home to an apartment behind a garage, with no furniture except a futon and a phone. I eat spaghetti almost every night. There is a yard outside my back window, where I put in the occasional pleasurable hours clearing weeds and planting flower beds. I think I have a crush on my landlady, which strikes me as simply sad.

Meanwhile, you are abuzz with your holy projects. Like Abbot Hackley himself, you want to "transfuse the world with a revitalizing monastic spirit, to offer the fruits of contemplation" like apples in a basket. But surely you are prepared to see the irony of your ambition, and our reverend abbot's. As cloistered monks, you both have let go of the world and striven to be free of its enmeshments, yet somehow you feel compelled to insist that your renunciation is cost-efficient, and that its fruits are marketable. How do you manage, keeping one eye on the meter of love and peace? Does it not grow tedious? The sweatshop of your prayer seems very small to me.

In any case, my best moments at Our Lady of Bethany came when all our revitalizing monastic activities seemed irrelevant and far away, like a hectic dream, and a perfect silence came upon me. It seems to me that all I ever really did in prayer was stay with that silence, while my grand religious career crumbled into ruins around me, while Abbot Hackley cracked the whip of good works above my head and the choir sang incessantly, proclaiming God's loud glory. It seems to me that I have never gone anywhere except deeper into that silence, which is a kind of nowhere.

Even now, once in a long while, the grace of that silence comes upon me anew, at the heart of my broken morning prayer, and everything seems all right. I sit quite still, with nothing moving in me and nothing, blessedly, wanting to move. It is a feeling so quiet that to call it joy seems a kind of distortion. It is peace. There is nothing else: no direction, no desire, no particular clarity about my place in the world. Just peace.

I don't see how I could possibly offer that peace to the world, Brother James. It is only in dying to the world that such peace comes. Nailed to the rude cross of our inevitable failings, helpless and abandoned, we see

the world slip away, in spite of our best efforts to cling to it . . . and that
peace comes. Tell that to your seminars, proclaim it from the mountain-
top: God is the nail that splits our palm to break our grip on the world.
He is an unfathomable darkness. He's not what you want to hear.

Meanwhile, I've got to get to work. We're having a big special this
week, two Quarter-pounders with cheese for $1.99. You'd be amazed
at the kind of crowd that draws.

Yours in Christ,
  Michael Christopher

For weeks after the gathering at Stinson Beach, Rebecca
didn't see Michael Christopher at all. The backyard continued to develop; beds of violets and petunias appeared,
along with a border of lavender and yellow slipperwort. The
patch along the back fence exploded into poppies, a glorious
orange sprawl. But she never saw her downstairs tenant at
work. Sometimes late at night she smelled cigarette smoke, but
she never managed to catch him outside. She lingered over her
own evening cigarettes on the back porch, hoping he would
stick his head out and say hello at least, if only to take the edge
off the awkwardness. But Christopher had snapped back into
his hole like a spooked gopher.

Rebecca blamed herself. She was sure that he had somehow
picked up on her fantasies, even in their relatively undevel-
oped form. Of course he wanted no part of secular intimacy;
he was still involved, however morbidly, with God. At best, he
was on the rebound.

She realized that she had begun to think of him as "Mike." That was disconcerting. It had been easier when he was just some down-and-out monk to her, an object of amused compassion at best, or the guy renting the in-law apartment, "Christopher," an opaque label for a relative stranger. But "Mike" was someone she could miss.

There was little time to brood, in any case. She was suddenly intensely busy at work. On the Monday following the baptism, wearing her best red suit, she had bluffed her way through the preview of the lightbulb man cartoon with the representative from PG&E. With twenty-three seconds of mediocre video in hand, Rebecca had relied on her sketches and emphasized the first-draft nature of the animation. The clinching moment, she was sure, was when Marty Perlman, the PG&E rep, looking a little uneasy as "This Land Is Your Land" blared and the lightbulb man did his herky-jerky waltz, had started patting his pockets unconsciously. Rebecca had turned the volume down at once and taken him out on the loading dock for a smoke break.

"I'm not so sure about that sound track," Perlman had confessed, when they were alone with their cigarettes. He was a small man with angelically curly blond hair, a slight stammer, and a Stanford tie. The sound track, Rebecca knew, had been his idea.

"I'm only leaving it in at this point to keep Jeff happy," she told him shamelessly.

"It seemed so much . . . I don't know, *hipper*, at the brainstorming stage."

"We may have been aiming too high. But I think we can still create an endearing character."

"I'm afraid Jeff's attached to the incongruity."

"*Fuck* the incongruity," Rebecca said.

Perlman met her glance and smiled uncertainly. She was left to wonder whether she had gone too far. But when they got back into the conference room, Perlman had said he thought they could go forward with the project, with a tweak here and a tweak there. Like maybe they could change the music.

"But I thought you liked the incongruity," Jeff had said, with a trace of his own relief.

"Fuck the incongruity," Perlman told him cheerfully. "I'm thinking 'Singing in the Rain.'"

Meanwhile, Bob Schofield and Bonnie Carlisle had started dating. Bonnie was downplaying it, but she could not hide her happiness. The new development had not been a total surprise, after the way they had romped together at Stinson Beach. Still, it had been a little awkward at first for Rebecca, who squirmed recalling her own months of snideness while she had been dating Bob, all the laments and exasperation she had dumped on Bonnie in the confidence of their chats.

That awkwardness aside, Rebecca found herself teased at moments by melancholy, glints bittersweet like autumn light. It wasn't that Bonnie's going out with him had suddenly made Bob more attractive, nothing so embarrassing as that. But the two of them getting together had somehow made the notion of a healthy compromise real. They were actually doing things by the book, straight out of Bob's library of Relationship, and it was working wonderfully. Bonnie's serene sanity in the relationship was a revelation, as was her . . . *satisfaction*. Not smugness, there was too much humility in Bonnie's attitude and too much respect. Bonnie was treating Bob as something precious; she was seeing the best in him and being clear-eyed and forgiving about the worst. It made Rebecca fear that she herself was somehow ruined, incapable of real relationship.

That she was asking too much and giving too little. In her own mind, real relationship happened in a place where Bob had never even showed up. She had waited there, hopefully enough at times, right there at the center of everything, quiet and still and perfectly willing to be met, while Bob had blundered around somewhere far away, somewhere loud and hectic. If only he had been able to *stop,* she had always thought. Or even slow down a little. But Bonnie wasn't asking him to stop. Stopping seemed to have no part in what Bonnie and Bob were doing, which was all very get-up-and-go. Maybe that was what real love was, being willing to charge toward the busy, noisy place that someone else inhabited and find what comfort there you could.

The success of the presentation to PG&E caused a brief panic among everyone involved in the project. Jeff had apparently been half resigned to losing the gig on the basis of the terrible animation alone, and his renewed faith had a slapdash quality. There were hasty conferences and meetings, flowcharts scrawled on blackboards and storyboards pinned on cork. There were urgent e-mails cc-ing everyone in sight. There was more talk of a dress code, which was greeted by a dangerous rumble from the graphics artists and the techs.

Complicating the office atmosphere was the fact that Jeff's marriage seemed to be falling apart. He had moved out of his house on Potrero Hill and was living in an apartment near Civic Center. He told Rebecca that his wife and he were "just giving it a rest," but late one Wednesday afternoon he lingered in her office with an open bottle of Glenlivet and two coffee mugs, talking about his woes suggestively enough for Rebecca to understand that he was quietly making her an offer, that he was ready for a fresh set of woes. She knew Charlotte, Jeff's wife, a gifted, perky woman from Minnesota who had come to work at Utopian Images at about the same time as Rebecca. Charlotte had been the artist Jeff had slept with after Rebecca, in the days when they all seemed to be making the rounds. Now, it seemed, he was working his way back in the other direction, reconsidering missed opportunities. Later that day, after she had let him know as gently as possible that it was all way too messy for her, Rebecca saw Jeff at Moira Donnell's station, sitting on the edge of the receptionist's desk with the same bottle of Scotch, the liquid level much diminished, swinging his leg and confiding his woes with the same air of melancholy alertness. Moira, in a thin phase, looked like she might go for it. She had missed the free-for-all atmosphere of the company's early days and so would have less of a sense of simply being the new Charlotte.

As the first deadline loomed, the job grew more demanding. Rebecca was late picking up Mary Martha from day care several days in a row. When the phone in her office rang on Friday at a quarter of six, Rebecca looked at the clock and sighed, thinking it was the poor woman at Bee-Well again.

"Rebecca Martin," she said, picking up.

"Now, Becca, don't get mad——"

Even if she hadn't recognized his voice, there was only one person in her life who started conversations that way. Her ex-husband should have known better by now. But of course, that was part of why he was her ex. "Rory, whatever this is, I haven't got time for it."

"This is serious, Bec. I'm in jail."

"What!"

"Two lousy ounces," Rory said. "And the guy came up to *me*. It's fucking entrapment, is what it is."

"What is it that you want from me, Rory?"

"They've set the bail at fifteen hundred."

"Can't Miss Green Fingernails come up with that for you?"

"I can't call her about something like this. She's . . . you know, *delicate*."

"You mean broke. And unreliable. And a little too stoned."

"What I've always loved about you, Becca, is your ability to skip the crap."

Rebecca looked at the clock. If she left this minute and everything went perfectly with the trains, she was going to be half an hour late picking up Mary Martha. But it was hard to picture facing her daughter after leaving Mary Martha's father languishing in jail. And harder still to picture explaining to Mary Martha where Rory was when he failed to show up tomorrow for his regular weekend with her.

"You're at the city jail?" she asked resignedly.

"Mere blocks away. I'd owe you big time, of course—and you know I'm good for it—"

"Oh, God, Rory, if I were keeping accounts . . . Do these people take MasterCard?"

"As long as it's within your credit limit."

"I've got to make a few phone calls, get somebody to take care of Mary Martha, close out here—"

He laughed. "Take your time. I'm not going anywhere."

That laughter stung. Rebecca could hear in its carefree note how sure of her he had been.

"No, you're not, are you?" she snapped. She slammed down the phone, reached for her address book, and began to rummage through it looking for someone who could pick up Mary Martha. She could feel the resentment halfway down her throat, a bone of helpless rage. She'd worked so hard to clean up her own act, to do right by Mary Martha, but what was the use? All it took was one phone call from Rory to drag her back into his mess. As if love were a blank check she'd signed all those years ago.

She called her regular baby-sitter, but the girl had a date. Rebecca's backup baby-sitter wasn't home, nor was her number three. Bonnie Carlisle wasn't home either. No doubt she was out with Bob somewhere, enjoying a relationship with a man for whom she would never have to post bail.

Even Phoebe was out. It was Friday night, and everyone had a life.

Rebecca stared at the phone for a moment, knowing that she was going to have to call Michael Christopher. It felt like squandering something precious. She'd been savoring her anticipation of their next conversation; the weeks of unnatural silence had been a kind of marinade, and she had looked forward to tasting the result. But to call this way, in prosaic need, just ground the subtlety into hamburger.

Still, she was out of options. He answered on the second ring. "Hello?"

"Uh, Mike?"

"Rebecca!"

She took comfort in the fact that he had recognized her voice and that he sounded genuinely pleased. She could hear music in the background, a Bach mass playing on what sounded like a boom box. The poor man lived in the last bubble of serenity in the Western hemisphere, and she was here to burst it. "Mike. I'm so sorry to be disturbing you like this—"

"No, no, I'm glad you did. I've been meaning to call *you,* in fact."

"Really? Why?"

"Well, you know. Just to thank you for the lovely outing last weekend, and so on. To say what a nice time I had."

Rebecca laughed in spite of herself. "That was two weeks ago, Mike. Almost three."

"Well, yes, but—"

"Plus, if I remember correctly, you ended up feeling like the whole thing had been a giant mistake. I had the impression that you were just glad to have survived it and that all you wanted afterward was to be left alone."

There was a silence, and she cursed her own big mouth. But Mike persisted wryly, "And yet still, I've been meaning to call you. Or at least to hang around suggestively in the backyard with a cigarette."

Clearly, he had been recovering. He was a solitary man, and his sense of social time was flawed. But it was nice to know he had been thinking of her, however ineffectually.

"Well, that just makes me feel worse to be calling you up for a huge favor," she said.

"A favor?" he repeated.

She hesitated at the sudden guarded note, decided to ignore it, and plunged on. "I'm stuck downtown with a crisis on my hands, and I'm not going to be able to pick up Mary Martha at her day care before they close the place. I've called everybody I know and—"

"Uh-huh," he murmured vaguely.

"—and honestly I wouldn't have called you if I weren't at my wit's end."

Mike was silent, for just long enough that she was about to tell him to forget it, it had been a bad idea. But in the nick of time he said, with passable sincerity, "Well, of course. Of course. I'd be glad to."

"It's only a couple of blocks away, on 38th, just past Irving," she said, ashamed to feel so relieved. "You can walk over and back in ten minutes. I'll call and tell them you're coming. And of course Mary Martha will be ecstatic. She thinks you're wonderful."

"Well, I think *she's* wonderful."

It was all so genial and love-thy-neighbor. She would much rather have had an uncomfortable conversation with him about what those two weeks of silence had meant. *That* was a relationship. This was glorified baby-sitting arrangements, and even then he'd only agreed after a truly unnerving hesitation, when she'd backed him into a corner.

But apparently she needed a baby-sitter, even a slightly unwilling one, more than she needed a relationship. "Well, *thank* you," she said. "You're a lifesaver. You're a *saint*."

Mike laughed, so easily dismissive of the extravagance that she felt reassured. "Hardly."

"I'll be home as soon as I can, but if you could cook her up a box of macaroni and cheese or something—?"

"Consider it done."

Rebecca gave him the address and thanked him again, then dialed the long-suffering woman who ran the Bee-Well Kindergarten Day Care to tell her the cavalry was on the way. The woman's reply was clipped short with a you're-a-bad-mother tone. Mary Martha was amusing herself nicely, she said, as if to underline the child's heroic adjustment to a life of appalling neglect.

Rebecca rolled with the punches and got through the call, but as soon as she hung up she began to cry. She cried for almost ten minutes, which seemed like a tremendous luxury, given all the things she had to do.

She walked the five long blocks down Bryant Street to the city jail amid the remnants of the rush hour. The Friday evening happy hour was in full swing, but the bars soon gave way to discount mattress stores, boarded-up storefronts, and cheap cell phone outlets, the edgy waste of Bryant Street between the freeway entrances, a little too far south for comfort even in full daylight. Rebecca walked briskly, keeping her eyes to herself, trying to look like a woman who had a gun in her purse. She knew she'd been foolish not to take a cab. But she'd been so mad at Rory when she set out that she'd felt bulletproof.

The shacklike shops of the bail bondsmen, hawking their services in lurid neon, announced the specialized country of the law. The street around the Hall of Justice was three-deep in police cars. Here too the weekend crush was just getting started: along with the uniformed men with guns, people in trouble came and went, with businesslike briskness. And people involved with people in trouble, Rebecca thought, people like her, people not really dressed for this—how *did* one dress for this?—all of them coming and going in the great democracy of trouble.

She entered the main doors self-consciously, passed through the metal detector, and floundered briefly in the lobby before spotting the large sign directing her. The desk where bonds were posted seemed remarkably like the returned merchandise counter at a department store. Rebecca had been hoping for a touch of dark humor, for some shared appreciation of this aberrant transaction—a wink, at least, toward the sheer weirdness of this Friday night. She felt like making sure that the man behind the counter knew that she was no longer sleeping with the person she was bailing out, that that was over, done, finito, long ago. Sure, she had loved Rory once, but what did that *mean?* There were a host of subtleties and qualifications to be conveyed.

But the clerk receiving her money seemed bored to the point of surliness, and she held her tongue. He dragged her credit card through the scanner, tapped some mundane data into his computer in a dry, pained way, and hit "Enter." She signed off on the credit card slip. The printer beside him chattered and spewed a single sheet, and he stapled the yellow second copy of the credit card slip to it.

"That's it?" she asked as he handed her the receipt. It felt like a dentist visit that had gone too easily.

"That's it. Waiting area's to your left."

"Don't you at least have to call someone and let them know that—?"

"It's computerized. . . . Next!"

Rebecca felt the flimsiness of those electronic impulses, the unlikelihood of anything so feathery tickling the machinery of justice into opening its jaws. But then, the whisper of duty and compassion that had brought her here seemed flimsier still. A hint, merely, like the residual background static of the big bang, imperceptible to normal instruments. And yet Rory had relied upon that fading buzz completely. Was that faith? The implicit trust in a genuine connection? Or was it simply cunning?

Sitting in the waiting area with half a dozen other unhappy women, clutching her receipt, Rebecca suspected the worst. She was in the grip of a compulsive response. Her life consisted of a series of compulsive responses. She was just a big kneecap waiting to be tapped by a rubber hammer.

By the time Rory appeared some forty-five minutes later, ludicrous in his baggy beach shorts, grinning his unfazed grin, clutching a plastic bag with his watch and wallet in it, she had worked herself into a furious state.

"I thought you might have decided to just leave me to rot in there," he said cheerfully.

"Believe me, if it weren't for Mary Martha—"

"You're an angel, Bec."

"I'm sure that angels do this sort of thing without wanting to kill the person they're doing it for."

Rory just laughed, which only made her angrier. The depthless innocence of his blue eyes was untouchable. She had once seen animal joy in that pure blue. Now all she could think was that his T-shirt needed washing.

"Are we done here?" she asked. "Is there anything else you have to sign?"

"No, I'm all set. I've been surprised by the lack of paperwork. There's no hard copy! I have the sense that if I could just hack into their computer and delete a file or two, I could make this whole thing disappear."

"It's just a big damned romp for you, isn't it?"

"I can't see any point in getting grim, if that's what you mean."

"No, you never could," Rebecca conceded wearily, feeling the uselessness of her spite. The institutional clock on the wall read 8:45 beneath its grate. With a little luck on the bus transfer, she could be home by ten. She headed for the exit, with Rory trailing her.

She was unwillingly conscious of his physical grace. She had cherished Rory's sense of effortless balance long after she had begun to suspect that he would never grow up. It had been like believing in God because a sunset was beautiful. A faith that cheap could not endure for long. But even now, long after she'd seen how little his grace could actually redeem, the languid poise of Rory's animal amble beside her soothed something in Rebecca.

On the sidewalk outside she turned toward Ninth, with Rory still beside her. At the bus stop, she lit a cigarette.

"You really ought to quit that," Rory said.

"Let's not talk about lifestyle right now, Rory."

He shrugged and subsided. They stood together in silence. He still wanted something, Rebecca noted, though she couldn't imagine what. She felt cleaned out.

When the 19-Polk bus appeared in the distance, she turned to him and said, "I'm not going to tell Mary Martha about this."

She had guessed right: Rory looked relieved. "Gosh, thanks, Bec—"

"For her sake, not for yours. But I don't know what I'm going to say once you're actually in jail."

"I'm not going to jail. This won't stick. They set me up."

The bus pulled up. Rebecca dropped her cigarette on the sidewalk and crushed it out.

"Whatever," she said. "Goodnight, Rory."

He touched her arm. "Thanks a million, Rebecca. I won't forget this. I owe you."

That meant something to him, she knew. She wondered how he was getting home. But Rory was never at a loss. He'd probably already called his delicate girlfriend. She'd come whisk him away and they would have passionate reunion sex. It would be beautiful, like a sunset. It would cost them nothing.

"You're welcome," Rebecca said. And she climbed onto the bus. Real love cost so much more; and if Rory had taught her nothing else, it was to cut her losses.

When she got home, the house seemed strangely dark and silent. She usually walked in to a cheerful glare and din; her teenage baby-sitters curled up on the couch with every lamp burning, and they all lived and died by the *TV Guide*. But the living room was empty and the television wasn't on.

Rebecca took an anxious step inside and noted with relief that the kitchen was lit up. Looking down the dark hallway, she could see Michael Christopher sitting at the table, absorbed in a book. She paused instinctively, not wanting to disturb him. Framed by the kitchen door, the scene had a timeless quality; it might have been a study by Vermeer, a luminous domestic moment of contemplation. Mike was dressed in jeans and a rough plaid lumberjack shirt, sea green and blue, with the sleeves rolled up; in the stark light of the single ceiling bulb, the fine golden hairs on his forearms were visible. His angular face in silhouette was poised in the tenderness of concentration. He turned a page, and the crisp ripple only made the silence more real; the way he cradled the battered paperback in his big, homely hands made her think of prayer.

Rebecca could hear their old grandfather clock, the one that only ran in spurts, ticking in the living room. She didn't want to move; certainly she didn't want to speak. The labor of producing the usual noise seemed unbearable. She just wanted this silence to go on.

A floorboard creaked beneath her feet. Mike glanced up, gently indulgent, no doubt expecting Mary Martha. She stepped into the light and smiled at him, afraid that he would think she had been spying. But he just smiled back, a simple smile of welcome. He'd been reading a Joseph Wambaugh novel, which struck her as funny. She had the odd sense, as she often did with him, that their intimacy had somehow run on ahead of them, like a dog on a beach. It was all so natural and easy.

"I didn't even hear you come in," he said.

"You seemed so peaceful I hated to disturb you. Did everything go all right here? Mary Martha was no trouble?"

"Mary Martha was fine. We had a great time. And your crisis?"

"It was a little overbilled as a crisis, I suppose. My ex-husband had gotten himself arrested."

Mike smiled wryly. "That sounds like a crisis to me."

"More of an aggravation. We've been split up for years."

"But you're still friends?"

"I don't know if 'friends' quite catches it. An ex is really like another child. Rory is, at least. I can't help but feel responsible for the failures in his upbringing, in some dark way. And bottom line, he's Mary Martha's father. I bailed him out and sent him on his merry way."

"Just like that."

She glanced at him appreciatively. "Well, that and a few hours of helpless rage seemed like enough for one night." She set her sketch case down, shrugged off her coat, and hung it on the back of a chair. "I should go check on Mary Martha. Did she get to sleep all right?"

"She made me read to her from *The House at Pooh Corner* until she dropped off."

"That's my girl."

He had risen, apparently intending to leave. Rebecca hesitated. At this point, she would usually have paid off the babysitter and sent her on her way. But she hadn't wanted Mike to be a baby-sitter in the first place, and it was impossible to imagine pulling out her wallet and handing him a ten.

"Would you be shocked if I offered you a glass of wine?" she asked.

Mike laughed. "Why in the world would I be shocked?"

It always surprised her, the way his face lit up. She realized that she forgot something crucial about him when he wasn't laughing; the natural melancholy of his features allowed a grimness to seep into her image of him. She would find herself suspecting him of secret judgments, of morbidity, self-righteousness, the bleakest extremes of dour religiosity. And then he would laugh. It was as if a light turned on and she could see him clearly.

She said sheepishly, "Well, you know, with your having been a monk for so long and all—"

"Monks are pretty much unshockable, actually. It comes with the territory. At Our Lady of Bethany, we were far from teetotalers. We had our own vineyard. We even had a drunk or two."

"Drunken monks?!"

"Oh, yes. Monks drunk as skunks. Drunk monks in deep funks."

"Now *I'm* shocked." She was flirting, she realized, which was crazy. *He* was flirting. Wasn't he? Rebecca was pretty sure he was. Not that it could go anywhere. But it would be good for a giggle with Bonnie later.

"Well, I'm going to go look in on Mary Martha," she said. "There's an open bottle of wine in the fridge, and you can grab a couple wineglasses out of the left-hand cupboard . . . Unless you would rather just go home?" she added hurriedly, in case she had misread him.

He smiled unambiguously enough. "No, no, I'd be delighted to join you."

"I hope you don't mind rosé."

"Drunk monks drink pinks," Mike said.

★ ★ ★

Mary Martha was asleep, which was a good sign. With baby-sitters she didn't like, she would often stay awake until Rebecca got home, keeping the lamp on and surrounding herself with unicorns, chanting soft conversations to herself. But tonight only the night-light burned. By its faint glow, Rebecca could see that Mary Martha's eyes were closed and her breathing was easy. With her brow slightly knitted, as if in concentration, she looked just like Rory in her sleep. She would always look like Rory, Rebecca thought, and she wondered if that would always hurt.

Back in the kitchen, Mike was sitting quietly at the table with two glasses of wine, generously filled, arrayed before him like a still life. Rebecca noted that the open bottle was within easy reach. She wondered whether this implied that he didn't expect to stop at one glass; had she been setting the table, she would have put the bottle back in the refrigerator and faced the refill issue in its own time. It was already late, after all; and what if they only had conversation enough for one glass each? She had grown cautious, wary of half-glass conversations, sipping all those months away with Bob.

She sat down and reached for her wine; Mike reached for his in response, and they paused self-consciously over the lifted glasses. But even the pause seemed like a subtle kind of progress. Bob would have already declared, *"To us!"* Rebecca realized that her exhaustion was gone; the long day and its complications seemed far away. There was just this simple, interesting thing, this man she liked. This man she was just beginning to get to know.

"To ex-husbands staying out of jail?" Mike suggested wryly.

Rebecca laughed and almost agreed. It was the kind of toast she and Bonnie might have made, rueful and humorous, a toast to just having survived the day. But then she caught herself. "No. Let's drink to something new."

He inclined his head. "All right. To something new."

"To—" She floundered briefly. She could feel that old dangerous vagueness in herself, the sudden gape of longing, blind and fierce and ravenous for some impossible delicacy. For a music she had never quite heard but always suspected was there, if she could just listen right. For a love that did not fail. For the surprise of goodness. But it all sounded wrong, clumsy, fervid.

Their glasses were still raised. Mike seemed to be in no hurry. She was grateful for that. Their eyes met, a quiet look, and Rebecca realized that she didn't have a thing to say.

"God, I don't know," she laughed. "To a decent moment sneaking in once in a while, I suppose, against all odds."

"To decent moments sneaking in," Mike agreed, and touched her glass with his.

They sipped their wine. Rebecca was struck again by how easy it was to be with him. He was not like Fulmar Donaldson at all. He paid attention, he was right there. Like a grown-up.

"I feel like I should ask you about the monastery," she said. "I've been wanting to ever since you moved in. But I don't even know where to start."

"Ah, well, the monastery." He considered his wine. "I don't know where to start either."

"How old were you when you went in?"

"Twenty-three."

"Twenty-three." Rebecca tried to picture him: a young man, not a boy anymore. Someone who had had some to time to live, some time to sin. Meaning, she thought, amused with herself, time to have had sex.

"I had this on-again-off-again college career," Mike said. "I was a philosophy major, supposedly, but I kept dropping out and looking for meaning." He heard himself and shook his head, smiling. "I used to be able to say that with a perfectly straight face. 'What are you doing, son, now that you've thrown away your scholarship?' 'Well, I'm looking for meaning.' I was a dreamy kid, maybe a little spoiled. Academic philosophy really had nothing to do with what I wanted. I wanted Truth with a capital *T.* I was shocked by the suffering in the world. And I had an unhappy love, a long-term relationship that didn't work out, which really loosened my moorings for a while. It was all very Kierkegaardian, I suppose. To make a long story short, at around that time I spent a weekend at a Bethanite monastery in Mendocino County and had a big mystical experience. One thing sort of led to another from there."

"So God caught you on the rebound."

Mike laughed, clearly taken off guard. "That's one way of looking at it. At the time I believed that I had seen through the empty values of the modern world and exhausted my personal delusions."

"And now?"

"The values of the world still seem empty enough, on the whole. But I've begun to suspect that my personal delusions are inexhaustible."

Rebecca laughed. "And your tragic love? Did you ever get in touch with her again?"

Mike's gaze drifted to a point somewhere near the ceiling in the far corner of the kitchen. "I did, actually. I wrote to her several times from the monastery, during my probationary period." His eyes tracked memories for a long moment; Rebecca waited respectfully, and at last Mike's gaze returned to her face and he shook his head, as if to apologize for a lapse. "She even wrote back, very graciously. I'm afraid my own letters were in-sufferable—full of Thomas Merton on the ascent to God and the amazing grace that had saved a wretch like me. I mean, if you look at it from her point of view, it was mostly my life with her that I was crowing about being saved *from*. She never gave a damn for all my metaphysical tumult; she saw my spiri-tual searching as a kind of neurosis. But she loved me anyway. That was incomprehensible to me. I thought my metaphysical tumult *was* me."

"How did you finally leave it with her?"

"The last time I saw her was when she came to the cere-mony when I was accepted into the order as a novice. She looked exceptionally beautiful, I remember; she had gone to some trouble to look good. It's strange, but I think that the two of us still had a chance at that point. Or maybe that was just my hunger for drama, my way of sharpening the edge of my renunciation."

"Did you feel torn, seeing her there?"

"No, I felt very serene; it didn't shake me up at all. I remem-ber watching her walk back to her car, knowing that I was see-ing that self-possessed sashay of hers for the last time, and feeling . . . I don't know, *benevolent*. I'd just shaved my head, my vows were fresh; the robes covered up a multitude of lies, and the world seemed well lost. There was a sense of poignancy, at most. It was only later that the doubt crept in."

"Doubt has a way of doing that."

"I suppose I was hoping God would protect me, somehow. Reward me for all my glorious renunciations. But deep prayer, prolonged prayer, is a terrible mirror—kneel there long enough and everything shows. There's no way out of eventu-ally seeing your phoniness and dishonesty. Years later, decades later, I would catch myself during a meditation, running after her to the car in my mind's eye, seizing her shoulder, spinning her around and kissing her—"

"Making wild love in the backseat," Rebecca suggested.

Mike smiled. "Making wild love in the *front* seat. On the *trunk*. In the parking lot. Making love in the monastery visitors' room. You'd be shocked at the amount of sexual fantasy that goes on in prayer."

"Single mothers are pretty much unshockable, actually," Rebecca said, and they laughed. The wine was having its effect, she noted; everything seemed a little slower and warmer. She could smell a ripe peach, in the fruit bowl on the counter. The kitchen seemed like a tiny island of light in the night sea of the house. She could almost hear Mary Martha's heartbeat in the deep silence, a comforting pulse, like waves on a shore. She felt dangerously content.

On an impulse, she stood up and cut the peach into slices. The blade slipping easily through the luscious flesh seemed so blatant, so outrageously erotic that she almost giggled and pointed it out to Mike. But she caught herself. She wasn't that drunk, Rebecca told herself sternly. She was handling a knife, after all, she was being competent in the kitchen, entertaining a guest. All this talk about sex had just made her a little giddy.

She arranged the slices into a sunburst pattern and brought the plate back to the table a little self-consciously. She and Mike each took a slice. The peach was perfect, firm but yielding, juicy and sweet.

"Oh, God," Rebecca murmured. "To hell with sex. If I got stuck in prayer for years, I'd dream of ripe peaches."

"The monastery had an orchard," Mike said. "In season, I had all the ripe peaches I could eat."

This struck them both as hilarious somehow. They laughed as quietly as they could, stifling the noise like high school kids after curfew, conscious of Mary Martha down the hall. Mike's glass was almost empty too, Rebecca noted. She was seeing everything with a hypervivid clarity, a realness somehow realer than real. Superreality was as useless as unreality, of course, in the long run. But it was so much more satisfying while it was happening.

"Try sipping your wine with some peach in your mouth," she said. "You'll never long for sex again. Your existence will be complete."

Mike complied and made appropriately orgasmic sounds of appreciation. He was so loose, it was starting to feel like an evening with Bonnie, the girls on a tear. His brown hair had finally grown in enough to stand up ruggedly, and Rebecca suppressed an urge to reach across the table and rub against the bristly grain.

Instead, she reached for the wine bottle and filled both their glasses. The Bonnie analogy left a lot of leeway. This wasn't a date, after all. They were just two friends talking about life over a bottle of wine. Or, alternatively, she was getting drunk with the baby-sitter.

Besides, he was the one who'd left the bottle out on the table in the first place.

"So, she walks off into the sunset, leaving you to a life of deep prayer and all the peaches you could eat—" she prompted, after a sip of wine. "Or am I crudely distorting the religious life with all this emphasis on relationships?"

"If you don't get your relationships right, one way or the other, there is no religious life. There's no one nastier than a contemplative with a grudge."

"So—?"

"So it was easy at first to think I'd done us both a favor. I rode the monastic routine, and I cultivated my little epiphanies. I was a good monk; I stayed out of trouble, more or less, and I persisted in my prayer—"

"You 'kept your costume on and attended all the events.'"

Mike smiled appreciatively. "Exactly. And somewhere in the long course of getting to know myself it became clear to me that I hadn't renounced intimacy at all. I had simply failed at it."

"Oh, come on. That seems too harsh."

"At first, maybe. It's rough on the old self-image. But eventually there's a kind of liberation in a truth like that."

Rebecca considered this for a moment.

"I know what you mean, I think," she said at last, tentatively. "There *is* that lightness that comes when you realize that you're not going to be able to make something work, no matter how hard you try. When you finally let go of wanting, out of pure exhaustion."

"I never let go of wanting for more than fifteen seconds at a time," Mike said. "But oh, those fifteen seconds . . . "

They laughed.

"It's the other twenty-three hours, fifty-nine minutes, and forty-five seconds that will get you," Rebecca said. "I think single mothers are the real monks."

"To the fifteen seconds," Mike said, and they touched glasses and drank.

It really was just like being with Bonnie, Rebecca told herself. It was free and easy and jolly and occasionally deep; it was friendship. They told each other their stories, and they sympathized and commiserated; they laughed together and they drank together and they would go to bed alone.

"That's quite a collection of artwork you've got buried down there in the garage," Mike offered as he refilled their glasses.

Rebecca stiffened. He noticed at once and said quickly, "It's not like I've been pawing through it or anything. I just couldn't help but notice—"

"Oh, it's all right. I'm a little touchy about it. Embarrassed, I suppose."

"You're very good, from what I've seen."

"I thought you hadn't been pawing through it."

Mike laughed, acknowledging.

"It's kid stuff," Rebecca said. "I fought this big teenage war with my parents over it. My father wanted me to be an architect. Phoebe was 'supportive.' But she always treated my painting like a hobby, this cute little parlor trick—hang-it-on-the-refrigerator-level stuff, death through benign patronizing. It was something to do until I found a husband and had kids of my own. So I came to California."

"And?"

"Hooked up with Rory. Had a kid of my own. Found out Phoebe was right."

"Nonsense," Mike said.

Rebecca shrugged and let a pointed silence settle. Mike, clearly inclined to pursue the subject, reached for the wine bottle by way of reinforcement and found that it was empty. They looked at each other, humorously teetering on the brink of opening another one.

"It's been such a lovely night," Rebecca said at last. "I'd hate to spoil it by becoming an ugly drunk."

"That would be interesting," Mike demurred, but he rose amiably enough.

He seemed as pleased as she was with the way things had gone, Rebecca thought. Even this final prudence was a kind of acknowledgment, a refusal to force the evening's advance onto ground too uncertain. She put the wineglasses in the sink and walked Mike out to the back porch, where they paused to look up at the stars. The fog had not come in and the sky was clear. Over the ocean, a waxing half-moon seemed surprisingly bright.

"I really can't thank you enough for taking care of Mary Martha tonight," Rebecca said.

"That's all right. It was refreshing to feel useful."

"Did the woman at Bee-Well say anything? Like, what a terrible mother I am?"

Mike looked uncomfortable. "Not at all. You're a wonderful mother."

"What *did* she say?"

"Well, she was definitely unhappy. It was pretty late and the place was empty. She said Mary Martha was the last kid to be picked up, every day."

"That's not even true. Well, for the last couple weeks, maybe." She looked at the sky. "God, maybe it's finally happened."

"What's that?"

"When I first left Rory, I was terrified that I wouldn't be able to support Mary Martha without working so much that she and I wouldn't really have a life together. I could just see myself becoming this work machine that made the money to pay for her day care, where I would stash her so that I could continue being the machine. And so on—around and around she goes. Then I lucked into this job at Utopian Images—very low-key place, wonderful people, a bunch of artists, lots of slack. It was perfect."

"Sort of like McDonald's," Mike said.

Rebecca laughed. "Well, there were no free french fries or anything, but it was a pretty nice gig. But lately the company has been changing. We're hustling corporate jobs, with real deadlines, high-pressure work. I used to be one of the first mothers at Bee-Well every night—I'd cut out of work a little early and beat the rush. But this latest project just eats the hours up. I look at the clock and the day is gone and I feel like I should work all night too. I'm not putting in the time I should at work, but I'm still always late picking up Mary Martha. And then at home I'm preoccupied about what I'm not getting done at work." She caught herself and shook her head. "God, listen to me. A couple of glasses of wine, and you get the whole poor-poor-pitiful-me spiel."

Mike was silent for so long that she began to fear she had overwhelmed him. But at last he said, tentatively, "I could pick up Mary Martha any day you have trouble getting away in time."

Rebecca laughed. "No, no, that's not what I was angling for. I mean, it's very generous of you. Insanely generous. But really, it's just been one of those days, on top of one of those weeks, inside of one of those periods. I'll be okay. I just needed to complain."

"But seriously, I could—"

"No. Don't you see? That takes all the fun out of it."

"Out of what?"

"Out of *this*—" Her hand took in the kitchen. "You and me sitting here in the quiet after the fray. This luxury, this rare thing, a quiet moment. You pick Mary Martha up once, and it's a favor, and a novelty. You pick her up regularly, and it's a chore. If you only knew how much I hated it tonight, calling you—"

"I was glad you called."

"But will you be glad the next time? And the next? Or will you hear the phone ring at quarter of six and think, Oh, shit, I've got to go pick up that kid again?" She glanced at him. "Were you *really* going to call, by the way?"

"What?"

"If I hadn't called you tonight. Were you actually going to call me?"

Mike looked sheepish. "Well, I wanted the timing to be right."

Rebecca laughed. "Oh? And how is the timing now?"

Their eyes met. She was surprised by how close his face was, and by how easy it was to be this close to him. He was obviously thinking about kissing her, which seemed so fraught with complications that her mind flailed for a moment and then stopped working. She just stood there quietly, wanting to kiss him too.

"It seems about right," Mike said, and he did kiss her, tenderly and confidently, a kiss as fine and firm and ripe as the peach, spiced with rosé. She had been kidding herself, of course. It was not at all like being with Bonnie.

Chapter Six

Dear Brother James,

Please forgive the vitriol of my last letter. I have been feeling much too sorry for myself of late, and clearly I took it out on you. As I told a friend recently, there's no one nastier than a contemplative with a grudge. I "got plugged in," as they say out here in the big bright world, mechanizing the sin of anger. Or, as my colleagues at McDonald's put it, "My bad." I'm sorry I dissed you.

The ritual response to a penitential "My bad," incidentally, is a benevolent "It's all good." The drama of Christ's gift of forgiveness is reenacted a dozen times a day over the deep fryer and the grill, by teenagers, with refreshing succinctness.

Did I mention "a friend"? No doubt your ears pricked up at that, you who have been urging me to expand my social horizons. You may feel I have overdone it, indeed: I feel more than a little sheepish, after all my insistence on the emptiness of my existence, to report that I am in love.

I won't bore you with the details. She is beautiful, smart, talented, and funny, and I am a preposterous buffoon; it is the age-old story.

Our profession should have prepared us for miracles, but this one has taken me off guard. I thought I was finished with life, in some deep sense; I was prepared to spend the balance of my days perfecting my resignation, going round and round the center of God's silence like water circling a drain. There was even a kind of peace in that. But it appears that God will not let me off so lightly.

Forgive me if this all seems a bit abrupt. Like Lazarus, in the grave too long, I am afraid that I stink as I stagger forth into the glare of this unanticipated resurrection. But I find that doesn't matter. Jesus said that the first and great commandment is to love God with all your heart and with all your soul and with all your mind; and that the second is to love your neighbor as yourself. I have spent the better part of my life wrestling with that first commandment, and God alone knows what it has meant. But it is only recently that I have begun to love my (upstairs) neighbor.

Perhaps I have taken the New Testament too literally. You and I have exercised ourselves with our dialogues on what it means to be "in the world" and what it means to be free of the world; we've drawn all sorts of exquisite lines no prudent soul should cross; we've postured and professed. But one whiff of love makes all that seem like nothing. Heaven and hell are the merest sand for castles, Brother James. I'll take the living rose, wherever it may be.

Yours in Christ (as ever),
  Mike Christopher

Rebecca woke earlier than usual on Saturday morning, with a trace of a headache and a sense of bleak lucidity. I'm glad we didn't open that second bottle of wine last night, she told herself. It seemed like a very middle-aged thought.

She still wasn't sure whether she was glad that Michael Christopher had kissed her. She was unsure in theory, at least. Viscerally, she was delighted. Even now, she could savor the warm thrill of the moment, the small melting of surrender, the unexpected authority of Mike's lips. She could feel the bristle of his late-night growth of beard and smell his weirdly comforting male smell. His hand had come up to her cheek, in a tender, tracing gesture. She had felt buoyed and enveloped; everything had stopped. It was the moment she had secretly been longing for. But the moment she'd been longing for was just a moment. This was the next moment.

She felt like making phone calls: to Bonnie, to her mother. The situation called for consideration at length. But she suspected that both women would be unreservedly supportive of the kiss and its potential consequences. Bonnie believed that love could be competently assembled from available elements like a casserole, and Phoebe believed in destiny; this made both of them a little rash in matters of the heart, in Rebecca's opinion. Certainly she didn't have Bonnie's confidence in her own cooking skills. She had believed in destiny herself, of course, once upon a time; but Rory had been her destiny then. You looked at your destiny differently after a slightly messy divorce.

Am I spoiled for life? Rebecca asked herself. Ruined by cynicism? Truly, I don't think that I am. I am a woman who bailed her first husband out of jail last night. I am a realistic single mother with too much to do already. Love is all very well, but the bathtub hasn't been scrubbed in weeks.

She resolved to keep her balance. In all likelihood, Christopher would pull a Fulmar Donaldson on her anyway and act like nothing had happened. And maybe that would be for the best. She needed the downstairs rent more than she needed half-drunken high school make-out sessions. If anything, she was sorry to have blown what seemed like a promising friendship.

But she kept thinking about the kiss. The weight of Mike's lips on hers appeared to have sunk right to the center of her body, where it spun imperturbably on an axis of its own, exerting its own dense gravitational field. It was embarrassing; she was a black hole of romance. Had she learned nothing since her sophomore year of high school?

Still, it had been a lovely kiss.

The sound of Mary Martha dragging a chair to the counter in the kitchen so that she could reach the cereal cupboard brought Rebecca out of her reverie. She climbed out of bed and pulled on her coziest terry cloth bathrobe. In the kitchen, Mary Martha had already settled in at the table with her Cheerios. She seemed pleasantly surprised to see Rebecca up so early, which cost Rebecca a pang of her recurrent weekend guilt.

"Good morning, Miss Bright-and-Early," she said, giving her daughter a kiss. "I missed you last night."

"Something important came up," Mary Martha allowed, so precisely that Rebecca realized her daughter must be quoting Mike. Apparently he had taken a minimalist line in explaining her absence.

"It sure did," she said. "But it's all taken care of now. Did you have a nice time with Mike?"

Mary Martha nodded happily, her mouth full of cereal.

"What did you do? Did you watch *The Little Mermaid?*"

Mary Martha hesitated, then confided, "Mike didn't know how to work the VCR." Clearly she felt that this reflected badly on him.

Rebecca laughed. "I guess they didn't have VCRs in the monastery."

"They had *one,* but Mike never had to work it. He didn't know how to work the microwave either."

Her daughter's tone of generous indulgence was touching. Rebecca asked, "So what *did* you do?"

"He cooked some spaghetti on the stove, and we played unicorns. He was the big unicorn and I was the small one."

"Was he a good unicorn?"

"Of course," Mary Martha said, as if this went without saying.

"And how was the spaghetti?"

Mary Martha rolled her eyes.

"Oh, *Mom,*" she said, with the slight exasperation she showed sometimes when Rebecca was just a little too slow. "You can't mess up spaghetti."

Later, after her daughter had gone to her room to prepare for Rory picking her up, Rebecca stood at the sink washing the dishes. She was just starting to rinse the second wineglass from the night before when Michael Christopher came out the garage door into the backyard below her, dressed in his usual jeans and wearing a light jacket against the fog that had come in overnight.

She leaned forward expectantly, to make herself as visible as possible in case this was some kind of bashful reconnaissance, but Mike kept his eyes averted from the kitchen window. He was carrying a pair of clippers and seemed prepared to go to work in the garden as he often did on Saturday mornings, as if nothing had happened.

Though she had told herself it would be this way, Rebecca felt a bleak thud of disappointment somewhere in her abdomen. She was surprised by how pained she was. He was a Fulmar type after all; there was nothing but awkwardness ahead. And now she was going to have to recover from that delicious kiss as if it were a case of food poisoning.

But Mike, moving briskly, spent a few minutes clipping poppies, nasturtiums, and a sprig of lavender; and once he had a bouquet assembled he mounted the back steps without hesitation. Rebecca was so startled by his approach that she was slow to respond, and he knocked on the back door before she could move to open it.

"Good morning," Mike said shyly, when she did finally get to the door. The confidence of his ascent had vanished sometime between his knock and her answer. His eyes were lowered and he held out the flowers without quite looking up. "For you. I'm afraid they're not exactly up to professional standards—"

She took the bouquet. "Not at all, they're beautiful. Thank you."

"I hope I'm not being . . . presumptuous."

Rebecca laughed. "You were presumptuous last night. This is common decency."

Mike met her eyes for the first time, saw that she was teasing, and gave her a tentative smile.

"Would you like some coffee?" she asked, conscious suddenly of her bathrobe, her bare feet, and her uncombed hair, but thinking, What the hell, here he is. The collision of high courtship and dowdy domesticity was disorienting, but she felt quietly elated. What good was all her prudence if it disappeared at the first sign of actual danger? She felt pleased enough to make all sorts of wild mistakes.

"I'd love some coffee," Mike said.

She stepped back to let him in. He entered the kitchen diffidently, blinking as if at a brighter place and looking around as if he had never been there. This sudden advent of Relationship was as vertiginous for him as it was for her, Rebecca realized. Maybe even more so: she'd had one eye out for intimacy all along. That empty half of the bed could seem like a failure or a promise, but in any case she had often imagined it being filled, while Christopher's celibacy all these years had been voluntary. It had been part of who he was. He probably felt like he was jumping off a cliff.

Mike sat down at the table, settling into the chair he had used the night before as if he were afraid someone had sawed halfway through the legs in the meantime. Rebecca found an empty vase for the flowers, filled it with water, and set the arrangement at the center of the table. Then she moved to the cupboard and stretched to take two china coffee cups and saucers off the top shelf. Phoebe had given her a complete set of Messen chinaware as a wedding gift, no doubt with visions of family dinner parties in the genteel tradition, but Rebecca hadn't laid a single setting during her entire marriage to Rory, whose catch-as-catch-can meals seldom called for more than paper plates or eating Chinese takeout from the boxes. After the divorce, she had used the china for everything for a while, china bowls for breakfast, china salad plates for lunch, the whole china array for defiantly elegant dinners, complete with candlelight, while Mary Martha sat across the table in her high chair and ate her mashed peas and carrots out of a china finger bowl. But that routine was exhausting, once Rebecca had started working again. Also, the casualty rate on the finger bowls was very high. Eventually the china had been relegated to the highest shelf and more or less forgotten.

"I hear you failed the VCR test last night," she said as she poured the coffee.

"It was a bad moment," Mike allowed. "Mary Martha was incredulous, like when I had no swimsuit. I felt very third world. But she was tolerant, in the end. We ended up playing with her unicorns. Did you know they all have two names?"

She brought the coffee to the table. "Milk's in the carton, sugar's in the bowl," she said. "Two names? You mean, like first and last names?"

Mike busied himself with his coffee. She had suspected he would take it black—monastic austerity down the line. But he used an unascetic splash of milk and a truly worldly amount of sugar.

"No," he said, stirring. "More like a public name and a secret name."

"The unicorns have secret names?" Rebecca repeated uneasily, adding her own milk, no sugar. She prided herself on keeping up to date on Mary Martha's unicorn lore.

Mike looked uncomfortable. "I hope I haven't been indiscreet."

"No, I'm glad she felt she could confide in you." Rebecca shook her head. "She's a deep kid. She scares the hell out of me sometimes. Just when I think she's surprised me for the last time, a whole new angle opens up."

"I don't think people are ever done surprising each other."

Rebecca laughed. "Well, *that's* for sure."

Their eyes met. Mike flushed. "I didn't mean—"

"I did," Rebecca said. And, as he still seemed flustered, "It was a *very* good kiss."

"That's a relief. I mean, I thought so too—" he added hurriedly. "But I was afraid there had been . . . you know, changes in fashion, or something, in the meanwhile. New techniques developed."

"No, no, the fundamental things apply."

They sat for a moment, looking, inevitably, at the flowers at the center of the table. The bright orange of the poppies and the deeper orange-red of the nasturtiums worked surprisingly well together, Rebecca noted. It had seemed like such a naive bouquet when he brought it up the steps.

"Questions of technique aside—" Mike began resolutely, if a little reluctantly.

"It was just a kiss," Rebecca said. "A relationship doesn't stand or fall on a single kiss."

"But it changes with one."

"Only if you want it to."

"No, it changes," Mike insisted, and she felt a warm thrill pass through her, because he had insisted, and because he had caught her in a kind of slickness. She realized that she had been giving him a handicap in her mind, making allowances for a monk's presumed ineptness, playing things casually and a little too broadly. But he was very precise.

She said, "I suppose that what I'm really trying to say is that I don't think we need to be in a big hurry to decide What It All Means. I just got out of a relationship with a man who had everything mapped out from the get-go, and let me tell you, I'd much rather endure a little creative uncertainty."

"That's Bob?" Mike asked, with just enough endearing relief that she realized he had been worried about her availability. "The guy I met at your mother's party?"

"He's dating my best friend now, and I couldn't be happier for them. I expect a wedding invitation by the end of the month. He's a single-minded man."

"And you don't want a single-minded man?"

Rebecca groaned. "That's exactly what I'm talking about. Don't start asking me what I want, as if I'm ordering a pizza and you're the only place in the Outer Sunset that delivers. I want reality."

"Pot luck. Whatever the delivery guy has in the box."

"To strain the analogy."

They were silent for a moment, and she was sure that she had been too brusque. But after a moment Mike offered, tentatively, "I'm pretty clear that *I* don't want anchovies."

Rebecca laughed, surprised and pleased. She had noticed before that Mike didn't so much roll with her punches as he turned them into something else. It was a kind of droll conversational judo.

"Or *pineapples,*" he went on, heartened by her response. "Have you ever had one of those so-called Hawaiian pizzas? I mean, it's like a beach after a typhoon, with pineapples and coconut and all sorts of other tropical debris—"

"You make a good point," she conceded. "In fact, I think we can rule out fruit on pizzas in general."

"Well, there, you see? That's all I'm looking for, a few broad principles to start with."

Rebecca started to reply, but a movement in the doorway caught their attention. They turned simultaneously. Mary Martha, dressed for the beach with one of Rory's West Coast Surfing Championship T-shirts billowing around her like a poncho, stood quietly contemplating them with her bright blue eyes.

"Are you going to have pizza for breakfast?" she asked, disapproving but intrigued.

"Of course not, sweetheart," Rebecca assured her.

"Not if it has anchovies on it," Mike said. He was really very firm about it.

Rory showed up to pick up Mary Martha half an hour later, just after ten o'clock, which was very early for him. But he had somehow found time to get a disconcertingly bad haircut since the night before. His ponytail had been lopped off with the crudeness of a battlefield amputation and the rest of his hair hacked short with no clear plan. It was a haircut like a kind of punishment, or a penance. Rebecca suspected that he had done it himself.

"How do you like my new look?" Rory demanded at once, subdued but defiant.

"It's terrible, as you must know. Did you have a fight with your girlfriend or something?"

"I just thought it was time for a change."

Rebecca decided not to rub it in. The arrest had obviously shaken Rory more than he'd been willing to let on. Maybe this was his way of backing toward maturity, a transitional phase, the sloppy molting of a used-up adolescence. Or maybe it was just another childish gesture.

She tried to keep Rory in the front hall while she went to get Mary Martha, but his animal sense led him straight back into the kitchen and she had to introduce him to Christopher. The two men nodded to each other genially and chatted about the weather, which they agreed was dreary. Rory was surprisingly civil, and Mike paid grave attention to his small talk. Rebecca noticed that Mike had stayed in his seat, while Rory lounged awkwardly by the sink. She liked it that Mike had held his ground.

"China cups," Rory noted laconically. "Well, la-di-*da*."

"Would you like some coffee?" Mike offered, before Rebecca could wave him off.

"No thanks, I never touch the stuff," Rory said. "I believe that caffeine is part of a government conspiracy to keep the zombies working."

"It works for me," Mike conceded, cheerfully enough.

Mary Martha came in with her little overnight bag. She kept her eyes downcast, a dinghy riding out a storm of adult politeness. She was markedly cool toward Mike, Rebecca observed, with none of her usual flirtatious sparkle. But no doubt Mary Martha felt her loyalty to Rory as a constraint.

Rebecca hurried father and daughter toward the front door before anyone's goodwill could falter.

"You might have mentioned . . . " Rory said, pausing on the porch while Mary Martha skipped down the steps toward the Rambler.

"It's none of your business. But he's just a friend."

"Yeah, right."

The sarcasm had no bite to it, though. Rebecca realized that she felt sorry for Rory. He looked so bedraggled and discouraged, and he clearly thought that Mike had spent the night. What was more interesting to Rebecca was how impersonal her pity was. Some secret balance had tilted, just since last night; whatever she felt for Mike, wherever that kiss took them, she felt free of Rory in a way she never had before. Not free of longing—she had been done with wanting Rory long ago. But free of bitterness, able to take him lightly.

And Rory felt it too. She sensed his groping for the abrasive grip of their usual exchanges and sliding off this sudden new equanimity. He seemed disoriented without her exasperation, and strangely diminished. How conscious had he been, all these years, of needing that morbid friction? How conscious was he, now, of what had actually changed? She had done a cruel thing, it seemed. She had moved on emotionally.

Mary Martha, waiting in the Rambler's front seat, honked the horn impatiently.

"Oops, Her Highness awaits," Rory said.

"Have fun. Bring her back in one piece."

He started down the stairs, then stopped and turned. "By the way, you were right about me having a fight with Chelsea. I swear you're psychic sometimes."

Rebecca recognized the old pattern. Rory never talked about anything serious without at least one foot out the door and his escape route clear; their most important conversations had often taken place with his car motor running. "Because of the arrest?"

"She says it's time I cleaned up my act. The same old crap."

"Is that what this haircut's about? Cleaning up your act?"

"I was so pissed off at her this morning that I cut it myself." He gave her an odd, appealing look. "Be honest now. You really don't like it?"

"It's the rough draft of a haircut, Rory. It's got great potential."

"I look like a fucking loser."

"It's nothing eight dollars at Supercuts won't fix."

"It's like Samson and Delilah, except I cut it off myself," Rory said bitterly. "I fucked *myself*. As always. It should be on my tombstone: A helluva surfer, but not so great on dry land."

"Don't make a bigger deal out of this than it is."

He shrugged and turned toward the car, then stopped again. "Thanks again for springing me last night. I'll never forget that."

"*De nada,*" Rebecca said, uncomfortable with the swing from self-pity into mawkishness.

Rory hesitated, then offered, frankly rueful, "I see that you finally took the guitar pick off."

Rebecca blinked in surprise. It was true. The guitar pick necklace, that absurd token of their funky engagement, was sitting on the back of the toilet, where she'd set it while washing her face the night before. It was the first time in ten years that she'd been up and around without it.

Mary Martha honked the horn again. Rory looked like he might have had more to say, but he grinned and held up his hands in a what-can-you-do? gesture. He turned and bounded down the last few steps and across the sidewalk to the car with something more like his usual energy. As he started the engine, Rebecca could hear him giving Mary Martha a mock hard time for her impatience; freed of conflicting adults, Mary Martha was laughing easily. As they drove off, the Rambler gave one sharp backfire, and Rebecca ducked instinctively, then sheepishly straightened.

She watched the station wagon until it was out of sight, then turned back into the house. Mike gave her a smile as she came into the kitchen. She would have poured herself another cup of coffee and sat down, but he stood up and took her in his arms.

At least they weren't going to talk about metaphorical pizza anymore, Rebecca thought as he kissed her. She wasn't going to sit down at the computer, and she wasn't going to vacuum or do the laundry. She wasn't even going to finish washing the breakfast dishes. It was a different kind of Saturday for sure, with a man waiting in the kitchen.

"There's so much I should be doing," she told Mike, when they came up for air.

"I think this is very important too," he said.

They kissed and kissed, standing there in the middle of the kitchen floor like revved-up high school kids with nowhere else to go. In a way, it was true: the house was dense with passion-resistant domesticity. It was inconceivable to Rebecca that they could walk from this kitchen, with the breakfast dishes still soapy in the sink, past the entryway's overloaded rack of coats and jumbled pile of shoes and sandals; through the living room, strewn with unicorns, the VCR loaded permanently with *The Little Mermaid* and the TV default set to Nickelodeon; down the hall, its walls lined with crayon masterpieces; past Mary Martha's pink bedroom and the bathroom with the tampon boxes on the back of the toilet and Rebecca's recently washed tights hanging from the shower curtain rod; and finally into Rebecca's own bedroom, furnished with absolutely no one else in mind, plain and cozy and purged of the erotic, a soft-edged fortress against loneliness, filled with novels by women, for women. Apparently she had really believed her amorous adventures were over. The place was as sex-proof as a fifties' sitcom set.

Mike, however, seemed perfectly content to make out in the middle of the kitchen all day long. His kisses had a wonderful, unhurried quality. Rebecca found herself relaxing, persuaded by his tender absorption. It was all very simple. She felt like a fish, swimming upstream against the current of his tongue.

And then she was leading him down the hallway after all. She couldn't remember which of them had moved first, but she was holding him by the hand, his gentle, ungainly hand, so different from all the hands she had known. The house offered surprisingly little resistance, when push came to shove. She had a sense of moving without particular effort, at just the right speed. Things were very clear at the right speed. It was not intimacy the house resisted, it was falseness: the home she'd made with Mary Martha demanded something real.

When they got to her bedroom, she moved self-consciously to straighten the unmade bed. Mike lingered discreetly by the window, looking outward with an air that somehow allowed for the possibility that they still might call this off. She liked it that he didn't assume he'd bought a ticket on a train that couldn't stop.

"You can see the ocean from here," he marveled when she had finished with the bed. He sounded genuinely delighted, a man who lived in a basement glimpsing the broader world. Rebecca walked right up to him and kissed him, because she was afraid that he was going to start talking again about what love meant. She didn't want to talk about what it meant. He knew damn well what love meant, he'd spent twenty years in mortal combat with it. Whether he could handle it or not remained to be seen. But they both knew what it meant.

PART IV

Word I was in the house alone
Somehow must have gotten abroad,
Word I was in my life alone,
Word I had no one left but God.

ROBERT FROST, "Bereft"

Chapter Seven

They made love through the afternoon, something Rebecca had not done in more years than she cared to count. She was intensely self-conscious at first, afraid that she might catch herself in some ridiculous imitation of herself at twenty or twenty-five. There'd been a time when she was as slick in bed as a performing seal. But there was nothing of the practiced performance in Mike's tenderness. It seemed to take him forever just to get her bathrobe open. She'd tied the knot loosely, for ease of access; the merest pressure would have done it. But Mike kept clear for what seemed an impossibly long time, concentrating his attentions on her face and neck, on her hands, on the V of skin the robe left open at her throat and the muffled contours of her body beneath the material, treating the terry cloth as a kind of absolute barrier, so that when his hands did finally slip to her waist and the subtlest tug unloosed the belt, Rebecca was actually surprised. The move seemed like such a daring escalation by then. As her robe fell open, she heard his breath catch, a gratifying little gasp, part pleasure and part awe.

It helped that Mike was self-conscious too, an endearing self-consciousness that bordered on shyness, on modesty. When she finally got his shirt off, he muttered something embarrassed about the slight bulge at his waist and his monastic paleness, and she caught a glimpse of an American guy who'd grown up playing basketball and going to the beach, of the tanned and lanky kid he'd been. Rebecca could sympathize with his chagrin at that kid's submergence in middle-aged flesh. They were both rediscovering their bodies after long intervals of neglect, assessing the damage of the years through each other's eyes. There was an odd camaraderie in such vulnerability.

She kept waiting for the Big Stupidity, the turnoff that too much dreary experience had trained her to expect, but it never came. Mike in bed was simple, warm, and direct; he was grateful without soppiness, generous without being cloying, and he could be unexpectedly, thrillingly decisive at just the right moment. Through the course of the afternoon, Rebecca found herself beginning to trust the suppleness of their rapport. It was like finally dancing with someone suitable after years of hearing her partners counting under their breath.

She cooked them a breakfast of Texas eggs and scallions at sunset. They ate the meal off china plates while sitting on the couch in the living room and watching the evening news. They both were languorous, spent, and ravenously hungry; and it was a sly pleasure, after so many hours in bed, to note that the world had gone on with business as usual.

After supper, Mike did the dishes with a naturalness that was as endearing to Rebecca as any of his more acrobatic moves over the course of the afternoon. She sat at the kitchen table and watched him at the sink. He wore some ugly white boxer shorts and a white T-shirt that had no messages or slogans on it. That was one more lingering aftereffect of his life in the monastery, she supposed, that none of his T-shirts said anything. His knees were bony and his feet were enormous, but he had very nice legs.

"Fulmar," she said contentedly. "I should call you Fulmar."

"Oh?"

"Fulmar Donaldson was the resident philosophy geek at my high school. You reminded me of him a lot when I first met you."

"Uh-oh," he laughed. "And now?"

"So far, so good."

Mike rinsed the frying pan and set it in the drainer. He sponged off the counter, then rinsed the sponge and reached for a dishtowel to dry his hands. Through the window behind him, the twilight sky over the ocean was the deepest purple Rebecca had ever seen. It was a color like a gift, a color to wrap yourself in and savor.

"I could believe in God on a day like this," she said.

"It's easy, on a day like this," Mike agreed, and she could hear the layers in his tone, the shadings and the promises of nuance, like echoes in a canyon at night. But she didn't even want to start, on a day like this.

"I think I'm going to have to buy you some underwear," she said.

Rebecca woke in the dark from a dream of being back in high school, electric with anxiety at some fiendish algebra test complicated by nakedness and no pencil, and instantly, acutely conscious not only that she was in bed with a man for the first time in literal years but that the man was praying.

The bedside clock, level with her nose, read 4:06 in glowing red numerals. She wasn't sure exactly how she knew that Mike was even awake. His breath was steady and even; spooned up against her back, with one arm draped gently around her ribs and the back of his big hand brushing against her breasts, his posture was that of a sleeping, sated lover. But it was as obvious to her as if he were reading under the covers with a flashlight that he was absorbed in prayer.

Rebecca wondered what the etiquette was for such an un-precedented situation. She would have liked to have gotten up and gone to the bathroom, but that seemed rude, if not sacri-legious. Perhaps she should pray herself? But all she could manage was a variation on a thought she had had the night before, seeing her careworn hand resting on Michael Christopher's chest: that she needed badly to get her nails done. The weird simultaneity of the longing for prayer and for a manicure produced a sort of hybrid in her still-sleepy mind, with sprawling imagery of holy polish sliding down hands folded into the supplicatory steeple, of crimson fingertips wav-ing in the air to dry their lurid plea and red blobs of inept prayer blossoming like measles on the nearest stainable surface. Another botched makeover, in short. She'd never been partic-ularly good in churches or in beauty shops. She needed her beautician, a deft Vietnamese woman with a firm grip, an emery board, and a brush stroke like Matisse, to make her hands presentable at all, and God knows what it would take to get her prayer life in shape.

Mike stirred, and Rebecca felt the hand across her ribs ease subtly upward to cup her breast. Taking this as a sort of

"Amen," she moved her hand to cover his and half-rolled so that they faced each other.

"Good morning," she said.

Mike made a gratifying little noise, not quite a chuckle, not quite a murmur, a lover's noise. "Oops. Did I wake you?"

"I was having the weirdest dream."

"Oh?"

"I was getting felt up by a guy who prays in bed."

Mike laughed appreciatively, as if to say, Busted. She already loved his laugh, with an intensity that seemed way ahead of the relationship's actuality.

"Odd," he said. "Yet strangely suggestive."

"What would Freud say, do you think?"

"That prayer is sublimated sex, of course."

"Oh?"

Mike shrugged. "I don't think Freud prayed much, to tell you the truth." His hand was still on her breast, and as she became conscious of this, Rebecca felt her nipple stiffen beneath his fingertips. Mike felt it too and smiled in the dark. "The apostle Paul, on the other hand, exhorted us to pray unceasingly."

"That horny old bastard."

Mike chuckled and began to pay serious attention to her nipple. After a moment he bent and added the fine, flickering pressure of his tongue. His hand slipped across her belly to the pointed bone of her hip, then found the curve of her waist. Rebecca closed her eyes and arched slightly toward him, surrendering to the slow rhythms of their intimacy, a rising warmth already familiar, like the first touch of dawn in the sky behind the hills.

Somewhere down the hallway, a floorboard creaked and they both paused, instantly alert, listening to see if it was Mary

Martha. She liked that about Mike too, his instinctive, un-grudging parental consciousness. But it had just been the house shifting. They smiled at each other.

"All clear," Rebecca said.

"Thank God. I was afraid for a moment it was Abbot Hackley doing a bed check."

Rebecca laughed. "Did he *do* that?"

"Oh, yeah. Though not for the usual reasons. Most of the monks were capable of getting home from the bars on time."

"So what was he checking on, then?"

Mike shrugged and traced his finger thoughtfully along the line of her collarbone and then down between her breasts. Rebecca thought for a moment that he was going to just let the question go unanswered, but at last he conceded, "He wanted to make sure I wasn't praying."

She smiled uncertainly. "You're kidding, right?"

His hand found her belly and rested lightly there. "Nope."

"But isn't that—I mean, what else is a monastery *for?*"

"We weren't technically a contemplative order. The Bethanite charism is a graced balance of service and prayer, Martha and Mary, the active and the contemplative sisters of Lazarus in Luke 10. Abbot Hackley always felt I gave short shrift to service."

"And?"

"I felt he gave short shrift to contemplation, obviously."

"And that's why you left?"

Mike's hand drifted down her belly, as if in reply, his fingers filtering tenderly through her pubic hair. Rebecca drew a breath as a fingertip found her vaginal lips, still wet from the earlier play around her breasts. He stroked her gently, penetrat-ing, and she softly moaned.

"I suppose that we could discuss the relative merits of the life of service and the life of passive prayer," he said.

"I suppose we could let that discussion wait," Rebecca breathed, and closed her eyes as his fingers moved. He was actually pretty deft for a guy who gave short shrift to service.

The telephone rang on Sunday morning at precisely ten o'clock, startling Rebecca out of a deep sleep. She and Mike had been awake until just after dawn, talking in hushed, intimate tones, exchanging life histories and rapturous confidences like children at camp after lights-out. She knew now that he had in fact played basketball in high school and that if he had had a better outside shot his religious vocation would have had to wait. He had first been kissed in the seventh grade by his best friend's cousin from Philadelphia. He could play the clarinet. She was the fourth woman he had slept with, and she knew the stories of the previous three disasters, which all sounded mild enough to Rebecca, even the star-crossed affair that had led him into the monastery. They still had not talked much about God, which was a relief in a way, because Rebecca could not imagine talking about God without sounding stupid and crude. But she was afraid that they were avoiding the topic the way you would avoid discussing the wife while having an affair with a married man.

"It's my mother," she told Mike as the phone continued to ring. "Like a German train, the Sunday morning 10:01. I've finally trained her to not call before ten. She wakes up at six and starts tapping her toes."

"Let the machine get it," Mike said languidly.

"I can't do that. She'll fret."

"Let her fret," he said, and buried his nose in her hair just behind her ear, which seemed like an excellent argument indeed for letting Phoebe fret.

The phone rang for the fourth time, and the answering machine kicked in. They could hear Rebecca's recorded voice in the kitchen, too far away to make out individual words but sounding excruciatingly chipper. Peppy, even, Rebecca thought. How had her machine greeting ended up sounding like a high school cheerleader's? She vowed to change it at the first opportunity to something with a more existential tone.

The hideous *beep* sounded, and Phoebe's voice came on, droll and indulgent.

"I'm afraid I'm going to have to talk to her," Rebecca told Mike. "She'll imagine the worst otherwise. She's perfectly capable of hopping into her car and driving over here to administer CPR."

"I was hoping to do that myself," Mike murmured, continuing with his attentions to her neck.

She smacked him affectionately. They were already getting silly with each other. It was wonderful. "I just wonder how I'm going to tell my mother I'm sleeping with a guy who works at McDonald's."

Phoebe was still chattering blithely away. Even from the other side of the house, it was clear that she was speculating on all the things that might be keeping Rebecca from the phone. Rebecca picked up before the theories got embarrassing.

"Hi, Mom."

"*Were* you in the shower?" Phoebe asked, without missing a beat.

"Nope," Rebecca said, amused at how smug she sounded.

Phoebe picked up on the note instantly. "My goodness, Rebecca, you're in bed with a man."

Rebecca smiled at Mike, who smiled back. He had a rumpled, drowsy air and needed a shave, but he seemed perfectly content to lie back on the pillow and watch her deal with her mother. She marveled anew at how easy it was to be with him. She had expected some awkwardness, first thing in the morning, passion's sober backlash—a belated attack of celibate conscience, maybe, the bad moment in Eden. But Mike was simply acting . . . well, *happy*. It was almost disorienting.

"It appears that I am," she told Phoebe.

"Do I know him?"

Rebecca covered the phone's mouthpiece. "She's onto us already. Are we keeping this secret for any reason?"

He hesitated, and her heart gave a little thud of dismay. No, she thought. No, no, no, don't say it. But he said, "Maybe that would be best, for now."

She stared at him for a moment in frank dismay. It was probably too late for him to take it back, but she still hoped he might catch himself and try. But Mike looked away. Rebecca was keenly aware, suddenly, of the mass of him, of the sheer volume of his flesh beside her. A big naked man, she thought ruefully. A nakedness that could only get more awkward now.

"No, you don't know him," she told her mother. "I barely know him myself."

"Oh, dear, is that really wise?"

"We all make mistakes," Rebecca said.

As soon as she had hung up the phone, Rebecca slid out of the bed and grabbed her bathrobe.

"I'm sorry—" Mike began as she was furiously knotting the belt. She had known he would begin that way. She had a sense that she knew everything, actually, from here on in.

"Sorry for what? That my mother is sure now that I'm a slut? I wish you'd told me sooner that I was in bed with someone anonymous."

"It just came up so quickly."

"Life is like that. Real people with real lives, telling other real people who they're sleeping with. How long did you think we were going to be able to stay in bed without the phone ringing? At what point were you going to tell me that what we were doing wasn't real?"

"It *was* real," Mike said, clearly pained by how lame that sounded. "It *is* real." She could see how much he wanted to get out of the bed and deal with this as a man with clothes on. He was eyeing the ten-foot stretch of floor between him and his pants like someone about to try fire walking. If she'd had any compassion at all she would have handed him his boxers at least. But she wanted him to suffer now.

"Let's just say it was a mistake, then," she said. "I suppose that's the Christian thing to do." And she turned on her heel and walked from the room.

She already had a pot of coffee started when he got to the kitchen about thirty seconds later, dressed now, shirt untucked, carrying his shoes and socks. Despite her rage, she was dismayed to see those shoes in his hand. He was way too ready to leave, and that only made her angrier.

"This is not for you," she said of the coffee.

"Of course you're angry—"

"Don't pull that monastic psychobabble on me."

"It was just too much, too fast," he said. "Don't you see that?"

"I see Rory, heading for the hills whenever life gets real. I see Fulmar Donaldson. I see every man on the planet, actually."

Mike took a deep breath. "I'm going to put my shoes on."

"Suit yourself."

He sat down and tugged a sock on. His feet in the morning light were extraordinarily ugly. How could she ever have imagined she could live with feet like that? She'd been desperate, apparently. She'd been so lonely.

"You would have been such a lovely friend," she said.

"Okay, I'm scared," Mike said. "Is that so hard to understand? I'm afraid that I'm spoiled for real life. I've been pretty sure that I was spoiled, actually, for a long, long time. And suddenly with you it seemed for a moment that I might not have to be spoiled completely."

"I don't care if you're spoiled, for God's sake! *I'm* spoiled. We're all spoiled, life does that. It's what you do with yourself after you realize you've been spoiled that matters. It's the life you make in the ruins."

"That's a cheerful thought," he said. It had actually perked him up.

"It's not like it's rocket science, being a decent human being."

"Actually, I don't think anyone appreciates what a miracle a decent human being really is." It was a joke of sorts, an offer of lightness, but she refused to smile. "A moment of terror," Mike persisted. "One moment of terror, and you're never going to talk to me again."

"What are you saying? That you've gotten over it? That we should call my mother back and tell her who Zorro is?"

He hesitated, an echo of his first hesitation that would have been comical if she had not been so enraged. Rebecca realized that she'd gotten her hopes up again, just that quickly, and she hated herself for that. She snatched the still-filling pot off the coffeemaker and dumped its contents into a cup as coffee dribbled onto the hot plate and sizzled. The smell of burned coffee filled the room. She jammed the empty pot back into its spot.

"Put your other goddamned sock on," she said.

Instead, he took the first sock off. They stared at each other. It was so spectacularly absurd. She could feel the corner of her mouth twitching; she was close to laughing. Rory had used to do the same sort of thing; she'd spent a decade of her life being mollified by simple existential charm.

"I'm not young anymore, don't you see?" she said. "I can't do the secret, complicated things anymore. I can't do the half-ass things. I've got a wonderful, pathetic little life that is precious to me. I'm not looking for an affair."

"I thought you wanted to keep things undefined."

"That's just something single mothers say when they're not sure whether a man is worth telling their daughter about."

"Ah," he said, receiving it, endearingly, as information. She found herself feeling a dangerous compassion for him.

"Look, I like you," she said. "You got in over your head, so did I. Let's just let it go at that. No harm, no foul. You just do what you've always done: head for the hills. Slip away into God, and think about me once in a while when you pray and feel . . . *benevolent.*"

"Just like that."

"Mike—" she said gently. "It wasn't me who flinched."

"It wasn't you I flinched from."

"No, it was just my life."

He met her eyes briefly, then looked down and began to put on his socks again. And then his shoes. He was ashamed, she saw, and also strangely resigned. She thought of Rumpel-stiltskin: named and dismissed. But she did not have a sense of having actually named a complete truth. She had named his fear, and hers. But that seemed to be enough. She stood there with her coffee, which was way too strong, still hoping he would find the right thing to say. It was so much harder now that she wasn't angry.

For the rest of the afternoon, Rebecca wandered around the house tidying up halfheartedly, feeling bereft and disoriented, trying to balance the impassive mass of all the ordinary things of her life with her sense that everything had changed. Inevitably, the weightless moments with Mike began to seem unreal. All her furniture said that love was a bubble and a fluke.

Rory dropped Mary Martha off at six o'clock that evening, right on time, which was unprecedented. Rebecca had braced herself for another tricky conversation; Rory's snide insinuations that she was sleeping with Mike were bound to be complicated now by the fact that she had. In a weird way, she had lost the high ground. But Rory didn't even get out of the car, just watched Mary Martha up the steps to the front door. When Rebecca let her daughter in, Rory gave them both a glum wave and drove off in a staccato flurry of backfires.

Mary Martha came into the house cautiously, peering around like a deer stepping into a clearing. She obviously suspected that Rebecca would not be alone; she checked all the rooms, one by one, as she and Rebecca sometimes checked the place for monsters after a scary movie or a bad dream. Clearly, Rory had put his own spin on the Mike situation while he had his daughter's ear. But Rebecca held off saying anything. She didn't want to come across as nervous and defensive or to blunder into any booby traps Rory might have laid. It always took her a while to get back on Mary Martha's wavelength anyway.

She cooked pigs-in-blankets, one of Mary Martha's favorite meals, in her usual Sunday night attempt to invoke their customary intimacy; and Mary Martha, as usual on a Sunday night, barely touched her food. Rory had let her have two ice

cream sandwiches late in the afternoon, an outrageous violation of their nutrition treaties even by his loose standards. After
dinner, Rebecca ran a bubble bath with extra soap, another
flagrant treat. Mary Martha, still preoccupied, sank deep into
the foamy cloud of bubbles until only her face was showing.

"Is Mike going to sleep here?"

"What?" Rebecca asked, caught off guard.

"Rory asked me if Mike sleeps here."

Rebecca weighed her response. Obviously Rory, true to
form, had been as subtle as a train wreck. "Sometimes when a
man and a woman are in love, they sleep together."

"Are you and Mike in love?"

"No," Rebecca said. "He's just a nice man who lives downstairs."

Dear Brother James,

*Please forgive my last, crazed note. I'm afraid I succumbed for a
time to the exhilarating delusion that I had a chance to be a decent
human being. But I have been purged anew of all such fantasies. I
have looked through the open door into the garden and found myself
unable to take the simple step.*

*The hideous truth is that I do well enough in my little hole. I am
that absolutely spoiled thing, a "spiritual" man. I can't convey how
horrifying it is to come upon the crippled ego at the heart of all my furious devotion, after all these fervent years. It was never about God,
I'm afraid. It was about hiding. It was about incapacity. I renounced
things I never had the guts or the heart to properly pursue in the first
place. My religious life amounted to the building of walls around a*

bubble, and now the bubble has burst and I am left with the walls, and the sticky emptiness.

Again, forgive my babbling. I did not think it was possible to despise myself more than I did when I left the monastery.

Michael Christopher

Chapter Eight

In the weeks after the fiasco with Michael Christopher, Rebecca avoided the back porch and the backyard completely. She was cautious even in taking out the trash, and she found herself letting bottles and cans pile up instead of recycling them because recycling meant an extra trip to the blue bin in the garage. She didn't want to take a chance on running into her downstairs tenant under any circumstances; she was afraid he would try to explain himself, and if he tried to explain himself she was afraid she would hit him with a wine bottle. There were probably all sorts of deep religious reasons for Mike's sudden recoil from intimacy. He'd been worked over by a life-denying church and had bought into all sorts of morbid medieval attitudes about the body, love, and normalcy. And of course, he was a *man,* his twisted monastic scruples aside. You didn't need a theology to explain emotional gun-shyness in men. Maybe Christopher had been too close to his mother, or not close enough; maybe his faltering was neurotic or sadistic or just plain self-absorbed. No doubt he had Issues.

But she just didn't have time for that kind of battlefield psychotherapy anymore. Once a man started talking about why he couldn't commit, the fun was over. For the duration of the relationship, he would make fresh vows, ask for slack, and generate theories. That well was bottomless.

In any case, Mike seemed as inclined to avoid her as she was to avoid him. He had stopped going out into the backyard to tend the garden, even when she wasn't home, and the flowers and shrubs he'd planted were dying. Watching the summer's aberrant burst of color withering day by day into the old familiar drab, Rebecca tried not to think of her breasts against Mike's ribs and his thigh between her legs. She could still feel the slow rise and fall of his chest beneath her hand; in her mind, she could nuzzle her nose against his neck and breathe him in, the smell of him blunt and strangely comforting, the scent of their intimacy. And she could still go over and over their conversations, wondering how she'd missed the clues, wondering if she could have said something to make it turn out differently.

At the office, she tried to lose herself in her work, but it was hopeless. The mass of sketches, notes, and memos on her desk seemed like debris from a previous tide. The sense of unreality in things she had previously believed to be urgent was unnerving. Day after day, Rebecca turned on her computer and stared at the screen, waiting for Jeff to charge in and ask her how the PG&E project was coming along. She was going to be forced to admit that she hadn't given the lightbulb man a moment's thought. She had fifteen e-mails to answer, and then twenty, and twenty-five; they multiplied like Tribbles. She thought of Mike, beyond the reach of e-mail. He had heard of the Internet while he was in the monastery, he'd told her, but he hadn't realized it was that big a deal.

Rebecca promised herself that this was the last time she was going through this ridiculous junior high school recovery process in her life, but such melodramatic vows only sharpened the pain. It seemed saddest of all to believe she was done with love. She had been much better off before she fell for Mike, believing she didn't care. He'd blown her cover, with his sly contemplative charm; she hadn't ever been a reconciled single mother after all, she'd been a love accident waiting to happen.

She would have liked to commiserate with Bonnie, but her best friend had just announced her engagement to Bob Schofield. She was so happy that Rebecca couldn't find an opening to talk about her woes. She and Bonnie had built their friendship on the seemingly unshakable ground of the impossibility of men, but the ground had shifted. Bonnie now sounded like an infomercial on the seven habits of highly effective couples; all she could talk about was her great communication with Bob, the little things they did for each other, their mutual tenderness and respect. Rebecca found herself longing for a glitch in the relationship—nothing fatal, she assured herself, just enough to initiate a gripe session. But Bonnie sailed on happily and Rebecca was left feeling ashamed of herself, mean and false and lonelier than ever.

The two of them hardly ever had time to talk these days anyway. Bonnie had taken to showing up at the office later and later. Bob believed that breakfast was the most important meal of the day, and Bonnie was cooking him lumberjack extravaganzas every morning. She would rush in half an hour late smelling of bacon and sausage, with pancake batter spattered on her blouse. She would also slip out early at the end of the workday—apparently dinner was crucial too.

Meanwhile, the office rumors had solidified into fact: Jeff Burgess and Moira Donnell were officially sleeping with each other. Not long after the affair began, Moira sought out Rebecca to ask for her advice.

Rebecca said carefully, "Moira, if you really want my advice on sleeping with your married boss—"

"No, no, I think I can handle *that* okay," Moira said. "It's basically just a matter of being clear and up front about your needs. But Jeff's got a birthday coming up—"

Rebecca laughed. "Ah, well, a birthday present. That's a little easier. . . . How about some discretion?"

"Those ties of his are terrible," Moira said. "I think I might get him a decent tie."

At home, after Mary Martha was in bed, Rebecca sat in the kitchen with her evening glass of wine instead of going to the back porch. She had all but quit smoking outside; she couldn't bear the thought of Mike catching her unawares, and she would shut herself in the bathroom instead, blowing the smoke out the window and burning incense afterward to skirt Mary Martha's wrath. Rebecca suspected that Mike was practicing a similar avoidance: she hadn't smelled smoke from below in weeks. There was probably something amusing in that, she thought, something about love and bad habits, but she was beyond finding comfort in ironies.

The main thing, she told herself, was to just keep going. Her life was not really bleaker than it had been before, as a room was not darker after a flashbulb popped. It was just going to take a while for her eyes to readjust.

Dear Brother James,

Thank you for your letter, which I took as an attempt to cheer me up. But I am beyond being cheered by reassurances that I am "a good person at heart" and that "God will provide." That kind of stuff just makes me suspect you aren't really paying attention. I am a futility. The life of prayer begins with that. And God is not a comfort, to be offered like Kleenex. God is a poisoned sea, with broken syringes washing up on the beach. God is shopping malls stretching to the horizon and warplanes in the sky. God is a flat tire in a rainstorm and beer cans in the ditch, a bottle shattered on a highway overpass and the taste of gunmetal in your mouth. God is dying children.

Have you forgotten, cultivating your pleasantness? Or have you really never known that terrible enormity? You talk of faith as if we were not desperate men; you prescribe it like an antacid. But real faith is a failure and a defeat, vomiting blood; real faith is a morphine drip; it is plastic bags whirled by the wind in an empty parking lot and a cigarette butt in dirty sand. It is possums squashed by trucks, and the slaughter on the evening news.

You consider me a project, clearly—community outreach or something, a target for your well-meaning nonsense about God. You walk around passing out hope like theological Monopoly money. But your colorful bills are no good here, Brother James. I am traveling in the desert, as you are; I'm off the game board. If we go on together, let's go on like men who are lost, crying for love as men cry for water. Let's not pretend we're doing anything else.

Yours in Christ,
    Mike

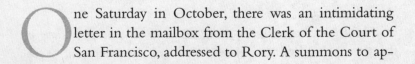

One Saturday in October, there was an intimidating letter in the mailbox from the Clerk of the Court of San Francisco, addressed to Rory. A summons to appear: his trial date had been set. Rebecca felt a brief surge of her old irritation, that Rory had given the city her address, no doubt to avoid the inconvenience of police officers at his real door. But Rory's troubles seemed far away. That was one of the lingering side effects of her encounter with Mike.

She drove out to Ocean Beach that same afternoon to drop off the summons, just to get it out of the house. Rory's Rambler was parked in its usual spot toward the north end of the beach; Rory liked the better waves near the rocks. The car was unlocked, as she had known it would be. Rebecca reached in through the open window to set the envelope on the driver's seat, then straightened hastily, feeling a sense of trespass. She glanced uneasily toward the ocean. There were half a dozen surfers in the water, backlit by the late afternoon sun, but she could still recognize Rory instantly, from years of practice. He was sitting up on his board, seal-like in his black wet suit, looking out to sea with the quiet, poised alertness she had believed he could bring to everything in his life.

As she watched, he pivoted the board and paddled hard to catch a rising swell, then popped to his feet with that easy, almost nonchalant air he had on even the most dangerous waves. He worked the three-foot break lovingly, cutting back and forth to generate a little excitement before he found a smooth long line in the heart of the curl and leaned into it, effortlessly, racing the collapsing edge.

He was so beautiful in his element, Rebecca thought. It was the moment she had married him for, the weightless glide that promised to go on forever, right up until it crumpled into churning foam.

She turned away as the wave gave out and Rory pointed his board back out to sea. He would do the same thing twenty or thirty times before the day was through, she knew; he would be out there for hours yet. But she wasn't waiting anymore for Rory to come ashore.

When she got back to the house, Michael Christopher was in the backyard. Her heart gave such a glad spontaneous leap that Rebecca realized she had been fooling herself. She wasn't over him; she wasn't resigned. She hadn't been hardened by life to a durable toughness. She wanted love and she wanted it now and she wanted it with this dear, fallible man on his hands and knees in her backyard, pulling up brown clumps of expired petunias.

"It's Mike!" Mary Martha exclaimed. She had been keeping an uneasy eye on the abandoned backyard for weeks. She ran toward the door, and Rebecca drew a breath, thinking to stop her, then let her go. It felt almost like cheating, letting Mary Martha break the ice. But she was in no mood to play by the stupid rules.

She gave her daughter ten minutes, then followed her down the stairs. When she got to the backyard, Mary Martha and Mike were discussing pumpkins. Mary Martha wanted to grow a pumpkin in the two weeks before Halloween. Mike was saying he didn't think that would be enough time.

"It *might* be," Mary Martha insisted.

"We might be able to grow a small pumpkin by Christmas," Mike said and turned to acknowledge Rebecca. "Hello," he said, careful but pleased.

"Hello," she said, conscious of his physical closeness. Mike hadn't shaved that day, and she could almost feel the stubble rasping on her own cheek. It seemed unnatural not to touch him. They'd had such great sex that her body still felt the world should have rearranged itself.

"We're going to grow a pumpkin for Halloween," Mary Martha told her.

"I heard Christmas," Rebecca said.

"The seeds may not even sprout, this late in the year," Mike admitted. "I suppose we could set up a cold frame."

"There's no need to go overboard."

"It's not overboard!" Mary Martha exclaimed.

"It's no trouble at all," Mike agreed.

"I'd hate to see you get too involved," Rebecca insisted. She met his eyes, pointedly, and after a moment he smiled, conceding. Her heart leaped again because the gesture was perfect, wryly acknowledging and yet dogged, the shrug of a man prepared to pay full price.

"It would be my pleasure," he said.

They all stood for a moment looking at the shabby beds of dead plants.

"I thought you'd given up on it," Rebecca said.

"Well, it's seasonal," Mike said.

"More like trial and error, it seems to me."

"Mike, can we plant the pumpkin today?" Mary Martha asked.

Rebecca said, "Mary Martha, why don't you run inside for a while and let the grown-ups talk?"

"Oh, *Mom*—"

"We can plant the pumpkin tomorrow," Mike said. "After I make the cold frame."

"What *is* a cold frame?"

"Mary Martha—" Rebecca said sternly.

"All right, all right," Mary Martha said. She turned and ran up the stairs, closing the door at the top with a distinct bang.

"How embarrassing it is sometimes to be a mother," Rebecca said. "I don't suppose you have a cigarette?"

"As a matter of fact—" Mike produced a box of Marlboros and lit one for her, then one for himself.

Rebecca breathed in and blew smoke toward the sky. It was a beautiful afternoon. She felt almost giddy. Everything suddenly seemed very easy.

"I'm sorry—" Mike began after a moment, resolutely, as she had known he would.

"I'm sorry too," she said. "I completely overreacted."

He looked at her warily. "I panicked."

"So did I."

"No, you didn't."

"Yes, I did. My panic manifested as rage. A preemptive strike. It's a lifelong pattern."

"My lifelong pattern is withdrawal. Also preemptive."

Rebecca took a drag and blew a perfect smoke ring.

"Look at that," she said. "There's a lifelong pattern for you."

"It's exquisite," Mike said. He hesitated. "I'm determined to go slowly this time."

"'This time'!" she laughed.

"If that's not presumptuous."

"Are you asking me out?"

"Do people still do that?"

"You were in a monastery, for God's sake," she said. "You weren't on the fucking moon."

T he next morning, Mike was out in the backyard again, banging together a large wooden box with transparent plastic stretched between the slats. He'd soaked a handful of pumpkin seeds in water overnight, and he and Mary Martha planted these solemnly in three little mounds, watered them again, and covered the bed with the frame.

After lunch, Rebecca dropped Mary Martha off at a friend's house for the afternoon, and she and Mike went for a walk.

By her reckoning, the outing counted as a date. He'd asked her to go, and she'd accepted. It felt very formal at first, like something out of a Jane Austen novel; she half-expected him to offer her his arm.

They strolled self-consciously into Golden Gate Park at 41st Avenue and walked along beside South Lake watching the slightly fanatical old women feed the ducks. It was a perfect Bay Area Indian summer day, with fluffy white clouds in a blue sky, and the park was packed with people. They had to keep stepping off the sidewalk to let roller-bladers, bicyclists, and joggers pass. It was all very distracting, and Rebecca was about to suggest that they leave the park and find a nice quiet bar when Mike took her elbow and steered her gently off the sidewalk into the woods. The path seemed overgrown and unpromising, but she was so glad for his touch that she went along without a murmur, and within a few minutes they were deep in a stand of fine old pine trees and the traffic noise had faded.

They walked along the sandy path. Mike had fallen silent, a comfortable silence that made their small talk amid the traffic seem a little forced, in retrospect. Rebecca was conscious anew of their recent fiasco. It was not an uncomfortable thought. There was even an odd intimacy in the memory, as if they had survived a shipwreck together. And soon enough it would be time to talk about what had caused the wreck and whether they would sail again.

"This is nice," she said. "Like a secret forest, through the looking glass."

"It's actually possible to get lost back here."

"That would be refreshing."

He laughed. "I'll see what I can do."

They walked for a time in silence. A gull wheeled in the sky above them, the sunlight gleaming on its white wings. The pines around them were alive with chittering finches.

"I thought you were just going to move out," Rebecca said at last. "Pack up your bags and go back to the monastery or something."

"I thought about it," Mike conceded.

"For a while there, I was even hoping that you would."

He shrugged. "You don't go into a monastery just because you haven't got anything better to do."

Rebecca felt an unwilling exasperation; the reasons one might or might not go into a monastery seemed irrelevant to her. The real issue was whether the two of them were going to be in love or not. It was embarrassing, to feel that so baldly; she would have liked to have been a deeper person, one who included the big cosmic factors in her heart's decisions. But she really didn't care about the big cosmic factors at the moment; the big cosmic factors seemed like a distraction, a cop-out, even. No doubt she'd burn in hell for that.

Mike seemed to have read something of this in her silence because he said quickly, "I didn't mean to sound sanctimonious."

"And I don't mean to seem . . . irreverent."

"All I meant was, there's God, and there's girl trouble. It doesn't do anyone any good to confuse the two."

Rebecca laughed. "And you feel like you've got girl trouble?"

"A guy can hope," he said.

They had reached a fork in the path. To the right, the trail was rutted with bicycle tracks, running downhill back toward the main road; the less-used left-hand path meandered beyond a fallen pine tree, into forest hedged with what looked like poison oak.

Mike asked, "Are you in a hurry to get back?"

"No," she said, and he led them off to the left. He stepped over the broken pine's trunk first, then paused and offered her his hand. She took it as she climbed over, feeling a crackle of electricity. Her body definitely remembered his body. He released her after she had hopped down to the other side. They skirted the poison oak and entered a grove of eucalyptus trees, their footsteps muted by the carpet of fragrant leaves.

She had never been in this part of the park before. Within the grove the autumn light was different, milder, steeped by the eucalyptus to a delicious blue-green. The air was cooler too, and Rebecca shivered a little. Mike, gratifyingly alert, offered her his jacket at once.

She hesitated; it seemed so intimate. If she let him put his jacket on her, there would be that moment when they looked at each other, that moment when she was warmer because of his action, enclosed in his warmth, safe and warm and silly with his sleeves dangling past her hands. It would be so easy just to kiss him then, to bypass all the negotiations. But she felt that the negotiations were important. She wanted to let him know that there would be hoops to be jumped through in this relationship, responsibilities, duties. She wanted him to assure her that he would be up to the challenges. That was what this walk was about. But she was chilly in her thin blouse, and he was wearing a flannel shirt. And she had to admit that the gallantry of the exchange was appealing.

She nodded, as casually as possible; Mike took off his jacket and held it up for her, and she slipped into it, one arm and then the other, with a sense of disappearing into warm depths.

Sure enough, as she made the little ballet turn to shrug on the second sleeve, their eyes met. She did want to kiss him, and she saw that he wanted to kiss her. They looked at each other for a long moment, and then Mike smiled gently and turned back to the path in a way that left the possibility of the kiss vividly between them, like the last cookie on a plate.

For the rest of the walk the kiss was there. She could feel it when they paused at views, when they stopped to look up at a hawk circling above the trees, when they sat down to smoke a cigarette on a fallen tree beside a horse trail: a promised sweetness growing more delicious with delay. The negotiations Rebecca had planned never really happened; they talked instead about late-season pumpkins, the delights of Indian summer, and what they had wanted to be when they grew up. Mike said that he had wanted to be a cowboy for quite a while, and then a deep-sea diver. Rebecca conceded that she had wanted to be a painter and that she had briefly owned a beret. It was all very charming and harmless, like the walk itself, a meandering intimacy lit with tender playfulness, two people quietly pleased with the fact that they were going to be kissing each other soon.

In any case, who could really say what might happen with an ex-monk who had wanted to be a cowboy? Rebecca suspected that Mike was determined to say what she wanted to hear anyway, that he had convinced himself he had learned something from the previous debacle, that he believed he was up to loving a single mother in a secular world. Her own gut sense was that he might be or he might not be. All she really knew for sure was that she liked the way his jacket smelled. She liked his laugh. She liked how easily they moved around together and the fact that he was willing to send pumpkin seeds on a kamikaze mission for Mary Martha.

They did manage to get lost for a few thrilling minutes, and they made the most of it, giggling and pretending to fret over the unlikelihood of ever being found; but inevitably they stumbled out of the trees onto the park's central bike path, beside a meadow where a vigorous volleyball game was in progress. They turned west again, walking past the polo field and the fly-fishing pond, and ended up at the windmill where the park opened out to the ocean. Rebecca made a quick call from a pay phone and established that Mary Martha could eat dinner at her friend's house, then she and Mike crossed the highway and stood on the concrete boardwalk, leaning on the wall. The sun was easing toward the sea, and the beginnings of a rose glow promised a spectacular sunset. A slight breeze had come up, and Rebecca was glad for the jacket. All along the boardwalk, sunset watchers were beginning to cluster. Beyond the breakers, a handful of surfers bobbed, none of them Rory. It was one more aspect of the moment's perfection.

"I'm not sure I could take it if we were to try again with each other and mess it up again," Rebecca said.

"We're not going to mess it up this time," Mike said, as promptly and as firmly as she could have hoped for.

The declaration had the ring of truth; there was a very dry, light serenity, almost a resignation in his voice. He sounded like a man prepared to embrace his fate.

"It's not all walks in the park and sunsets," she persisted, with a conscious effort to be sensible. "A real relationship is something that survives everything the world can throw at it, not something that happens instead of the laundry on my one free weekend this month."

"Bring it on," Mike said, which seemed crazy. She even believed him, in the dazzling moment, which seemed crazier still. But she kissed him anyway.

Walking home after the sunset, hand in hand, they stopped for dinner at a little Chinese restaurant on Judah. Mike ordered kung pao chicken, joked easily with the waiter across the language barrier, and proved surprisingly deft with chopsticks.

"You seem much too worldly to have been a monk," she told him as he filled their tiny cups from the pot of green tea. "Way too at home in Chinese restaurants. And in bed, for that matter."

Mike laughed. "Being a monk doesn't mean you don't know how. It just means that you don't."

"And now you do."

He smiled. "Eat Chinese food?"

"And the rest of your secular activities."

Mike busied himself with his tea.

"So what changed?" she persisted, dismayed by the faint note of truculence in her voice but needing somehow, however blindly, to probe this part of him. It was like throwing a stone into a lake at night, to hear it plop. "I mean, is this a sin, for instance?"

"Is what a sin?" he asked warily.

"*Us.* Is it some kind of fall from grace for you to be in a relationship at all? You once were found but now are lost?"

Mike laughed and shook his head. She was afraid that he would let it go at that and make her go after him again, but after a moment he said, "There was a guy who came into the monastery about a year after I did, a heartbreakingly sincere kid, Brother Mark. He was a passionate type, volatile, very mystically inclined, took everything hard. He used to weep during mass sometimes, especially during Lent. He'd beat his breast and rock back and forth moaning, 'I'm a sinner, I'm a sinner, I'm a hopeless sinner!' It was pretty unnerving, and whenever he started up, I would glance over at the older monks, to take my cue from them. And I would always see them nodding quietly—sort of amused, you know, but also very sympathetically."

"Meaning that the kid *was* a hopeless sinner?"

"Meaning, as I saw it, that we all were. Compunction 101." A strand of Rebecca's hair had fallen across her face. Mike hesitated, then reached across the table to move it back into place. They smiled at each other.

"*Anyway,*" Mike resumed, "this went on for quite a while, for years, off and on—I'm a sinner, I'm a sinner, and so on. It got so that you could count on it. And then one day Brother Mark stood up, right in the middle of the matin psalm, and started hollering, 'Holy, holy, holy! Everything is holy!' Which was also a little unsettling, to tell you the truth. But I looked over at the older monks, and, sure enough, they all were nodding."

Rebecca was silent for a moment.

"So it's a paradox," she said at last. "The moral of the story is that we're all sinners, and yet everything is holy? It's some kind of Zen thing?"

"You could read it that way," Mike said. "Personally, I think you just never could tell what Brother Mark was going to say next." He was silent for a moment, looking at the unopened fortune cookies on the plate. Then he said, "I suppose that what I'm getting at is that I don't think sin is the point with you and me."

"What *is* the point, then?"

"Redemption, maybe." She shot him a dubious glance and he laughed. "Maybe that's too glib. But I have this sense of having finally plunged into the real work of my life. Abbot Hackley used to say that real love doesn't sit around on its ass.

It gets up and *goes.* I always thought he was just saying that to get me to put in more time in the monastery vineyard. He wanted me out there stomping grapes and heaving oaken barrels around for God. He wanted me visiting the sick and praying novenas for the hungry and the lame, and all I wanted to do was let the Big Wheel stop. But I feel now like I might finally be getting it, like I might finally be *going.*"

"Going *where?*"

"I don't know. I'm not sure Hackley ever really said." They laughed.

"But seriously, folks—" Rebecca said.

Mike shrugged. "God, I don't know. I hate to think that I'm finally coming around, after all those years of fighting with the man about contemplation versus activity. I mean, I used to pray for an extra half an hour sometimes just to piss him off. He hated to see me kneeling there with my eyes closed; he was sure it was just a waste of time and that I was a lazy bum angling for a religious excuse to shirk my chores. And I always thought he was a rigid maniac without an inner life, covering over his existential emptiness with frantic hustle and bustle." He shook his head. "He would quote *The Cloud of Unknowing* to me: the devil has his contemplatives too. He said the silence that I experienced in prayer was just a natural quiet, not a divine infusion, and that I should work harder in mental prayer and keep my mind filled with holy words and images, or the devil would get me in the end."

"You guys both sound like a barrel of fun to me," Rebecca said.

Christopher laughed and attended to his orange slice. "I suppose the issues do seem a little obscure. Angels on the head of a nonexistent pin. A tempest in a monastic teapot."

"Let's just say it's not exactly the stuff that ends up above the fold on the front page of the *Chronicle*."

"It was my life. I was sworn to obedience, but I ignored him completely, of course, and just went deeper and deeper into the silence. It was pretty obvious to me by then that God had nothing to do with everything I thought about Him, that all my holy words were just getting in the way. And Hackley just seemed like a cartoon character to me. He was my abbot and my confessor, and I had to tell him about my prayer life and to endure his opinions, but he had about as much of a sense of the subtleties of contemplation as a plumber."

"And so you left, to prove him wrong."

"No, I left because my precious little silence finally went dead on me and I started to be afraid that he'd been right all along." Mike hesitated, then said, "I think that at some level I always thought of the monastery as a sort of nest. And so in the back of my mind I always figured that someday I'd get pushed out and it would be time to fly. I had all sorts of theories about what it would *be,* to fly—union with God, sainthood, glory. Whatever. But then when the time came, when I did leave the nest, I just dropped like a rock and hit with a splat."

Rebecca smiled. "Are those the technical religious terms?"

"A loose translation from the Spanish of St. John of the Cross." He met her eyes. "The point is, with you, I've glimpsed what it might mean to fly. That's all I'm saying. I don't give a damn about the rest of it. I just want to try to fly."

"Flying with me is going to involve a lot of walking, and a certain amount of time on buses and trains," Rebecca said.

"Okay," Mike said amiably, and reached for his fortune cookie, which said that all sorts of business opportunities were about to open up for him.

* * *

After dinner, which Mike insisted on paying for out of a battered old wallet without any plastic in it, they stopped to pick
up Mary Martha at her friend Patricia's house. Mary Martha, a
little giddy after a long afternoon of play and a Coke with her
dinner, chattered all the way home. At Patricia's house, she
said, they had Coke with their dinner all the time. They had a
big-screen TV that took up the whole living room. They had a
pool table.

"We're a milk-with-dinner family," Rebecca said. "We're a
small-TV family."

"Patricia has a hundred and seventeen Beanie Babies."

"That's amazing," Mike said, completely missing the parental
point. Rebecca suppressed a groan as Mary Martha turned to
him eagerly.

"I only have *eight* Beanie Babies," she said.

"Eight Beanie Babies are a lot," Rebecca said.

"Oh, *Mom,*" Mary Martha said exasperatedly.

"I doubt that Patricia is able to have the kind of deep relationship with her Beanie Babies that you have with yours,"
Mike offered.

Mary Martha peered at him warily, obviously suspecting
that he was crapping out on her.

"What are your Beanie Babies' names?" he asked.

"Dolphie, Zinger, Yogi, Bounder the Flounder, Hootie,
Specs, Percival, and, uh—"

"Elvis the Catfish," Rebecca supplied.

"—and Elvis the Catfish."

"You see?" Mike said. "That's special. I bet Patricia can't remember all hundred and seventeen names of *hers.*"

Mary Martha walked in silence for a few steps, then said
crossly, "Well, she can remember more than *eight.*"

* * *

Back at the house, the three of them paused in the driveway while Rebecca considered the complexities. She'd never had to deal with end-of-a-date dynamics and a cranky Mary Martha at the same time. It seemed precipitous to ask Mike in, but there was so much she still wanted to say. And she wanted to kiss him again. There was that.

"It's been lovely," she told him.

"Yes, it has."

"I know you said that you wanted to go slowly this time. . . ."

He smiled. "I've been very happy with our pace."

"I'm *freezing,*" Mary Martha said plaintively. "And I have to pee."

Rebecca decided to dispense with the formalities. "Would you like to come in for a cup of coffee or something?" she asked Mike.

"I'd love to," he said, not slowly at all.

"Is Mike going to sleep here?" Mary Martha asked as Rebecca tucked her into bed.

"I'm going to ask him if he wants to," Rebecca said.

Mary Martha hitched her big pink quilt more snugly under her chin and nodded uneasily.

"Come on," Rebecca said. "You like Mike. You've always liked Mike."

"Rory said Mike's going to be my new daddy."

"Well, that's not true. Nobody will ever be your daddy but Rory."

"Rory never sleeps here."

"You sleep at Rory's sometimes."

"That's not the same," her daughter insisted.

Rebecca sighed. There was no bluffing Mary Martha. She sat for a moment in silence, then said frankly, "Rory and I just don't get along that well, sweetie. We don't have a sleeping-together kind of relationship anymore. The main thing that we have in common is that we both love you."

Mary Martha considered this gravely.

"So are you going to be all right with this?" Rebecca asked.

"I guess so," Mary Martha said. It wasn't particularly enthusiastic, but it wasn't "No," and Rebecca thought it was good enough for now. She longed to tell Mary Martha that everything was going to be okay, but too much reassurance was probably as bad as too little for a child with Mary Martha's keen sense of bullshit. They were just going to have to take it one step at a time.

She kissed her daughter goodnight once, then again, and then a third time, an exorbitance that finally moved Mary Martha to give her a grudging smile.

"Mom?" Mary Martha said as Rebecca reached for the light switch.

Rebecca paused. "Yes, honey?"

"Can we make a photo album with pictures of Rory, like Grandma Phoebe has of Grandpa?"

Rebecca felt a stab of complex emotion, part chagrin, part poignancy, and part pride in her daughter's emotional loyalty, in the way she was laboring to balance the shifting loads.

"Of course we can, sweetheart," she told Mary Martha. "We have a whole shoe box full of pictures of your dad."

In the kitchen, Mike was waiting quietly with a pot of decaf coffee. He stood up as she came in, and Rebecca kissed him uncertainly, afraid of a false note. But his kiss was perfect, tender and somehow humble.

"This is not just about us anymore," she said. "If that still freaks you out, then please, please, bail now. Because if you're going to stay here tonight, you're going to have breakfast with my daughter. You're going to have to be a decent human being. You're going to have to be a man."

"I would love to have breakfast with your daughter," Mike said, and she believed him as much as she could believe a man at this point in her life.

Chapter Nine

At work on Monday morning, a dress code had been posted prominently on the bulletin board in the employees' lounge. A disgruntled crowd of technicians in jeans and graphics artists in variations on basic black milled and muttered over half-drunk cups of coffee.

"You're the only person here who's not going to have to buy a whole new wardrobe," Rebecca told Moira Donnell, who was looking spiffy and a bit smug today in a cherry red suit and a candy-cane-striped blouse with a ruffled collar.

"Jeff's all torn up about having to implement this," Moira said diplomatically. Since she had started sleeping with management, she seemed to feel a certain responsibility for policy decisions.

"I'm sure he is," Rebecca said. Jeff in fact had seemed miserable lately. He'd shaved off his mustache and started wearing quiet blue ties and better suits. It was hard to tell whether the changes owed more to the pressures of courting corporate accounts or to Moira, who had a distinctly *GQ* sense of style and a high-maintenance attitude, but the trend was clear.

Bonnie Carlisle wasn't in her office yet. Rebecca wrote *See me ASAP big news must talk* on a Post-it, stuck the note to Bonnie's computer monitor, and went on to her own office.

She was still staring at the screen, thinking about Michael Christopher, when Bonnie charged in five minutes later, waving the Post-it with a condescending air.

"If you think it's big news that Moira sleeping with Jeff is having a bad effect on this company, you are *sadly* out of touch," Bonnie said. "And don't even get me started on this dress code nonsense."

"No, no, this just in," Rebecca said.

Bonnie settled on the edge of the desk to indicate that she was all ears. "So?"

"Michael . . . Christopher."

Bonnie took a moment to place the name, and another to weigh the tone, and then her eyes widened gratifyingly. "You're *kidding!*"

"Nope."

"You and the monk?!"

"We pretty much spent the weekend together."

"Well, well, *well!*"

"We'd been kind of dancing around the possibility for a while, I think," Rebecca said, sensing a critique in Bonnie's exaggerated amazement and feeling compelled to present the relationship in its most favorable light. "It doesn't even feel like it happened fast. It feels like it all happened in this exquisite slow motion."

"That's a good sign," Bonnie allowed. "How is he in bed?"

"Very sweet. And . . . deft."

"Deft!"

"Pre-monastic flings. I guess it's like riding a bicycle."

"Has he gotten hit by the backlash yet?"

"The backlash?"

"Yeah, you know—guilt, morbidity, that kind of thing. Twisted religious scruples. Bad conscience."

"You're an expert on 'that kind of thing,' are you?"

"It doesn't take a rocket scientist, Rebecca. We've all read *The Scarlet Letter.* We all know the type."

"I was sort of counting on you for a little support."

"So you think it's got a future?" Bonnie asked dubiously.

"*He's* already talking about love. I feel like the designated driver. But yes, I do. I hope so, anyway."

Bonnie was silent for a long moment.

"*What?*" Rebecca demanded.

"Well, it's just . . . Are you sure you're not just on the rebound from Bob?"

Rebecca considered a range of nasty replies but managed to hold off. Bonnie, she knew, meant well. "I can do this with you or without you, Bonnie. It would be so much more fun with you."

Bonnie said stubbornly, "It's just so sudden. That's all I'm saying."

"You and Bob were sudden."

"Bob and I were both very clear up front that we were looking for a mature, committed relationship."

"Oh, come on. You met on a beach, he played Frisbee with your dog, and within a few days you were cooking him French toast, sausage, and eggs over easy."

Bonnie wavered in a way that amounted to a concession, then countered slyly, "Well, breakfast *is* the most important meal of the day."

It allowed them both to laugh. With the tension broken,

Rebecca leaned back in her chair and sighed. "I guess it *is* pretty sudden. Mary Martha seems a little wigged-out too. But things happen the way they happen. He's really wonderful, Bonnie. We talk and talk. We *laugh*."

"Oh, I'll get up to speed, I promise," Bonnie assured her. "Who made the first move?"

"He did, I guess. A kiss."

"Deft?"

"Very deft," Rebecca said happily.

"Another good sign," Bonnie pronounced, and it began to look like they were going to get through it after all.

On her lunch hour, instead of the usual sandwich at her desk, Rebecca walked up to Market Street and browsed through several men's clothing stores in search of the perfect underwear for Mike. She felt very serene and focused. The gay salesmen were all delighted with her, and one guy in particular entered immediately into the extravagant spirit of the mission. The two of them discussed Mike's size with a slightly raunchy enthusiasm for much longer than was strictly necessary. He led her through all sorts of wicked options from silver lamé to frank red briefs before finally showing her a pair of royal blue boxers that were just right, Burmese silk like a soft, dark breeze, with subtle gold threading.

The price was outrageous, but it seemed like cheating to flinch. The salesman found a stylish box with the store's monogram; he gift-wrapped the package in heavy gold paper with a royal blue ribbon, and when the crucial moment at the cash register came he gave Rebecca a wink and typed in his employee discount number, which brought the cost of the grand gesture down from inconceivable to merely prodigal.

On the street again, swinging her handled bag in the bright afternoon sunshine, Rebecca found a sidewalk table at a nearby café and ordered wine with her salad. She gave the bag its own chair. She felt free, light, and happy. The wine arrived. She lit a cigarette, wondering if that was illegal. But it felt so fine, it felt positively Parisian, and nobody said a thing. It was the middle of a workday, and all she felt like doing was basking in the sun. No wonder Bonnie was so worried. She'd just spent almost a week's grocery money on underwear. Love was a dangerous thing indeed.

Back in the office, she chewed some mints to get the wine off her breath and spent the afternoon trying to translate her pencil sketches of the lightbulb man into computer animation. The work was as maddening as ever, like trying to play a saxophone part on a kazoo. But she felt like she was finally starting to get the hang of it. By now she had about a minute and a half of the lightbulb man cavorting in his unwieldy, earnest way, with a touch of pathos and the hint of a self-deprecating smile, as if to say how ruefully aware he was that he was not Fred Astaire. It was a little ridiculous, Rebecca thought, how fond of him she had grown.

She wrapped up early, feeling reckless and come-what-may, and left at five o'clock on the dot, carrying the bag with the gold-wrapped boxers and leaving her sketch case on the desk. She was still feeling uncommonly serene. She and Mike had agreed to let Rebecca have an evening alone with her daughter, to ease the pace of change, but they were going to meet on the back porch that night after Mary Martha was asleep, and the thought of the rendezvous had been like solid ground all day.

The woman at Bee-Well was so surprised to see her on time that she didn't say anything snide. Mary Martha seemed to be back to normal, chattering about her day while Rebecca ordered a pizza by phone, as a sort of treat and bribe. They ate off paper plates at the kitchen table and didn't mention Michael Christopher once. That seemed like a very good sign, as did the fact that Mary Martha went to bed after an uneventful night of TV without insisting on any particular unicorn security measures. Rebecca read to her from *The House at Pooh Corner* with a sense of blessed ordinariness until Mary Martha dozed off.

As soon as her daughter was asleep, Rebecca hurried out the back door, feeling a little sheepish in her excitement. She and Mike had agreed to meet between nine o'clock and nine-thirty; it was just past nine. Mike was not outside yet, but the lamp in his apartment glowed behind drawn curtains, casting a square of muted light on a freshly planted jasmine at the base of the stairs.

Rebecca hesitated, then slipped in the back door of the garage. The in-law apartment was just to the right, past the garbage cans and the blue plastic recycling bin. The tiny, somewhat ramshackle door looked like the entrance to an elf's lodging in a tree. Rebecca knocked, feeling the plywood rattle beneath her knuckles.

There was a pause, a seemingly startled silence, and then she heard Mike's footsteps, the four strides it took to cross the apartment. The door opened and he stood before her, stooping to peer out. He was barefoot, dressed in a white T-shirt and khakis that seemed new; his hair was wet, with the comb lines showing, and his face was half lathered with shaving cream. A blue shirt, crisp on its hanger, dangled from the doorknob of the apartment's minuscule closet. Rebecca felt a small thrill at the thought that he had been preparing himself for her.

"No one's ever knocked on this door before," Mike said, which somehow struck her as utterly endearing. She flung her arms around his neck and kissed him, smearing them both with shaving cream. He met her lips, and then her tongue, amused at first and then passionately. She could feel the difference between the smooth, already-shaved parts of his face and the stubble beneath the shaving cream. She fumbled for the button at the waist of his pants, a little uncertainly, not wanting to presume. He responded by pulling her blouse over her head in one motion and unhooking her bra with an expertise that still seemed incongruous. Her breasts fell free, and he plunged his face between them and ran his tongue back up to the base of her throat.

There was shaving cream everywhere by now. She kicked off one shoe and managed to close the door before they staggered toward the center of the apartment. Mike's futon, the only furniture in the place, was neatly folded against the far wall, and rather than bother with it they sank to the floor, still entwined, shedding clothing haphazardly. The carpet was wonderfully lush, Rebecca noted in passing, with a landlord's pride. She had been afraid they wouldn't know what to do with each other, now that they had spent some time apart, immersed in what she still thought of as their real lives. But it didn't seem like that was going to be a problem after all.

Afterward, they lay together on the mud-colored carpet with their arms around each other, tender and disheveled, talking in whispers, conscious of Mary Martha asleep above them.

"I thought about you all day," Rebecca told Mike.

"Me too. I kept burning hamburgers."

She laughed. "Are we ridiculous?"

"I hope so."

"No, seriously."

"We are seriously ridiculous," Mike said.

A last smear of shaving cream under his ear lent credence to this. Rebecca scraped the white foam off his jaw and transferred it to the tip of his nose. He ran his finger along the ridge of her collarbone, to the point of her shoulder and back, and she closed her eyes, savoring the garden-toughened rasp of his fingertip.

"I want a painting," Mike said.

She opened her eyes. "What?!"

"I want one of your paintings from the garage. The pick of the litter. I think it would go great on that wall."

"No *way.*"

Mike smiled, unperturbed, absurdly dignified with the shaving cream on his nose. "Way."

He had gotten that from Mary Martha, Rebecca knew. She considered the bare wall uneasily. It was strange. Here she lay, naked on the floor with this man, but it seemed too intimate to let him hang one of her paintings in his apartment.

"I'm prepared to pay top dollar," Mike persisted, and Rebecca laughed in spite of herself.

"Bonnie thinks we're moving too fast," she said.

"Look who's talking."

"That's what I told her. But maybe she has a point."

"Of course she has a point. But this is how fast love moves."

"So what should we do?"

He mulled this mock-solemnly, then suggested, "I've got more shaving cream in the bathroom."

Rebecca laughed. "See, this is what I don't understand. You spent all those years praying and fasting and practicing God knows what kind of medieval self-denial, and yet you're a completely silly man."

Mike shrugged modestly. "I knew it would pay off eventually," he said.

She slipped back up the stairs soon after that, reluctantly, but not wanting to leave Mary Martha alone too long. As she readied herself for bed, Rebecca realized that she had forgotten to give Mike his present. The gift-wrapped box of underwear, still in its bag, sat on the floor by her closet. It seemed outrageously glitzy amid the rest of her mundane debris. But that was okay, Rebecca thought contentedly. It was a future of sorts.

Dear Brother James,

Thank you for your very frank letter in response to the news of my renewed relationship with Rebecca. I had not expected what you call my "most recent fling" to cause you such dismay; I had actually imagined that you would be pleased for me. But I realize now that you have continued to think of me as a renunciant, even as I suffered through the confusion of my faith—that you "believe in my vocation," as you put it, and that by falling in love I have somehow invalidated myself in your eyes.

It is true, as you point out (intending, I am afraid, to bring me up short), that "one cannot go far in prayer without being horrified by the poverty of the self." But there are richer fruits of prayer. Deeper than a sense of sin and unworthiness, deeper than the self-contempt, the dryness, and the futility of will, the truest revelation of the endless fall through the self toward God is a sense of genuine nothingness. This "humility" is no affectation; it is no false modesty calculated to ease the usual traffic of egos; it is simply realism. I am nothing. I have looked within, long and hard, for the soul that would hasten into God, and in the end I was not there. What is left when we get to the bottom of the self, when we have exhausted all our tricks? Real prayer is a disappearance, a surrender to the embrace of deepening mystery, in darkness. In that darkness, finally, God alone is. And God is infinite surprise.

So say that I have been surprised by love, surprised by desire, surprised by my fear of inadequacy and the fear of loss. Say that I have been surprised by the way a woman's hair falls across her eyes and by the tender movement of my hand to lift her hair away. Did we really expect to turn into beings of light? Did we really believe that radiance would be best? Say that I am surprised by how much I want to be a man now; say that I have finally found a reason to struggle with myself.

You insist that the image of my living "a monk's life in the world" had given you heart. But what is the point of the monastic life, in the world or out of it, if it is not perfect openness to the surprise of God? The monastery walls do not exist to protect your calling, Brother James; nor did I escape my calling in leaving those walls—or my celibacy—behind. The ancient monks, seeking quiet for contemplation, found the desert's emptiness perversely hectic, wild with inner demons, and were tempted to despair; the tidy faith they had brought with them failed before such overwhelming bafflement. But that failure eventually revealed itself to be the point. The faith the desert teaches is a faith that risks and trusts, a faith that survives in the wilderness of the world not through fortresses of routine and unassailable vows but through simple reliance on the mercy of God. And God in His mercy has made us human beings.

I know you wrote from the heart, in genuine concern for the state of my soul. And so I write back from the heart, to assure you I am well. You have mistaken me, I am afraid, if you believe that I am somehow taking the side of "the world" now while you represent "the transcendent." It is really so much simpler than that.

Yours in Christ,
  Mike

On a Thursday afternoon about a week and a half after she had started up again with Michael Christopher, Rebecca had lunch with her mother. She'd been preparing Mike for this all week, gently and a little uneasily, since it was the point at which the wheels had fallen off before. But Mike seemed prepared to take the announcement of their relationship in stride this time.

"There's still time to wig out, you know," Rebecca told him on Wednesday night as they sat on the back porch wrapped in a blanket against the night air. "This is your last chance before it all goes *really* public."

Mike smiled. "I respectfully decline the chance to wig out."

"She's probably going to want to have us over for dinner right away."

"Yikes," he exclaimed, endearingly.

She laughed. "I warned you."

"I'm still recovering from the last shindig at your mother's house."

"I could tell her you're just in this for the sex."

Their eyes met. She knew what he was thinking; she was thinking it herself. It was too soon to be performing as a Couple. It seemed like a lot of weight to put on something so new. But this was what he had gotten into. This was her life.

Mike, surrendering, said regretfully, "She's already seen my best jacket, I'm afraid—"

"Phoebe doesn't give a damn about your clothes."

"I'm not going to baptize anybody this time. I'm not even going to say grace."

"I'll be happy if you just get through the evening without deciding to renounce the world again," Rebecca told him, a little chagrined by the relief she felt at what struck her as perfectly normal in-law reluctance.

She and Mike sat quietly for a moment. Their time on the back porch together after Mary Martha was in bed had already evolved into a cherished ritual for them both. They would sit out here for hours at a stretch, sipping glasses of wine, holding hands and talking and smoking the occasional cigarette. It felt comically like dating, but dating without all the fuss and bother, the dinners out and the small talk, the events requiring tickets and costumes, heroic exertions in quest of a simple quiet moment with someone you could care about. She and Mike had cut to the chase somehow.

He had unerringly picked her favorite painting from the stacks in the garage, a modest study of the bend in the river where she had grown up in coastal New Jersey. She'd painted it for her mother not long after John Martin died: the view from their old back porch, golden marsh grass spilled against meandering blue, steadied by mud flats and sturdy green pines. Rebecca had called the work *Low Tide,* which in retrospect may have been too mordant; Phoebe, gently refusing the gift, had always said the picture made her sad. But Mike had gone right to it, and it opened inward now from the wall above his futon like an unsuspected window.

Rebecca gave him a sudden hug. "I don't trust it," she said. "It's too good to be true. You *are* going to want to go back into the monastery. Or you'll meet another woman—I'm just your transition relationship."

"My 'transition relationship'?"

"Between God and . . . whatever. The real world. I'm a scaffold, a temporary support during the construction of the actual building."

"Which is?"

"*I* don't know. It's just my paranoid scenario; I'm not a placement agency."

Mike laughed. "Well, I'm not going anywhere."

"People never are. Right up until the moment that they do."

But she didn't really believe he was going to leave. To consider the possibility was more like watching a horror movie for the thrill of being scared. What Rebecca really believed was that she had been given a miraculous second chance in love. And she was determined not to blow it.

She met Phoebe at one of her mother's favorite downtown haunts, an elegant place muffled in ivory and cream, too delicate to draw much of a business lunch crowd, on Fourth Street near Mission. Phoebe knew the waiter, who brought her a vodka tonic without asking; Rebecca had a glass of wine. The only other customers in the place were a man and a woman who were apparently beginning an expensive affair.

"Don't you look pleased with yourself," Phoebe noted as their salads arrived.

"Do you remember my mystery man, a while ago?"

"I'm sure it's none of my business," her mother said with a scrupulous nonchalance that made them both smile.

"It's Michael Christopher, Mom."

Phoebe gave a little squeal. "The monk!"

"He's surprisingly dissolute."

"Well, I hate to say it, but I told you so."

"You did *not* tell me so."

"I certainly did. I'm so happy for you, darling. You'll have to bring him over for dinner sometime soon."

"I told him you'd say that. He's half a step away from bolting at the very thought."

"It's how these things are done, dear. He's not in the monastery anymore."

"I think that's dawning on him."

"How's Mary Martha taking it?"

"A little grudgingly, I'd say. It's all moved pretty fast."

"She seemed fine with him at the baptism."

"I think Rory's put some kind of bug in her ear about it."

"Ah. Well, she'll be fine. . . . I truly am happy for you, dear."

"I'm just trying not to jinx it."

Phoebe rapped obligingly on the wooden table, then made a zipping motion across her lips.

Their meals arrived, and they talked of other things as they ate. Phoebe was thinking about a trip to Australia. Or maybe Kathmandu. It had something to do with Buddhism, but Rebecca could never quite keep up.

They skipped their usual coffee, as Rebecca had to get back to work. Phoebe insisted on paying, as she always did. The waiter brought her credit card back, and she signed off for her usual flamboyant tip.

"Shall we say Saturday then?" Phoebe said brightly as they stood to go.

"Saturday?"

"For dinner, dear."

"I'll check with Mike."

"Tell him I promise not to bite."

Rebecca laughed. "I'm sure that will help."

On the sidewalk, they kissed and parted, with Rebecca heading toward Fourth Street and Phoebe heading toward Fifth. At the corner, Rebecca glanced back affectionately and noticed that a small crowd had gathered not far from the restaurant entrance. Someone was lying on the sidewalk, a woman in a nice tweed suit. Her mother.

A jolt ran through her entire body, an electric horror. She raced back down the sidewalk and pushed through the bystanders. Someone had already put a jacket under her mother's head. Phoebe's face was slack and gray.

"Sthummled," she murmured, her mouth lopsided. She seemed distressed to be causing a fuss. "It's very odd."

Rebecca took her mother's right hand, which was unnervingly limp. "Are you all right, Mom? What happened?"

"So silly of me, really," Phoebe said, her words slurring. "I don't know wha—I don't . . . It's very odd." Her eyes drifted, seeking words, and her brow knitted in frustration. "I can't seem to . . . I'm *terribly* sorry . . ."

"Someone call an ambulance!" Rebecca screamed, but there were already at least three cell phones out. Everybody in downtown San Francisco seemed to be dialing 911.

"I'll be needing an aspirin, I suppose," Phoebe mumbled with an air of concession. "For the headache." Her gaze drifted again, and then she said, quite distinctly, "It's really most extraordinarily odd."

PART V

In the beginning Love satisfies us.
When Love first spoke to me of love—
How I laughed at her in return!
But then she made me like the hazel trees,
Which blossom early in the season of darkness,
And bear fruit slowly.

HADEWIJCH OF ANTWERP
(ca. thirteenth century)

Chapter Ten

At the hospital, despite the genuine urgency of the attendants, the check-in process seemed maddeningly slow. Phoebe, upright in a wheelchair, gave a fair impression of normality. But Rebecca knew something was very wrong. Her mother was being polite and trying not to cause anyone any trouble, but she couldn't seem to remember Rebecca's name, and she was serene in the belief that when her husband arrived everything would be straightened out.

"Your father has always been at his best in a crisis," Phoebe told Rebecca cheerfully. Her face was lopsided and her speech was still slurred, but there were three traffic accident victims and a gunshot wound ahead of her, and all that blood was undeniably more compelling than the fact that Phoebe believed it was 1973.

When Phoebe was wheeled away for a CAT scan, Rebecca hurried at once to a phone, conscious of juggling both Phoebe's purse and her own. There were calls to be made; she had a critical meeting with Jeff and Marty Perlman that afternoon; the lightbulb man was on the verge of going into final production. But she found that she didn't want to call anyone. It all still seemed unreal, and if she could put off that moment when she would have to say, "My mother has had a stroke," then maybe somehow, magically, the beleaguered ordinary world could still win out.

She rummaged through her purse and found a quarter and a dime, and as she raised the quarter to the slot she began to cry. Because the coin was going to make that little rattle when it fell, because the dime would drop after it, because the dial tone would hum its small demand. She was standing in front of a row of pay phones in a hospital hallway, and everything was going to be different now.

Phoebe's doctor was a smooth-spoken man named Pierce, incongruously dapper in a pink silk shirt, crisp slacks, and tasseled Italian loafers, smelling of mouthwash and cologne. Rebecca distrusted him instantly; she would have preferred a doctor more disheveled, someone more obviously in the fray. But Pierce seemed unruffled by the horror of her mother's damaged brain.

"The CT shows evidence of an ischemic stroke, with obstruction of the carotid artery," he told Rebecca. "We did an MRI, and there's no indication of intracranial hemorrhage—"

"And that's good?"

Pierce looked briefly disconcerted, as if such a notion would never have occurred to him. "It's certainly less bad," he said. "I'd like your permission to administer a tissue plasminogen activator—a thrombolytic agent, a sort of clot-busting drug. Often a t-PA can help with the restoration of circulation to the damaged areas, if it's administered within three hours of the onset of the attack. But there's a danger of increasing any undetected intracranial bleeding."

"If you think that would be best," Rebecca said.

"Definitely."

"Then do it." She hesitated. "How *is* she?"

"It's very hard to tell at this point how much permanent damage has been done. There is definite hemiplegia—"

"'Hemi—'?"

"Paralysis, on the right side. There is confusion, some aphasia or loss of speech function. It's impossible to say for sure how much can be recovered through therapy." He hesitated. "I wouldn't be honest if I didn't tell you that sometimes it gets worse before it gets better. And often the worst thing in the case of a stroke like this is the patient's reaction to diminished capacity. There's a tendency toward deep depression. She's going to need a lot of support."

"My mother is a fighter."

"I'm sure she is."

"Can I see her?"

"She was asleep when I left her. And—" Pierce hesitated again. "It's often upsetting."

"Then I might as well start getting used to it."

He met her eyes fleetingly then shrugged. "It's up to you. I'll see to the t-PA. We'll keep her in the ICU for at least twenty-four hours and monitor her closely—hopefully she's through the worst of it. As for the rest—time will tell."

"Thank you, Doctor."

Pierce made a little gesture, almost embarrassed, with his manicured hand, and hurried away. Rebecca walked up the hallway and found her mother's room. The placard in the slot by the door already said MARTIN in brisk blue hand lettering. Like the coins dropping in the pay phone, it was another ratcheted notch into the new reality. Rebecca took a deep breath and entered the room.

The curtains were drawn, blocking out the late afternoon sun completely. The room's bathroom jutted into the central space, and it was not until Rebecca cleared its corner that she saw her mother in the hospital bed. Phoebe, who had always looked like a vigorous sixty-year-old, had aged twenty years in a couple of hours. She seemed heartbreakingly frail amid the array of tubes, racks, and monitors—a crumpled bit of gray debris, like a sparrow that had smacked into a windowpane. The oxygen tube beneath her nostrils looked alien and imposed, a grotesque plastic smiley face. Her hair, which Phoebe kept clipped short in an elegant silver bob, was mussed and wispy.

Rebecca moved to the bedside and reached uncertainly to soothe her mother's hair into place. Phoebe stirred beneath her touch, which was heartening. The IV unit clicked like a weird metronome; the oxygen tank hissed softly. On the monitor, Phoebe's heartbeat showed in jagged pulses of green light.

"You're going to be okay, Mom," Rebecca whispered. "I'm here now."

She called Mike at McDonald's half an hour later. There was no way around it; someone had to deal with Mary Martha. But she dreaded Mike's reaction to the crisis, to her need. It had been a phone call like this that had essentially ended her marriage with Rory, on a day when she'd been caught at work and unable to pick up the infant Mary Martha. Rory had flaked out on her, as he always did, for the usual lame reasons; she'd had to pick up Mary Martha herself, and she'd lost her job. She'd taken the baby and moved out the next day.

Someone absurdly young answered the phone at McDonald's. "Hello! Stanyan Street McDonald's! How can we help you today?"

"Is Michael Christopher there?"

"Who?"

She could hear the fast food chaos in the background. Someone was hollering something about french fries. "Michael Christopher? He works the grill, I think—"

"Oh, sure, Mike. Hey, Mike! . . . *Mike!* Telephone!"

The receiver clattered to some hard surface. A moment later Mike picked it up, sounding tentative, as if he suspected a mistake had been made. "Hello?"

"Mike—"

"Rebecca?"

To her horror, she began to cry. It was the last thing she had wanted to do. She wanted to sound brisk and cool, to let him know there was no pressure, that she just needed a small favor, this one small thing, that she had no intention of burdening him with too much of her life.

"Rebecca, what is it?" Mike asked. She could hear that he had moved someplace quieter.

"I'm at the hospital. It's my mother. It looks like a stroke."

"Oh, God. Do you want me to come down there?"

"No! No, no, there's nothing to be done here. She's sleeping now. But Mary Martha—"

"Of course. I'll go get her right away."

"Is this going to get you in trouble at work?"

There was the briefest of pauses, and then Mike, gently incredulous, said, "I'm sure these hamburgers will get cooked without me."

"There's no food in the house, I'm afraid. I was going to do some shopping on the way home. I was going to buy milk, cereal, rice, fish, broccoli. . . ." Her throat was tightening again, and she tried to choke back the sob. "I was going to buy peanut butter," she said pathetically.

"I'll see to it."

"I don't know when I'll be able to get home."

"We'll be fine. You do what you have to do." He hesitated. "What are the doctors saying?"

"That we'll have to wait and see how bad it is."

"Okay," he said, and she felt him pause, groping to say something supportive.

"Don't you talk to me about God," she said. "I don't want to hear a word about God right now."

P hoebe surfaced briefly, just before seven o'clock that night. She obviously recognized Rebecca, giving her a fond, weary smile, but she still couldn't remember her daughter's name. She thought she might be in a hotel and seemed disconcerted by the liberties the room service personnel took with her. She still expected her husband to show up. But there were flashes of a Phoebe who knew what was going on.

"Is it very, very bad?" she asked Rebecca after a nurse had taken her blood pressure, refused a tip, and left the room smiling.

"They say we'll have to wait and see," Rebecca said, wondering what would constitute very, very bad for Phoebe at this point. Was it very, very bad that she couldn't move her right arm and leg, that her vocabulary was hit-or-miss, that her face was drooping and she was talking out of one side of her mouth like Jimmy Cagney? Somehow these things seemed more manageable than Phoebe believing John Martin was still alive. Rebecca was dismayed by the rawness of the grief she felt each time Phoebe mentioned her father; a wound she thought had healed had been torn open as if it were new. She didn't have the heart yet to tell Phoebe her husband was dead. She wasn't sure she ever would.

"Could you see to my orchids?" Phoebe asked, an encouragingly pragmatic turn. "They'll need water."

"Of course."

"You're a good girl, um—"

She smiled sadly. "Rebecca."

"Of course. Rebecca." Phoebe sighed. "This isn't as easy as it looks."

"You're doing great, Mom."

Phoebe met her eyes, an eloquent, doleful look, blurred by exhaustion.

"You're doing great," Rebecca repeated. She took her mother's good hand, and they sat quietly for a while until Phoebe fell asleep.

A nurse came by half an hour later to add a sedative to the IV mix; the doctor wanted Phoebe to sleep through the night. Rebecca stayed for another hour, then kissed her mother's cheek and made the long journey to the Sunset. She fell asleep on the train and rode all the way out to the ocean before she woke up, and rather than waiting at the turnaround for the train's inbound run, she walked the ten blocks back up the hill to 38th Avenue. The neighborhood seemed weirdly normal; she realized that she had half expected dramatic changes everywhere she looked. But the TVs glowed gray through the usual windows, the Vietnamese restaurant at the corner of 45th did its usual brisk business, and the usual crowd of tough teenagers milled and whooped in the parking lot of the 7-Eleven. Rebecca walked slowly, conscious of the dim stars above her, beyond the streetlights and the city's glare. It seemed like a very long time since she had noticed the stars.

The house was quiet when she walked in, with only the kitchen light on, but the kitchen was empty. The table was strewn with crayons, scissors, and scraps of colored construction paper—Mary Martha and Mike had been making get-well cards for Phoebe. Rebecca picked up her daughter's effort, a bright blue card with a big, smiling yellow sun on the front. Inside were three stick figures with the wild hair that denoted females in Mary Martha's art, holding hands. One was big, one was medium, and one was small. The card read, in Mary Martha's laborious lettering, I LOVE YOU GRANDMA. I HOPE YOU FEEL BETTER SOON.

Rebecca felt a brief, unwilling chagrin; she was not sure she would have thought of such a constructive way to focus her daughter's reaction. It seemed petty to resent the fact that Mike had managed to break the bad news so well, but she could feel a twinge of grudging, along with an uneasiness, a sense of a big event in Mary Martha's life having happened without her.

She realized that there was activity in the backyard—a bright light, and movement. She went to the back door and saw that Mike and Mary Martha were huddled over the pumpkins' cold frame, adjusting some kind of lamp on a tripod stand. Rebecca hesitated; the two of them seemed so content and she hated to be the party pooper; then she told herself that was ridiculous, that she was just feeling sorry for herself.

She stepped outside. Mary Martha ran to her at once, aglow with somber excitement. She was wearing her pink nightgown, her bunny slippers, and Mike's jacket, which hung down past her knees, but she clearly felt the gravity of her mission.

"We're going to give the pumpkins to Grandma now," she told Rebecca proudly.

"You're up way past your bedtime," Rebecca said. "And you shouldn't be out here in your slippers and nightgown."

Mary Martha's mouth made a startled little O and then snapped shut into a frown at the injustice of this.

"I'm sorry," Mike said, a step behind her. "I guess we got carried away by the special circumstances."

"What in the world *is* all this?"

He looked sheepish. "A grow light. These plants are going to need some help."

"The pumpkins think it's August," Mary Martha offered, with a conspiratorial glance up at Mike, who winked at her.

The look of adoration on her daughter's face sobered Rebecca somewhat. She took a deep breath and said, as mildly as she could, "Well, this is all pretty amazing, I'm sure, but it really is time to get you to bed, young lady."

"Did you see the cards we made for Grandma?"

"I sure did," Rebecca said. "They're beautiful. I particularly liked the picture of you and me and Grandma."

"It was my idea to cut out yellow paper for the sun," Mary Martha said.

The durable ceremonies of normality were soothing. Mary Martha washed her face, brushed her teeth and hair, and insisted on her usual bedtime reading. Rebecca read an entire chapter from *The House at Pooh Corner* while her daughter listened with quiet absorption.

When Rebecca set the book aside, Mary Martha said, "Is Grandma going to be all right?"

"I think so. She may be a little . . . different. A little confused. She may not be able to walk as well."

"I lit a candle for her."

"What?"

"At the church. Mike lit one too. And we said a prayer for
Grandma to get better."

Rebecca was silent for a moment, absorbing this. She realized that she was furious. It seemed absurd, and petty, to be
so angry. Nothing was more natural. Mike had spent most of
his adult life in prayer; she should have been grateful that he
was able to offer her daughter something of the comfort of
faith. But somehow it only sharpened her own sense of
helplessness, her outrage at events slipping out of control. It
made her daughter seem, to a tiny degree, like a stranger to
her.

She controlled herself and bent to kiss Mary Martha's forehead.

"We all want Grandma to get better," she said.

In the kitchen, Mike was washing the dinner dishes. He'd made
Mary Martha pancakes, a dinner of pure comfort food. Somehow this only enraged Rebecca more. Her mother had had a
stroke, and Mike was making a party out of it. He was pulling
the same kind of thing that Rory always pulled and making her
be the bad guy, the nasty representative of reality. It was all
pumpkins in the wintertime and God will make Grandma better, and meanwhile Phoebe was slumped in a bed at S.F. General, with three kinds of plastic tubes in her and a useless arm
and leg, her mind skidding sideways like a truck on ice.

"Have you eaten?" Mike asked.

"I'm not hungry."

Mike picked up on her tone at once. He finished rinsing

the plate in his hand and set it carefully in the drainer, then turned to face her.

"Mary Martha said you took her to the church," she said.

"It seemed like the thing to do. She was pretty upset."

"Did it even occur to you to ask *me* if it was 'the thing to do'?"

He met her eyes. "It honestly didn't."

"You had no right to lay that kind of trip on a little girl."

Mike took a deep breath. He was angry, she noted with a little thrill; he was struggling to be patient. "She asked me what we could do for her grandmother. I told her what people have been telling each other for thousands of years when they're confronted with their helplessness in the face of life and death. I told her we could pray. And I think it helped her."

"So it's happy lies. Twenty years in a monastery, and all you've got to show for it is happy lies for six-year-olds."

He ducked his head stubbornly, refusing to meet her glare.

"And if Phoebe dies? If the mumbo jumbo doesn't work? What are you going to tell her then?"

Still he would not look at her. Rebecca waited for a long moment, then said, "You really had no right."

Her purse was on the table. It diluted the effect, but she paused to rummage through it for her cigarettes before she turned and stalked out the back door.

On the porch, she plopped down on the top step and lit up, venting the smoke at the waning quarter-moon over the ocean and taking another savage drag. From inside the kitchen she could hear the sound of running water, equally furious. It took her a moment to realize that Mike was finishing the dinner dishes. That was a novelty, in the midst of a domestic dispute. Rory would have been smashing plates by now.

The clatter of wet dishware ceased. There was a silence, long enough for Rebecca to suspect that Mike had slipped out the front door and gone back to his own apartment, but then the door opened behind her. Mike stepped out onto the porch, sat down beside her without ceremony, and reached for her cigarettes. She liked that, that he felt free to help himself, that he didn't make a big deal out of it. He had brought two glasses of wine with him, she saw, as a peace offering perhaps, but she didn't feel like reaching for one yet. It seemed like giving away too much.

In the yard below them the ridiculous pumpkin lamp glared above the makeshift cold frame. It looked like an archaeological dig down there, or a weirdly abandoned movie set.

"How much did that damned thing cost?" she asked.

Mike shrugged.

"Too much for a guy making minimum wage, I'll bet."

"I got a raise. I'm the main man on burgers now."

"I'm serious."

"Mary Martha is really into this pumpkin thing. She says she and Phoebe carve them every year."

This was true. Phoebe had a grand, New England notion of the rituals of autumn, and she and Mary Martha had always shared a rowdy Halloween. The two of them would drive down to the fields near Half Moon Bay and pick out several of the biggest pumpkins they could find, then come home to Phoebe's backyard and spend hours drawing wild faces on them in Magic Marker before the messy hilarity of the gutting. Mary Martha's loyalty to the tradition was undeniably moving.

Rebecca stubbed her cigarette out and reached for a wineglass. Mike waited a judicious beat, then reached for his own. They sat for a moment without speaking.

"God, what a nightmare," Rebecca said at last. "I turned

around and there she was on the sidewalk, crumpled up like a beer can. She couldn't move her right side, her face was drooping like a bloodhound's, and she was trying to pretend that nothing had happened. Like it was bad form, somehow, to have had a stroke. A faux pas."

Mike smiled. "She's got a fierce sense of style."

"She thinks my father is still alive. I just want to lie down and cry every time she asks for him."

"Have they said anything more about her long-term prospects?"

"I've been dealing with this doctor named Pierce, who looks like the smoothest guy in a singles bar and smells like a cologne counter. He seems very uncomfortable telling me anything except the names of the chemicals he wants to run through her. I'm hoping that tomorrow I can find a human being who'll give me a straight answer."

"Sometimes they really don't know. They gave my mother six months, at most, when she was diagnosed with ovarian cancer, and she lasted almost two years. Toward the end, they gave her six weeks, and she died three days later."

Rebecca glanced at him. "I'm sorry, I didn't know."

"That was five years ago. I didn't want to talk about God then either. But I was always amazed by how good it felt to light a candle." He hesitated. "Look, I'm genuinely sorry, if I overstepped—"

"I know you meant well. You're wonderful with Mary Martha. There's no one I would rather have her with."

"I was just glad that you felt you could call me."

She sat in silence for a long moment, afraid he would reach out and touch her. Bob would already have tried to take her hand. Rory would already have been out the door. But Mike held off.

"I'm so afraid I'm not going to be able to do this," she said.

He did take her hand then, and somehow it felt right.

"Someone's going to have to go out to Phoebe's house tomorrow and water her orchids," she said. "Someone's going to have to be with Mary Martha. I don't want her at the hospital for a while yet, until Phoebe's a little more presentable. But I'm going to have to be with Phoebe."

"Okay," Mike said.

"I know this isn't what you signed up for."

He smiled. "It must have been in the fine print somewhere."

"I'm serious. I mean, isn't that what the monastery was all about? You haven't had to buy groceries for twenty years. You haven't had weeping women calling you on the phone."

"I'm here for you," he said. "I know that doesn't sound like much."

"You haven't had to make a six-year-old eat green vegetables," she said. "But you are really going to have to get that kid to eat some vegetables."

As they readied themselves for bed, she felt the quiet solemnity of it, the inevitable suggestion of marriedness. He'd had his chance to bolt and he hadn't taken it, and now they were standing here in their boxers and T-shirts, brushing their teeth together after a very bad day. She reached for the dental floss afterward, which she had not done since they had been sleeping together, feeling it was unsexy. But Mike took a stretch of floss too, with the slightest smile, acknowledging the new territory.

In bed, she slipped into his arms and they lay quietly together. She could feel the tension in her body, clenched against the comfort of darkness. She'd left the curtains open, and the low glow of the pumpkin's lamp in the yard below threw a patch of light high on the wall near the window.

"Does that thing stay on all night?" she asked dubiously.

"It's on a timer, set for an eighteen-hour day," Mike said sheepishly, but with a trace of pride at his gadget. "There's a photoelectric cell—it will click on on foggy days too."

"You're a maniac. You realize that, don't you?"

He chuckled, conceding the point. Somewhere in the near distance a siren started up, and they listened in silence as it drew near, the urgency building to a wail, then passing on.

When the noise had faded, Rebecca said, "It was such a wild scene in the ambulance. The EMS guy was trying to get Phoebe to say, 'The sky is blue in Cincinnati,' to check her speech, I guess. And Mom was just trying to keep up the conversation as best she could; she thought he was making small talk. She said, 'I've never been there, but I hear it's beautiful.'"

Her voice caught slightly. Mike kissed her forehead. Her leg was thrown across his, a comfortable entwining, but she couldn't relax yet. She could see her mother in the hospital bed when she closed her eyes; she could hear the hiss of the oxygen.

"She looked so frail," she said. "Like the last leaf on a tree. Like a little puff of wind could come along and just send her spinning away."

Mike was silent for a moment, weighing something out.

"What are *you* going to tell Mary Martha, if Phoebe dies?" he asked at last.

Rebecca stiffened, but his tone was true. It wasn't a continuation of their earlier standoff; he really wanted to know.

"I don't know," she said.

He let it go at that. They lay quietly, his nose in her hair, her face against the warm solidity of his chest, and she began to cry. She cried for a long time, and it felt wonderful, to just be crying.

The light in the garden clicked off sometime after midnight, and not long after that she felt his breathing turn slow and steady. She must have slept herself, at some point, because the night passed. But she was awake when the pumpkins' lamp clicked on again, as the darkness softened.

Chapter Eleven

Dear Brother James,

   Thank you for your generous letter, and for your words of comfort for Rebecca's mother. Her prognosis is still murky, but it appears that she will survive. We have been extraordinarily preoccupied, as I'm sure you can imagine—to have survived something like this is barely to have begun. But Phoebe's spirit has always seemed indomitable to me.

   I am sorry to hear of Abbot Hackley's illness. It may surprise you to hear that I feel genuine fondness for the man. We fought on and off for the entire fourteen years he was my superior, and there were certainly stretches when my feelings toward him were less than charitable, but I never doubted the bedrock of his good intention.

   There is real irony in the fact that he has, as you note, come to a greater appreciation for pure contemplation in recent months. He was always so oriented toward heroically active virtue. He and I went round and round about the true interpretation of Luke 10: Jesus arrives in "a certain village"—we know it to be Bethany—and Lazarus's sister Martha receives him into her house. She hurries to

show him every hospitality, while her sister Mary simply sits at Jesus'
feet and "hears his word." At last Martha, "cumbered about much
serving," overworked and perhaps feeling unappreciated, comes to Jesus
and says, "Lord, dost thou not care that my sister hath left me to serve
alone? Bid her therefore that she help me." And Jesus replies—fondly,
one imagines, even indulgently—"Martha, Martha, thou art anxious
and troubled about many things: but one thing is necessary, and Mary
hath chosen that good part, which shall not be taken away from her."

For inward types like you and me, this story is the gospel text of
choice, a manifesto for the relationship between the vita activa, *the life of*
compassionate service, and the vita contemplativa, *the life devoted to*
the contemplation of God. The obvious interpretation is the one Origen
gave to it as early as the third century—that Jesus' praise of Mary's choice
signifies the preeminence of contemplative love. But most interpreters have
also given Martha her due and insisted that only in a balance of the two
types is a genuine spiritual life achieved. Meister Eckhart goes so far as to
insist that Martha is the spiritually mature sister, that Mary in fact needs
to get up off her butt, and that Jesus' words to Martha are not chiding at
all but rather reassuring: that Mary too will eventually mature sufficiently
to let go of the intoxication of his simple presence for the true spiritual
work of an activity rooted in God's love.

Abbot Hackley, obviously, was a Martha man, while I was just as
clearly inclined toward Mary's way. He wanted us teaching and preach-
ing, serving and sweating, laboring in the vineyard, literally and figura-
tively; he had no patience for the consuming Quiet of the deeper reaches
of prayer, and as that Quiet became prominent in my own prayer we
were often at odds as to what my priorities should be. He was my abbot
and my confessor, and I had taken a vow of obedience, but I fought hard
for what I believed to be the deeper value—for "that good part," the
one thing necessary, the heedless repose in the loving consciousness of
God. And it was easy for me to feel righteous in my obstinacy, for years
on end, when the rewards of contemplation were vivid and all activity

seemed like a kind of distraction. Ruusbroec castigates the "natural emptiness" of certain mystics of his time, their tendency to rest in a silence that is merely avoidance. But who is to say, at any given moment in a soul's journey? By their fruits ye shall know them, as Father Hackley always insisted; but fruits ripen slowly, especially the fruits of silence. Push too hard along Martha's busy path and you may wake one day to find that you don't believe in anything anymore. Your own dry will has made every effort arbitrary. Abide too stubbornly in Mary's quiet and you risk morbidity, mere inertness, a nothingness as arbitrary and willed as the nothingness of Martha's driven and empty activity.

Obvious truths, perhaps. But it was not until I passed into the desert country of my own dark night, when the joy of contemplation withered into emptiness and dread, that the conflict reached its crisis for me. It was no longer a question of balancing Martha's claims against Mary's; the seed of love at the root of both the active and the contemplative life seemed to have died in me. I told Rebecca, when I first came here, that I had left the monastery because of my arguments with Abbot Hackley, but that wasn't true. I left the monastery because those arguments had come to seem terrifyingly irrelevant. I was as incapable as ever of plunging into Hackley's vigorous life of service, whistling as I worked, yet I could no longer feel that I sat smugly at Jesus' feet, ensconced in the one thing necessary. I had simply lost my way.

These are the baffling ways of God. Abbot Hackley now is dying, and finding his joy in the prayer of quiet presence; I have no doubt that his meditations will be rich. And I have fallen in love with Martha and bent my will to serve with her at last. I hope the abbot finds a peaceful moment to smile at this; I hope the man can know the gratitude and love I feel now in my heart for him, the sweet fruit of all our battles. Will you let him know he is in my prayers?

Yours in Christ,
  Mike

Friday passed uneventfully into Saturday at the hospital, and Rebecca settled in through the weekend. Phoebe was seldom awake for more than half an hour at a time, which was a sort of blessing because it was painful to be with her as she slowly discovered the things she couldn't do. She had finally realized that she couldn't move her right arm and leg. Rebecca would catch her looking at her limp right hand with a kind of wistful reproach, as if it were a favorite child who had let her down. Phoebe couldn't find words for the simplest things, and tears would come to her eyes as her mind came upon another blank, another unnerving gap. There was a small clock on her bedside table, the time showing in red digits, and she couldn't read the clock. She kept asking Rebecca what time it was, until Rebecca finally went out and bought a small old-fashioned clock with a big hand and a little hand. Phoebe looked at it, and tears came to her eyes again.

"Quarter of three," she said. But she still didn't know what year it was.

Dr. Pierce was off for the weekend. His replacement was a neurologist named Al-Qabar, a brisk Iraqi with a rapid way of speaking that Rebecca found hard to keep up with after slowing down to Phoebe's speed. Dr. Al-Qabar said that the first few days were often the worst, that some brain cells might be only temporarily damaged, not killed, and could resume functioning. Sometimes another region of the brain would take over the functions of the region damaged by the stroke. It was very hard to say.

"Ten percent have almost complete recovery," he said. "Twenty-five percent survive with minor impairments, forty percent with moderate to severe impairments. Ten percent, unfortunately, require long-term care, in a nursing home."

"She can't read a digital clock," Rebecca said.

"Fifteen percent die," Al-Qabar said, finishing his thought. "Your mother has not died."

She found that she was jittery after talking with Al-Qabar; the man affected her like strong coffee. Alone with her mother after a conversation with the doctor, Rebecca could not keep herself from finishing Phoebe's sentences, from asking her leading questions, trying to coax her toward the privileged percentages of the less impaired. But any sign of haste or impatience just pained and exhausted Phoebe, who knew enough to know she was not performing well. She would grow increasingly distressed, striving to say something scintillating. Once she said, "The sky is blue in Cincinnati," which she had apparently retained from the ambulance ride as a sentence of deep import. But usually she just floundered for a while and fell asleep, at which point Rebecca would flee to the elevator and smoke cigarette after cigarette on the sidewalk in front of the hospital, standing there with the people in their slippers and pajamas who had dragged their IV racks down from their rooms to cop a smoke.

Mike and Mary Martha had gone out to Phoebe's house on Saturday to water her orchids, and they returned with two days' mail. Leafing through the substantial stack at home that night, Rebecca felt a wave of despair, a sense of the full burden beginning to register. There were bills, bank statements, postcards from Europe, appeals from the many causes Phoebe supported, and an inscrutable but definitely threatening letter from the Marin County tax assessor that seemed to be part of an ongoing dispute.

Rebecca sorted the mail into two stacks, items that seemed to require immediate attention and items that could be deferred. It occurred to her that she could not ask Phoebe what to do about any of this stuff. She had already begun to worry about money, after missing so much work, and the thought of paying Phoebe's bills until her mother could get her finances straightened out was overwhelming.

It was almost midnight. Mike was in the shower; he'd seemed as drained as she was. Mary Martha had been asleep long before she got home. Mike said that she'd been crying earlier, asking about Phoebe; she wanted to go see her grandmother. She had also wanted to go to the church again, he'd conceded unhappily, but he'd managed to distract her.

He'd managed to distract her from praying for her grandmother, Rebecca thought. That was great. Score one for my motherly guiding hand. Score one for shaping the souls of the next generation.

The kitchen's shelves were full of unfamiliar products. Mary Martha had talked Mike into buying Count Chocula instead of Cheerios and an inferior orange juice substitute that was basically just colored sugar water. He'd bought brussels sprouts, which there was no way Mary Martha would ever eat, white bread instead of whole wheat, white rice instead of brown, and hamburger with all the fat. He'd bought milk, a quart instead of a gallon, with 4% fat instead of the 2% Rebecca always bought, which was really not that big a deal except that it was more clear evidence that everything was slipping out of control.

Mike had also bought something called Little Debbies, individually wrapped oatmeal cream pies with an obvious appeal to the six-year-old palate, and Rebecca ate four of these now, one after the other. She was trying to remember the last time she had eaten, and she could not. The lunch with Phoebe, sixty hours earlier, seemed like another lifetime.

Mike came into the kitchen as she was unwrapping the fifth oatmeal cream pie and adding the plastic wrapper to the little pile on the table. His eyebrows went up, but he could see she was in no mood for jokes, and instead he sat down across from her and took a Little Debbie of his own.

"I don't know how long I can keep this up," Rebecca told him.

"There's milk to go with those," he said.

On Sunday, Phoebe seemed much worse. She was worried about Goldwater and nuclear war. She was extremely agitated and even tried to get up at one point, though it was pitifully easy to keep her in the bed. She dictated shopping lists, the steak-and-potato shopping lists of Rebecca's New Jersey childhood, heavy on the gin and menthol cigarettes. The rose-bushes needed to be pruned, with an urgency equaled only by the need to get out the Democratic vote.

Dr. Al-Qabar seemed unreasonably cheerful about this sudden, basically incoherent flurry. He said that Phoebe was stabilizing nicely, that her energy level was up and her vital signs were strong. She was trying to put her world back together. He thought they could start her physical therapy soon.

That night Rebecca called Jeff Burgess from a hospital pay phone to tell him she wouldn't be coming in to work the next day.

"This is not about the dress code, is it?" Jeff asked uneasily.

"Jesus, Jeff. My mother can't feed herself. She's trying to shake off her IV lines to vote for Lyndon Johnson. She wants to buy martini fixings for my dead father."

"I'm sorry," Jeff said. "The company's gone nuts lately. The techs and graphics artists are pulling some kind of sick-out to protest the dress code. And Moira's all over me to get hair implants."

"Hair implants?"

"She says I'm going bald."

"Well, thinning out a little, maybe."

"That's what Charlotte used to say. She was always very gentle about it, even said that it was sort of cute. We would joke about aging gracefully together. But these younger women are so . . . *intolerant*."

"About this life-and-death situation of mine, Jeff—"

"Of course, of course, take as much time as you need. It's no big deal." He hesitated. "How much time are we actually talking about here?"

"I don't know. I'm barely keeping my head above water at the moment. I haven't slept in three days, I'm spending all my time at the hospital or on the train."

"I covered for you at the meeting on Friday, but they're all over me for a finished product. And with this sick-out there's no way I can slide your work over to somebody else—"

Rebecca groaned.

"I mean, I want to be as sensitive to your situation as I can, but—"

"God, I suppose I might be able to get in for a few hours . . . Wednesday, maybe?"

"Wednesday would be *great*."

She thought of the first job she had done at Utopian Images, a series of posters for a little crew of hippies in Humboldt County who wanted to sell organic produce in inner cities. She could still remember the mangoes from those posters, the lush smear of watercolor orange and the wispy red. She'd put in a hundred hours on the project, and the hippies' check had bounced. Jeff had laughed that day and given her the afternoon off; they'd gone out to the beach and drunk tequila shots, watching the sun go down. He'd written the whole thing off to karma then.

"We've become the people we never meant to be, Jeff," she said.

He was silent for a long moment. In the background, she heard Moira's voice, a little plaintive, "Jeffie, honey, come on back to bed."

"Come in when you can, Rebecca," Jeff said at last. "Seriously. Come in when you really feel that you can. I'll get it covered somehow."

"Okay. Thanks."

Jeff sighed.

"Plugs," he said.

"What?"

"Plugs. That's what these hair implant thingies are called—plugs. Moira wants me to get a head full of plugs." He sighed again. "Take care of your mother, Becca," he said, and hung up.

Driving down Oak Street through the Panhandle on the way to the hospital on Monday morning, Rebecca's car broke down. The transmission had been making ominous grinding noises for several weeks, so the breakdown didn't come as a complete surprise, but the timing was maddening. Someone with a cell phone stopped to help, and she called AAA. The tow truck arrived forty-five minutes later and towed her to a garage in the Haight, where the mechanic seemed optimistic enough.

"We'll just need a credit card imprint to get started," he said.

She handed him her MasterCard, and he came back a moment later with an embarrassed look on his face.

"I'm afraid this card is maxed out, ma'am," he said.

Rebecca began to cry. Of course it's maxed out, she wanted to say. My mother is in the hospital, I'm my ex-husband's bail bondsman, and my kid's day-care provider charges extra after 5:00 P.M.

The mechanic wiped his hand off on his coveralls and patted her shoulder awkwardly.

"Why don't I just get the car fixed, and we'll figure you're good for it one way or another," he said, and he called her a cab.

Rebecca arrived at the hospital half an hour later to find that Phoebe had suffered "a setback," as Dr. Pierce, back from a weekend skiing in artificial snow in the Sierra, put it delicately. Her mother was on a respirator, unconscious, her breathing labored and her brows knit as if in furious concentration. Pierce was as chary with details as ever, but she had apparently almost died overnight.

"Was it another stroke?" Rebecca asked him, in the hallway outside her mother's room. Phoebe's original hand-lettered sign had given way by now to a neatly printed one. It did not seem like progress.

"It was an event," Pierce said carefully. He was wearing one of those blue shirts with a white collar, which Rebecca had never liked, and his face was deeply tanned except for a distracting goggle-shaped area of paleness around his eyes.

"An 'event,'" she said, trying to focus.

"Obviously something happened. The brain is very mysterious. The CT and the MRI are not showing any new damage. It may be a reorganization of some kind."

"Her brain is reorganizing into a coma?"

"One step forward, two steps back, that kind of thing," Pierce said feebly. It might have been an attempt at humor. He was clearly unhappy to be baffled. "It's not a coma, per se. Her EEG indicates that she's asleep."

Rebecca told herself that none of this was the doctor's fault, that her anger was misplaced, that his silly shirt was not the point. But that goggle patch made the man look like some kind of demented raccoon. And it felt good to be mad. It felt like doing something.

She realized that Pierce probably got a lot of this, and she took a deep breath.

"I know you're doing everything you can," she said as mildly as she could.

"There's not that much we can do at this point. That's the hell of it. We're just going to have to wait and see."

"Then I guess we'll wait and see."

Pierce hesitated, a basically decent man with a misguided sense of fashion. "Is your mother a religious woman?"

"Are you saying I should call a priest?"

"It couldn't hurt," he said.

She called Mike at work instead, and he arrived less than an hour later in his McDonald's uniform, with his name tag still on. She began to cry as soon as he came into the room, and they embraced without a word. Mike smelled of hamburger and grease, a seasoned rankness like an old camping blanket's that was oddly comforting after Pierce's cologne.

He turned to the bed, and Rebecca saw her mother through his eyes for a moment, shriveled and flimsy, almost a stranger, collapsed inward like a spoiled apple. Her brow was still contorted in that unnerving, private scowl of effort or of pain, and Mike reached at once to soothe it, as Rebecca had. Phoebe's features relaxed for a moment, and then, as if recovering from distraction, she frowned again.

Mike glanced at Rebecca, who nodded at the chair by the bed. Mike sat down and took Phoebe's hand. Rebecca realized that he was already praying. It was something that had happened without perceptible transition, a different air. His long, sad face simply settled into an almost Byzantine repose, a calm like a penitent's in the fringes of a Giotto, and suddenly the silence was alive.

She drew the room's other chair over and sat down beside him. Phoebe's respirator wheezed and clicked; her mother's lips were chapped. For some reason it was impossible to keep her hair combed. Do you want me to be good, God? Rebecca thought. Do you want me to keep her hair combed? What do you want from me?

"She's fighting," Mike noted quietly, and Rebecca stirred, half unwillingly, resurfacing to speech.

"Yes."

"What did the doctor say?"

"He said that I might want to call a priest."

He met her eyes, then looked back at Phoebe. For a long time he said nothing, but Rebecca waited patiently. She could feel a strong, strange calm of her own now; she felt that there was time for everything important.

At last Mike said, "Wouldn't she want the real thing?"

"She thought you were fine for the baptism."

"That was different."

"Was it?"

"You know that it was."

Rebecca stood up and circled the foot of the bed to the window at the far side of the room. She had been keeping the curtains drawn to protect Phoebe's eyes, but Phoebe's eyes were closed now and she didn't want her mother to die in bad light. She eased the heavy drapes open and was surprised to see that it was raining outside, a quiet, steady rain, the first of the season. Dr. Pierce could ski on real snow soon. The mid-morning traffic on Potrero Avenue, five floors below, was vigorous in an unreal, distant way, with cars and buses cleaving swift-fading wakes on the wet black pavement and the sidewalks mushrooming with umbrellas.

Rebecca turned back toward the bed. It seemed to her that Phoebe's face had shifted slightly, seeking the gray light like a plant. Mike had let go of her mother's hand and was watching Rebecca closely.

"Are you saying you won't do it?" she asked.

"I'm sure the hospital has a priest on call."

"I don't want some goddamned stranger in here!"

Mike stood up. "Maybe we should talk about this outside."

"Phoebe's heard me yell before," Rebecca persisted combatively, but she followed him out of the room. Mike continued five steps up the hallway, an oddly touching discretion.

When she had caught up with him, he said, "What you're talking about is a sacrament—Extreme Unction, now called the Anointing of the Sick."

"Okay," Rebecca said, as unencouragingly as she could.

Mike took a breath. "Okay. The Catholic Church teaches that a sacrament is an outward and visible sign of inward and spiritual grace and that its value stems from its divine institution, 'from the work already done,' *ex opere operato,* by the saving action of Jesus Christ. The sacrament properly performed by a presbyter of the Church is seen to convey God's grace independently of the moral character of its celebrant or recipients. Another school of thought would have it that the value

of the sacrament does in some way depend on those who cel-
ebrate and receive it, *ex opere operantis,* from the work being
done in the particular instance. But any way you look at it, I'm
not qualified—"

Rebecca said, "Mike, if my mother dies while I'm out here
with you discussing how many angels can dance on the head
of a pin, I'm never going to forgive you."

"You're asking me to do something very serious and very
real. Something I'm no longer authorized to do."

"You did the baptism."

"The baptism was a circus stunt. And a mistake."

"The baptism was beautiful. I loved you that day. You're the
only person I've ever met who could have brought a grain of
dignity to that scene. That's all I'm asking you for now—a
grain of dignity. I don't want some canon lawyer in here filling
out the proper forms."

Mike looked at her unhappily.

"Listen—" she said. "My mother is a good Catholic. She
married my father in a church, forever. She raised me right—
Baptism, Confession, First Communion, confirmation. I mean,
it *pained* her when Rory and I got married on a beach. She's
lived a wonderful life, by any measure, and it's certainly not her
fault that I've turned out the way I have. Are you really going
to tell me that God of yours is checking your license at this
point? That's he's going to let her die in this stupid little room
with a daughter like me and a tube down her throat and no
one to do the right thing? Because I'm not going to call some
standard-issue priest. I'm so mad at your fucking God right
now that I could bite through steel. It's a goddamned miracle
that I'm asking you to do this at all. But I'm asking you to do
it for Phoebe. Because it's what she would want."

Mike had ducked his head during this tirade, like a man in a rainstorm; when she was finished he continued to study the floor at their feet for a long moment before he looked up and met her eyes.

"Okay," he said quietly. "I'll need to go get a few things."

"It's a fragmented culture," Rebecca said, astonished by how relieved she was. "We don't need the whole nine yards."

He was back within twenty minutes with a small brown paper bag from the corner store, a Dixie cup with holy water from the hospital chapel, and a sprig of jasmine. He had even rounded up a Bible somewhere. Sitting by Phoebe's bedside, holding her mother's hand again, Rebecca watched him make his preparations, impressed by his quiet gravity. Mike went into the room's small bathroom and washed his face and hands at the sink, then cleared off Phoebe's bedside table and covered it with a white cotton towel. He took two votive candles, one mauve and one cream colored, out of the bag and lit these with his cigarette lighter. Rebecca smelled vanilla and some other, sweetly indefinable fragrance.

"What's that other smell?" she asked, amused in spite of herself.

Mike rolled his eyes. "Raspberry. Lucky for us, the Council of Trent never got around to pronouncing on the use of cheap scented candles." He took his rosary out of the pocket of his McDonald's uniform and set it on the table between the candles, with the crucifix visible. From the paper bag he drew an eight-ounce bottle of Bertolli's olive oil. He'd brought a glass of water and a clean washcloth from the bathroom, and he arranged these on the table; he blessed the olive oil and poured some into a second Dixie cup. Then he took a deep breath and let it out slowly.

"Okay," he said.

"Should I kneel down or anything?" Rebecca asked.

"You're fine where you are." Mike picked up the sprig of jasmine and dipped it into the holy water, then made the sign of the cross over Phoebe. "In the name of the Father, and the Son, and the Holy Spirit—"

Rebecca crossed herself self-consciously, feeling the cool drops on her left hand, which was still holding Phoebe's. Mike began to pray in the firm, straightforward voice she recalled from the baptism, an Our Father and then a Hail Mary, prayers straight out of the Sunday mornings of her childhood. Her family had always risen early for the nine o'clock mass, because her father didn't like the priest who said the ten-thirty and didn't want to miss the start of the one o'clock football games if they went to the mass at noon. They would skip breakfast, in accord with the stricter rules of fasting then in effect, and Rebecca remembered how solemn she had felt in her hunger as a little girl, the fierce, secret joy of it, as if that gnawing in her belly were a private communication from God. That had been as real as God had ever gotten for her, that hunger and the ringing of the bells during the canon, the silence that had seemed so palpable and pregnant as the priest, his back still to the congregation in those days, lifted the bread and then the wine. She had always tried to convince herself that the bread and wine were God now, by some holy magic, though she'd never quite been able to pull that off. But it had been easy to believe that God was in those bells.

"... *and forgive us our trespasses, as we forgive those who trespass against us ...*"

After mass, the family would stop at a nearby pancake house, and there would be immense glasses of fresh orange juice and the smell of the grown-ups' coffee, stacks of steaming pancakes and a cheerful, post-mass crowd at the tables all around them. Phoebe had loved blueberry syrup, Rebecca remembered; they had never had anything but Aunt Jemima's maple at home, and the silken purple sprawl of the blueberry syrup, the way it mingled with the slabs of melting butter and slid down the fluffy stacks to fill the edges of the plate, had always seemed like a continuation of the mysterious mass itself, an integral part of their faith, and a privileged thing she shared with her mother while her father teased them about their penchant for the exotic and stuck to good old Vermont maple.

". . . *Holy Mary, mother of God, pray for us sinners, now, and at the hour of our deaths. Amen.*"

Mike paused, his head bowed; then he took a deep breath and reached for the Bible, flipping through it toward the end.

"*Be patient, brethren, unto the coming of the Lord. For behold, the husbandman waiteth for the precious fruit of the earth, and hath long patience for it, until he receive the early and latter rain. So be ye also patient; strengthen your hearts: for the coming of the Lord draweth nigh.*"

Mike glanced tenderly down at Phoebe, as if checking whether he still had her attention. He seemed at ease now, collected in the ceremony, solemn and gangly in his blue McDonald's uniform, his bright plastic name tag glaring, HI! MY NAME IS MIKE! YOU DESERVE A BREAK TODAY!

"*Is any sick among you? Let her call for the elders of the church; and let them pray over her, anointing her with oil in the name of the Lord . . . .*"

Rebecca began to cry quietly. She wasn't even sure why; it just seemed suddenly that there was room for it, as if a space were opening up within her, a vast, quiet place with room for grief.

Mike set the book down and turned to the altar. He wet his hands from the glass of water and dried them with the washcloth. He laid his hands briefly on Phoebe's head, formally and gently; then he turned and dipped his fingers into the oil. He traced the sign of the cross on Phoebe's forehead.

"Through this holy anointing may the Lord in his love and mercy help you with the grace of the Holy Spirit." He traced a second cross on her hand. *"May the Lord who frees you from sin save you and raise you up."*

"Amen," Rebecca murmured. She realized that she was waiting for her mother to open her eyes, that some part of her expected a miracle, as she had at her first communion, when the priest laid the host on her tongue. After so many months of preparation for a holy thrill, the unleavened bread had seemed disconcertingly stiff and dry, unwieldy as a piece of cardboard. She had rolled it on her tongue, wondering if she was doing something wrong, and the wafer had softened and stuck to the roof of her mouth. The girls in line behind her had made their own communions, knelt beside her, and moved on; the congregation had finished the communion hymn and fallen silent; and still she had knelt at the altar rail, trying to work the obstinate bread from the roof of her mouth with her tongue and waiting for something, for something very special. For a sign.

She realized that Mike had been silent for some time.

"Is that it?" she asked, and he nodded. She looked at Phoebe and tried to tell herself that she looked more peaceful, at least. But what she really wanted to do was wipe that oil off her mother's head.

The door behind them opened, and a nurse came in.

"Oh dear—" the woman said with a trace of alarm. "I'm afraid we can't allow you to burn candles in here."

"I'm sorry," Mike said, sounding sincere enough. But he made no move to extinguish them.

The nurse hesitated, then bent and blew the candles out.

"And how's our girl today?" she asked, resuming her professional cheerfulness.

"She seems about the same," Rebecca said and reached instinctively to stroke her mother's hair into place. She could still smell raspberry in the air, a luscious hint, mingled sweetly with vanilla and edged with smoke from the snuffed wick. She wondered if Phoebe could smell it too. She wondered if you could get blueberry candles anywhere.

S he spent the night at the hospital on Monday, dozing in the stuffed plastic chair in the corner of her mother's room and waking every two hours when the nurse came in with her blood pressure machine and her thermometer. But Phoebe did not wake.

Mike had gone home Monday evening to take care of Mary Martha, and he returned the next morning after dropping her off at day care. Rebecca wanted to tell him that it was all right, that she could handle it, that he should just go to work, but her heart wasn't in it. She was glad to see him, and she liked the way he was with her mother, relaxed and attentive, always treating her as a presence in the room. Also, Mike had found a courtyard on the seventh floor, where they could slip outside and smoke. It turned out that the pysch wards were on the seventh floor too, and sometimes a subdued little group of patients from one of the locked wards would shuffle out in their bathrobes and frayed slippers. The shepherding nurse would issue them their cigarettes, one at a time, and

they would scatter desultorily to every corner of the courtyard, smoking assiduously for a precise ten minutes, then troop
back inside again.

Mike said Mary Martha wanted to see Phoebe, to bring her
card, to tell her about the pumpkins. But Rebecca didn't want
that yet. All she could remember of her own maternal grandmother now was a withered woman in a bed in a room that
smelled bad. It took a real effort to get beyond that image, to
recall the grandmother who had baked and decorated Christmas trees, the grandmother who had taken her to the zoo and
who had sung "How Do You Solve a Problem like Rebecca?"
in a takeoff from *The Sound of Music* when her granddaughter
got testy.

Mike simply nodded at this decision, though she sensed he
disagreed. But she didn't feel like pushing it, and she appreciated his tact. The two of them sat on either side of Phoebe's
bed and talked quietly about their days, like an old married
couple over cocktails. Mike had cooked the brussels sprouts
for Mary Martha's dinner the night before, with predictable
results. Rebecca suggested peas. He said they had finished *The
House at Pooh Corner* and started on *Beezus and Ramona,* which
Rebecca found painful. She and Mary Martha had been in the
Pooh phase for months; an era had ended without her.

When Mike went home that evening, Rebecca took a
shower in the hospital room's bathroom and then ate Phoebe's
dinner, which the orderly continued to deliver every day like a
newspaper to a family on vacation. Then she settled in beside
her mother's bed.

The odd thing was, this felt like reality now. This tiny room
with the drapes closed against the city's night glare and bustle,
this place where nothing really happened, where only patience
mattered. Where love was as simple as sitting here. The ritual

the day before had had its unforeseen effect, and Rebecca felt unexpectedly freed; she had done what she could, which amounted to nothing, and the rest of it was this vast immediacy, this halt, this drifting, dodging, denying mind of hers brought home again and again to the brute fact of her mother helpless in this bed. Her childhood was here, surfacing in odd moments like bubbles from a recent shipwreck; her furious adolescence whirled through like weather in the Midwest; and all the missed opportunities of her adulthood hurt her anew, all the moments when anything had seemed more important than loving this woman who had given her life. The good times were here too, the laughter in kitchens and the quiet moments halfway up the stairs, which for some reason was where she and Phoebe had often had their best conversations. And her father was here. Sometimes Rebecca even felt that he was in the chair beside her, strong and comforting, smoking his pipe, and that Phoebe was somewhere between them now, touching them both. All the precious dead were here.

Phoebe breathed and scowled and seemed at times to dream. The nurses came and went. Rebecca found herself feeling extraordinarily tender toward these cheerful or beleaguered messengers from a world that trundled on out there somewhere, a brisk reality where people hurried from task to finite task and kept appointments. Phoebe's room was like another country, with customs and a language of its own, an exotic climate and a terrain as forbidding and as beautiful as the Tibetan plateau. The air was thin and time didn't matter much. She wondered if the nurses felt that. She wondered if they knew how badly she had lost it.

When Mike showed up on Wednesday morning, Rebecca realized that she had forgotten all about him, which was scary. He looked harried; there had been a laundry crisis at home. Mary Martha had wanted to wear the red jumper outfit that

Phoebe had given her for her last birthday, even though she
had worn it every day that week. Mike had tried to wash it but
had used warm water, and it had bled and faded. There had
been tears—a lot of tears, Rebecca gathered. She could picture
the scene. Mike felt awful. He felt he had taken part of Mary
Martha's grandmother away from her. He felt that he had let
Rebecca down.

"It's okay," Rebecca told him. "I've done similar things myself."

"She insisted on wearing it anyway—it's all pink and
blotchy and a little tight on her now. I think the woman at
Bee-Well thinks I'm a bad parent."

"The woman at Bee-Well is a first-class pill."

Mike looked down at the floor. "I took Mary Martha by the
church again," he confessed. "We lit candles. It was the only
way I could get her to stop crying."

"It's okay," Rebecca said again. She wanted to tell him that
she loved him, that she thought he was a hero. It was hard to
imagine ever doing anything again except telling people she
loved that she loved them.

She took his hand. Mike glanced up at her, and she saw that
there were tears in his eyes.

"I love you," she said. "I'd be lost right now if it weren't for
you. And Mary Martha loves you too. In twenty years, all she's
going to care about is that you were here for her now. She's
going to remember lighting those candles."

"The tag said 'machine wash cold.' I don't know what the
hell I was thinking."

"I love you," she said. "I love you. I love you."

That afternoon, Dr. Pierce took Phoebe off the ventilator. He
was afraid that Phoebe would get "respirator brain," that she

wouldn't be able to resume breathing on her own. They all stood tensely around the bed for a while after he had taken the tube out, but Phoebe seemed to be breathing all right on her own. Dr. Pierce conceded that this was a good sign. He seemed a little abashed, even chagrined, and Rebecca realized that he had expected her mother to die right there.

Through the afternoon, Mike kept vigil with her, sitting beside her in the chair that Rebecca had come to think of as her father's chair. He caught her up on the news from home. Jeff had called, in a fresh panic, trying to find out when Rebecca might be able to come back to work. Apparently his nobility had faltered. There'd also been a message from Bonnie, expressing her sympathy and asking where some of the lightbulb man files were; Jeff had piled the job onto her for the moment. And Rory had called, twice. He'd pleaded no contest to felony possession and his sentencing hearing was in three weeks. He wanted Rebecca to show up as a character witness, to vouch for his commitment to good fatherhood, to say he was a nice guy and an asset to his community.

"That nervy bastard," Rebecca said.

"He seemed humbled."

"For as long as it takes to get what he needs. I hope you didn't commit me to being a nicer person than I am."

"I told him you'd be in touch."

"Good. Let him stew."

Mike had even managed to retrieve the car, which was running fine again. She was afraid to ask him how he had paid for it, but he showed her his shiny new credit card proudly, like a kid with a movie pass.

"You'd be amazed how eager these companies are to give plastic to an ex-monk with no visible means of support," he said.

"It's the American way, I guess," Rebecca said, but she was touched. She'd never had a man plunge into unmanageable debt for her before.

It was strange, watching Mike assume her errands and duties, like watching old 8mm family movies, the beloved figures a little speeded up and herky-jerky in a flickering light. She loved him for it, and yet as soon as he left that afternoon, to re-trieve Mary Martha, cook the dinner, and staff the phones, she was back into the all-absorbing immediacy of just being with Phoebe, alone on the special planet of her meditation at the bedside, sinking beneath the waves of what seemed to her now like a vast sea of grief.

Maybe this was why people went into monasteries, Rebecca thought, smoothing her mother's hair, the fine, soft hair so much like her own, which she'd always despaired was too limp. Maybe this was why monks embraced such fathomless silence: they'd glimpsed how deep grief really was and understood that to grieve properly they had to sink from sight. They'd discov-ered the love that lived at the bottom of grief, the love you couldn't bring to the surface because the daylight and the bright air and the business of everyday life twisted it into some-thing unrecognizable, something that inevitably seemed crude.

She had never allowed herself to grieve wholly before, she realized now. Not for her father, not for her grandparents. Not even for her marriage: she'd never allowed herself to face what it meant to fail in the central relationship of her life. To really remember that shining, innocent love she'd felt and everything that had happened to it. And this was why, of course: because some pragmatic, self-protective sense had told her that grief was bottomless. Skirting this sea, she had dipped her toes in; she'd wondered what would happen if she crossed the line, but it had always seemed that it could only be a kind of defeat, a drowning, a death. And so it was. But maybe it was not the end, to be defeated by life. Maybe that was even part of what it meant to be a human being: to recognize the ways in which life had finally defeated you, to accept the ways in which death had come, to stop looking away from the failures of love, and to grieve. To keep your heart open in the sea of this silence; to drift in it, surrendering to its currents, baffled and without recourse. And at the bottom of it, to be surprised anew by love's simplicity. To feel that nothing had been lost.

The little windup clock she'd bought for Phoebe ticked away the hours; Rebecca held her mother's hand and finally dozed, and dreamed. She was at the beach with her parents; she was Mary Martha's age. Her father lifted her up and carried her into the waves, with Phoebe beside them; and her mother dived beneath a breaking wave, her body slim and lithe and tanned. She surfaced, laughing, shaking her head in a spray of water droplets. Another wave rolled in, and John Martin lifted Rebecca over it, then eased her into the water, and she was paddling toward Phoebe, whose arms were stretched out toward her. She could feel how fast her heart was beating, but she was not afraid. It didn't seem so far to swim at all.

Rebecca woke. The room's heavy curtains glowed gray; it was light outside. She rose and crossed to open them, and the autumn light filled the room. She stretched stiffly and turned to find Phoebe squinting at her, blinking at the morning.

"Is that too bright?" Rebecca asked, amazed by how natural it seemed.

Phoebe shook her head.

"Boodifuh," she said.

"'Beautiful'?"

Her mother nodded contentedly.

"It is beautiful," Rebecca said.

PART VI

how should tasting touching hearing seeing
breathing any—lifted from the no
of all nothing—human merely being
doubt unimaginable You?

E. E. CUMMINGS,

"i thank You God for this most amazing"

Chapter Twelve

Three days later, Rebecca and Mike drove out to Phoebe's house in Marin to pick up a few essentials. Phoebe had started her physical therapy the day before and was demanding a decent bathrobe, some lipstick, skin cream, a toothbrush, and a hairbrush, a heartening array of necessities. Her condition since awakening continued to improve day by day. Dr. Pierce conceded that he had no idea what had happened. Somewhere deep in her brain, Phoebe had worked something out. Pierce fluttered around her bedside every day now, moving Phoebe's limbs and asking her questions, most of which she answered incorrectly. She still wasn't sure what year it was or what city she was in. She couldn't even consistently come up with Rebecca's name, but Rebecca had stopped being disturbed by this. It was plain enough that her mother loved her.

The day was bright and beautiful, real autumn now, brisk and crisp; Halloween had gone uncelebrated, and Indian summer had passed into November while Phoebe languished, and the northwest wind off the ocean had a bite to it. It felt odd to be out and about in daylight, to not be on her way to the hospital. Moving around the city the past few days, Rebecca had half expected strangers to walk up to her and ask how Phoebe was doing. But San Francisco bustled on heedlessly. At home, there were a host of new pictures by Mary Martha on the refrigerator and messages on the answering machine: Jeff Burgess, sounding frankly desperate; a sheepish Rory, still needing her to con the judicial system for him; and a surprising message from Moira Donnell saying that she was keeping Phoebe in her prayers. It was hard to picture Moira actually praying, but the thought was moving.

Beside her, Mike quietly smoked a cigarette, his window rolled down, his fine brown hair stirring a little in the breeze.

"I think you're going to need a real haircut soon," she said, and he laughed.

"That would be a novelty."

"I can do it for you, if you want. Unless you want something fancy."

"I liked the blue Mohawk that guy had on Haight Street."

"I can do a blue Mohawk. But then Mary Martha would want one too."

"I'm sure the woman at Bee-Well would appreciate that."

Rebecca laughed. The parental banter was one of a host of subtle changes she'd noted upon coming home from her long hospital vigil. The dish drainer, even now, was full of china plates and bowls; Mike, apparently under the impression that it was the mundane norm, had been using the Messenware, and she hadn't had the heart to disillusion him. The beds were all made differently, no doubt according to monastic standards, and there was a pile of freshly laundered clothes on the couch,

ineptly folded, with some of Mike's T-shirts, socks, and underwear mixed in. There was shaving equipment in the bathroom
and a battered copy of Thomas Merton's *Contemplation in a
World of Action* on the bedside table. There was a newspaper on
the kitchen table, open to the sports section. Mike, that devo-
tee of John of the Cross and Teresa of Avila, turned out to be a
49ers fan as well.

The ocean beyond Tamalpais was slate blue, seared with
whitecaps. The coastal mountains had already settled into winter dun, and Stinson Beach was deserted, with gulls milling in
the parking lots of the galleries and knickknack shops. An
SUV lurched by them at the stop sign, an avid couple with
binoculars around their necks, in search of southbound birds.
Rebecca let them roar off toward the lagoons beyond the
town and turned onto the gravel road to Phoebe's. As she
pulled up in the empty driveway, she was conscious of the
jagged edges of this journey to an abandoned house. It felt a
little like looting, like saving what could be saved from a sinking ship.

She and Mike entered the cottage in silence and moved
about separately for a time, gathering the items Phoebe had
requested and whatever else seemed relevant. A thin layer of
dust had settled on everything, and the answering machine
was full of outdated messages. There were dishes in the sink
and Rebecca washed them, wondering if Phoebe would ever
use them again. The VCR, programmed to record, had faith-
fully taped a week's episodes of *General Hospital* before the
tape ran out. Phoebe's book club had sent the automatic selec-
tion of the month, a fat multigenerational saga of an Irish family that Phoebe would have loved, if she had still been able to
read it, and Rebecca hesitated before putting it in the bag.
Maybe her mother would want it read to her.

She assembled a makeup kit from the array on Phoebe's vanity; she packed her mother's toothbrush and shampoo, her cold cream and silk dressing gown. Phoebe, newly able to sit up in bed, had visions of wandering the hospital hallways in style. Rebecca considered several sets of earrings, trying to decide what would go with the robe, before she realized that she was about to cry. For some reason, it was especially painful to accessorize.

She retreated to the kitchen and found an open bottle of 1989 Château Margaux red; even Phoebe's *vin ordinaire* was typically extraordinary. Rebecca poured herself a generous glass and took it out onto the deck. The beach was empty, a sweeping stretch of desolate sand that seemed to fit her mood. She'd just managed to get a cigarette lit in the brisk north wind when Mike, looking haggard, came out the sliding door with a bottle of Czechoslovakian pilsner in hand. He'd missed one of Phoebe's orchids during his previous watering run and it had died. He was near tears too.

"I broke down over the jewelry," Rebecca told him. "I think it's because so much of it is from my father."

"She can't remember anyone's name, but I'll bet she's got every flower clear in her mind," Mike said. "God, I feel awful."

Rebecca smiled in spite of herself; she knew perfectly well that Phoebe wouldn't give him a hard time over the orchid. Her mother was still sure that Mike was a priest. The first thing she had said to him when he walked into the room after her return to consciousness, in a conspiratorial whisper, had been, "Last rites?" Mike had glanced uncertainly at Rebecca, who had given him a trace of an I-told-you-so smile.

"We already did that," he'd told Phoebe. "But you're not going to die."

"Aren't *we* cocky," Phoebe had noted dryly, with a flash of her old wit, and the two of them had laughed together. It hadn't seemed particularly funny to Rebecca, but her mother's sense of humor had always been a little beyond her.

"She's not going to be able to come back here alone, you know," she said now. "I don't know *what* I'm going to do with her."

"She can move into the in-law apartment," Mike said.

Rebecca laughed. "And then what will I do with *you?*"

"You could marry me."

A line of half a dozen pelicans came into view just beyond the breakers, heading south, their big dark wings flapping stolidly. Rebecca watched them until they rounded the point and passed from sight. Beside her, Mike waited quietly.

"You want me to marry you to free up the in-law apartment?" she said.

"I want you to marry me because I love you and want to spend the rest of my life with you."

Her cigarette had burned down to the end. Rebecca looked at it uncomprehendingly for a moment, and Mike reached over, took the butt out of her hand, and stubbed it out on the railing.

"It's not always going to be as much fun as it's been the last few weeks," she said, and he laughed.

"It's so strange," he said. "All those years in the monastery . . . It always seemed like a particularly galling kind of failure to me, to just fall in love and live your life, to shop at Safeway and to watch TV. To say goodnight and good morning, to brush your teeth together. To buy turkeys at Thanksgiving and hams at Christmas. To worry about money and sign report cards and try to explain gravity to a six-year-old. All that stuff just seemed so overwhelming."

"All that stuff is life."

"I know. It's terrifying, isn't it?"

Rebecca laughed and reached up to run her fingers through his hair, savoring the ripple it made, like wind in a wheat field.

"You were such an awkward little gosling when you first showed up," she said.

"Is that a yes?"

Rebecca picked up her wine.

"I can't even settle on some jewelry for Phoebe right now," she said. "Give me a few weeks. Give me a month."

"A month!"

"Maybe two," Rebecca said. "And for God's sake, come help me pick out some earrings for my mother."

She had several more glasses of Phoebe's Bordeaux before she was able to decide on the jewelry and to pick out one of the photos of her father from her mother's bedside table. At sunset, as they walked out to the car to go home, laden with sentimental loot. Rebecca found that she was a little drunk.

"Maybe you'd better drive," she told Mike. "If you think you can handle it?"

"Sure," he said.

"You *do* know how to drive, don't you?"

"I hear it's like riding a bicycle," he said, accepting the keys with a wink and opening the passenger door for her. She was struck by the jaunty way he joggled the keys in his hand. It took her a moment to place the new note, but as he started the car and accelerated out of Phoebe's driveway, spinning the wheels ever so slightly on the gravel, she realized that he sounded just like an American guy. He was overconfident, macho, and showing off for his girlfriend. It was strangely reassuring.

Sure enough, his driving was fine. Between the work being

done and the abundance of wine she'd drunk, Rebecca found herself in a surprisingly celebratory mood. They rolled the windows down and played the radio—Mike had it tuned to an oldies station, which made sense, of course. This was a guy who probably hadn't heard any new music since the heyday of Wham. They wound up and down the twilit cliffs, the only car on the road, singing along to corny hits from the seventies and smoking cigarettes. She felt vaguely guilty, acting so carefree with her mother still in the hospital, but she couldn't imagine Phoebe begrudging her the moment. Mike had a lovely, modest baritone, which he attributed to twenty years of Gregorian plainsong. Rebecca loved the exotic feel of that. She was driving along on a clear cool evening with a man who had spent most of his adult life chanting psalms from the twelfth century but who could still remember all the words to "Piano Man." It had begun to seem to her that she might get through this after all.

She finally took Mary Martha to see her grandmother the next day, after first calling Bee-Well to let them know her daughter would not be coming in. The woman who ran the place was unprecedentedly warm. Mary Martha must have told her about Phoebe, because she said that her own father had recently had a stroke. This was offered almost casually, in the shorthand of the afflicted, and Rebecca suddenly glimpsed how vast it was, this secret society of domestic suffering into which she had been initiated. The revelation was a little disorienting. It made the world seem like a different place.

Mary Martha insisted on wearing the red jumper that Phoebe

had given her, which was showing real signs of wear by now; there was no dissuading her, and Rebecca had to smile, getting a taste of what Mike had been dealing with. She decided that as soon as her mother had recovered enough to consider such things, she was going to ask Phoebe to buy her granddaughter more clothes.

On the way to the hospital, Mary Martha was solemn and preoccupied, absorbed in the gravity of the expedition, clutching her cards and pictures for Phoebe in her lap. As they drove up Potrero, Rebecca tried her best to prepare her daughter, reminding her that Phoebe was still very sick, that she was a little confused and that she couldn't talk the way she had used to talk. Mary Martha nodded, not dismissively but with a dogged air, determined to make her own judgments.

Phoebe was sitting up in bed, trying to make sense of a straw and a glass of cranberry juice, when they arrived. She had already had a nurse apply some lipstick and rouge, and she looked undeniably more chipper. Mike, who had spent the night at the hospital, sat beside her, looking unshaven but cheerful. The curtains were wide open and the room was full of flowers from Phoebe's friends and cronies. Mary Martha hung back for a moment, but Phoebe spotted her right away and said brightly, "Hello, Mary Martha. Come give your old granny a kiss."

Mary Martha glanced at Mike, who nodded encouragingly and moved out of the way. She crossed to the bed and gave Phoebe a tentative peck on the cheek, and Phoebe hugged her with her good arm.

"Don't you look wonderful in red," she said.

"It's my favorite dress now," Mary Martha said. "I'm sorry you've been sick."

"Just a little speed bump," Phoebe said. "I'm feeling much better."

"I made you a card."

"Did you? You sweetheart!" Phoebe accepted the card and exclaimed over the artwork, then opened it and stared at the inside text for a while. Rebecca realized with dismay that her mother couldn't read it, and she was about to say something to dilute the moment's impact when Phoebe looked at Mary Martha and said quite naturally, "Maybe you could read it to me, dear."

Rebecca sat in the corner chair admiring her mother's grace under pressure. She was fairly certain that Mike had coached Phoebe in advance on some of the details, such as her granddaughter's name, but the old Phoebe charm was undeniably functioning. The discussion soon turned to pumpkins, and the rest of the visit went much better than Rebecca had expected. Nevertheless, in the car on the way home, Mary Martha began to cry.

Rebecca stopped the car and put her arms around her daughter. There didn't seem to be that much to say. If you loved Phoebe now, it was going to hurt you to see her. Like facing cold water, you just jumped in and swam anyway. But she was glad she hadn't taken Mary Martha to the hospital any sooner.

When Mary Martha had quieted, they drove on. Mary Martha was still preoccupied, looking out the window, but as they crossed Sunset, on Kirkham, she stirred.

"Could we stop at the church and light a candle?"

"What?" Rebecca asked, caught off guard.

"I want to say a prayer for Grandma," Mary Martha said, a little doggedly.

Rebecca drove in silence for a moment before she said, "Of course we can, sweetheart. We'll say a prayer for Grandpa too."

254 · TIM FARRINGTON

A week later, Rebecca drove downtown to the Hall of Justice for Rory's sentencing hearing. She was dressed in a blue power suit, as Rory had advised, and had even gone so far as to apply some lipstick and mascara. But even disguised as an upright citizen, she wasn't sure what she could possibly say to a judge to keep her ex-husband out of jail. *Well, Your Honor, it's true that for quite a while now he's taken his last hit in the car* before *he comes in to pick up Mary Martha....*

She met Rory, his girlfriend, and his court-assigned lawyer in the hallway outside the courtroom. Rory was outfitted incongruously in a navy blue suit and a gray tie sprinkled with little black anchors. He'd gotten a severe new haircut, flattering in a crisp, quasi-military way, and he looked surprisingly good, a young executive on the rise. Rebecca wondered who had tied the tie for him. Not his girlfriend, certainly, who was wearing the sort of dress that hippie girls often wore when compelled to ransack their closet on short notice to produce an effect of straightness: an old-fashioned calico print with a flared and pleated skirt and nonfunctional pearl buttons. She'd scrubbed off her usual savage crimson lipstick and painted her nails light pink. The overall effect was vaguely Appalachian, a simple girl just out of the hills, an impression heightened by the fact that she was at least four months pregnant. Rebecca realized that she was probably going to have to learn this one's name.

Rory's lawyer, an earnest, harried-looking kid himself, coached her briefly: Rory was a good father, crucial to Mary Martha's emotional development, unstinting in his support.

"'Unstinting'?" Rebecca exclaimed, as Rory looked uneasy. "What is this, a eulogy?"

"Judges love 'unstinting.' It sounds very family values."

"I'm not sure I can say 'unstinting' without snickering."

"No snickering," the kid lawyer said, alarmed. "Somber and

dignified. Mutually committed to the best interests of the child. Loving."

"Loving!"

"Fond, then."

"It's a goddamn miracle I'm here at all. I'm not going to say 'unstinting.'"

"You just say what you have to say in your own way, Bec," Rory said hastily. "We're so grateful to you for coming down here like this."

"I'll give you 'fond.' Intermittently fond."

"I know how much Rory values his friendship with you," the girlfriend said.

The lawyer took a deep breath, straightened Rory's tie, and led them into the courtroom. The place was crowded, and they seated themselves near the back; trailing the group slightly as they filed in, Rebecca found herself beside Rory's girlfriend, which was briefly disconcerting. She still could not recall the woman's name.

"When is it due?" she whispered.

"April," the girl said shyly.

"Rory never even mentioned it to me."

"We didn't want to tell anyone until we were sure I wouldn't lose it. I lost one about a year ago."

"I'm sorry. I didn't know."

"It's okay. I think it was even for the best. There's no way Rory was ready then."

They exchanged a knowing, female look, and Rebecca felt an unwilling camaraderie. Chelsea, she recalled suddenly. The girl's name was Chelsea.

"I hope he's ready now," she said.

"He's ready," Chelsea said. "He better be." She was clutching a packet of index cards in her lap—her plea to the judge,

Rebecca realized, written out in full in a rounded, surprisingly firm hand.

At the front of the room the court's business proceeded, a succession of grand theft auto and drug cases, domestic abuse and burglary, handled briskly by the presiding judge, a no-nonsense woman in her fifties with severe gray hair in a short cut reminiscent of Phoebe's. It was almost an hour before Rory's case came up, and as she sat there waiting, Rebecca tried her best to think of nice things she could say about Rory's moral character without rolling her eyes. But she kept thinking about a joke Mike had told her the night before as they discussed the situation in bed: A woman dies and goes to heaven, where she is met at the gate by Saint Peter, who tells her that to get in, she has to spell a word.

"What word?" the woman asks uneasily.

"*Love.*"

Relieved, the woman spells *L-O-V-E* and enters paradise. Some time later, in the normal course of things there, she is assigned to watch the gates herself, and while she is on duty, who should show up but her ex-husband, who has finally succumbed to cirrhosis of the liver.

"Well, well, look who's here," the woman says. "How've you been?"

"Pretty much the same," her ex-husband says. "So how do I get in?"

"It's very simple," she tells him. "You just have to spell a word."

"What word?" her absolute slimeball of an ex-husband asks, and the woman smiles sweetly and says, "*Pteridophytic.*"

Rebecca had laughed appreciatively the night before; Mike had a deft way of acknowledging her darker impulses without getting grim about them. But today in the courtroom, sitting beside Rory's pregnant girlfriend, it didn't seem so funny. Rebecca felt that she knew this judge already. She could see the wedding ring on the woman's hand; she'd noted the dry humor, the swiftness of the judge's moral intuition, and the impatience with bullshit. She didn't have to make Rory spell *pteridophytic;* she could have her revenge with an inflection, with the lift of an eyebrow and a strategic hesitation; the judge would grasp her point instantly. Rory would probably never even know what had hit him.

She recalled an afternoon at the beach, early in her relationship with Rory. There had been a shark scare, and everyone had come out of the water except Rory. Rebecca could remember the progression of her emotions that day, watching her lover bob nonchalantly on the empty sea beyond the breakers—her panic, her helplessness and rage, and finally, with the bittersweetness of acceptance, a grudging, impersonal admiration. The surf hadn't even been particularly good that day. But Rory was free. That had been his point to her, always. Free to make a mess of things and free to take full advantage of that fleeting moment of beauty when the wave curled right and grace was all that mattered. Free as a bird, she'd thought wearily: free as those seagulls that worked the trash cans along Ocean Beach.

There was a stir beside her; Rory's case had been called. The previous defendant was being led away through the door at the far side of the room, flanked by a sheriff's deputy. The four of them rose, and, as the last one into the row, Rebecca found herself leading them forward. She paused at the swinging gate that separated the spectators' section from the judge's bench and the attorneys' tables and glanced back. Rory, a step behind her, gave her a smile and a wink, and a nod to go forward. He was flaunting a determined cockiness, she noted, but he was scared.

She turned right and took one of the seats at the defendant's table, and the others arrayed themselves to her left, still standing. Rebecca hurriedly rose to her feet again. The bailiff read the details of *The City of San Francisco v. Rory Burke* and noted that a plea of nolo contendere had been entered. Rory's lawyer affirmed that this was so and they all sat down.

The assistant city attorney rose and asked for a sentence of three to five years; Rory's lawyer rose in turn and noted that while this was the defendant's third arrest, it was only his first conviction. His client had purchased the marijuana from the undercover officer without any intent to resell it; it had been for recreational use only. Moreover, he'd since gotten himself into rehab. He was a committed father to his daughter, maintained good relations with his ex-wife, and was the primary source of support for his new family.

"Let's hear from the women," the judge said, sounding unconvinced.

Chelsea rose and in a wavering voice read her little speech from her index cards. Rory was a good and loving man, she said; he'd never been anything but kind to her. And this arrest had changed him. It really had. He was sobered. He'd gotten a haircut and a job. He didn't want to be in jail when their child was born.

"Is he going to marry you?" the judge asked.

Chelsea bit her lip and glanced uncertainly at Rory.

"I am, Your Honor," Rory said.

"How romantic," the judge said dryly, but Chelsea's face lit up. She sat down with a pleased little flutter and reached for Rory's hand under the table.

"Do you have anything to add, Ms. Martin?" the judge asked.

Rebecca stood up, wishing she had thought to bring notes too. "Rory really is a decent guy, Your Honor. He has a generous spirit and he's been . . . unstinting in his devotion to our daughter. He's a truly loving father, and I think it would have a terrible effect on Mary Martha if he were to have to go to jail."

"Most loving fathers think of that *before* they commit the crime," the judge said.

Rebecca met the woman's cool blue eyes. This was the moment, she knew: woman to woman.

"Rory's been a little slow to grow up, Your Honor," she said. "But I believe him when he says he going to take this chance to do it."

The judge held her glance appreciatively; she had the picture. Rebecca sat down.

"The defendant will rise," the judge said.

Rory and his lawyer stood up hurriedly.

"Do you have any idea what a lucky man you are, Mr. Burke?" the judge said.

"I think I do, Your Honor."

"I don't think that you do at all. I think you're a long shot, and I think these women know it. But if they're willing to make that bet, then I am too. I am sentencing you to time already served in the city jail and a three-year period of probation. If you violate the terms of that probation, you will be prosecuted to the full extent of the law."

"Thank you, Your Honor," Rory said, in his best imitation of sincerity.

"I don't want to see you again," the judge said. "I don't actually like you very much." She made a note on the sheet in front of her, then tapped her gavel firmly. "Next!"

★ ★ ★

At the desk on the first floor, Rebecca completed the paperwork to have the bail she'd posted returned, minus a hefty administrative fee. To her surprise, Rory wrote her a check for the difference on the spot. He'd gotten himself into some kind of second-chance program for minor felons, and he really did have a job. Unlikely as it seemed, after a lifetime of creative unemployment, Rory was a lifeguard at the YMCA.

"If you could hold off cashing it for a week or two—" he said sheepishly.

"Of course," Rebecca said. She'd already decided that there was no way she was ever going to cash that check. There was no sense tempting fate.

She would have left immediately, but Chelsea gave her an unexpected, heartfelt hug, and Rebecca felt the swell of the girl's belly against her own, the firm reality of the next phase of Rory's life, the palpable demand.

"Is it going to be a boy or a girl?" she asked.

Chelsea smiled proudly. "A boy."

"Mary Martha has always wanted a little brother," Rebecca said, and turned to leave while everything was still going so well.

Dear Brother James,

Please forgive my long delay in responding. We have been extraordinarily busy here, as I'm sure you can imagine. But thank you, as ever, for your thoughtful letter. Despite the occasional indications to the contrary, I am glad that you have kept our embattled correspondence alive. Some-

thing of the best of the monastery revives for me still, in your dogged, earnest script. Even now, when I wake too early, in the old, automatic way, all dressed up and nowhere to go at 3 A.M., I think of you in the predawn darkness, shuffling through the dew to matins with your hands in your sleeves, your cowled head bowed. I still hear the murmur of lauds through the trees as the sky turns, the song unchanged for a thousand years. And on through the day, through prime and terce, I hear the plainchant and the prayer; through the noontime brightness of sext, through lazy none and the sweetness of vespers, and the final rounding tenderness of compline, I am reminded of the circling song, the never-ending dance, ancient and ever new. And I am grateful for it. I am grateful for it all.

There is a passage in John of the Cross's "Spiritual Canticle" that had always baffled me. It comes quite late in the poem, well after the "small white dove" of the seeking soul has built her nest in solitude with the One she sought. St. John says:

> *Let us rejoice, Beloved,*
> *And let us go forth to behold ourselves in Your beauty,*
> *To the mountain and to the hill,*
> *To where the pure water flows,*
> *And further, deep into the thicket.*

It was the thicket that I could not understand. My rosy notion of the life fulfilled in love did not include such exertions; I suppose that I pictured an eternal rest by a heavenly poolside, with umbrella drinks served in the unimpeded sunlight. But we do not serve that larger Love by renouncing our particular loves for some mystical lounge chair; we serve by being faithful to those loves, by suffering them wholly. We are born to love as we are born to die, and between the heartbeats of those two great mysteries lies all the tangled undergrowth of our tiny lives. There is nowhere to go but through. And so we walk on, lost, and lost again, in the mapless wilderness of love.

As I write this, Mary Martha is at the kitchen table with me, puz-zling out the intricacies of Dick and Jane. Phoebe is due to move in downstairs this week, and is already filling the backyard with zinnias and gladiolas in her imagination; she will no doubt wrest the garden from my control and turn it into a wonderland. Rebecca is on the back porch with her easel out, painting our view of Point Reyes, editing out the rooftops and TV antennas. She's on a sabbatical of sorts for the moment, and is thinking about starting her own graphics business and finding work on a scale that suits her.

And I? My résumé is as flimsy as ever. Still, I have let go of my po-sition at McDonald's and am seeking some employment that doesn't involve a grill. Perhaps I will work with the dying, somehow. It seems I have a gift for it.

Yours in Christ,
Mike

Bonnie Carlisle and Bob Schofield had scheduled their wedding ceremony for the second Saturday in Decem-ber. Rebecca spent that morning working in the in-law apartment with Mike, installing grab bars in the shower, a tub bench, a handheld shower head, and no-slip pads, prepar-ing the place for Phoebe to move in. Her mother was due to move out of the rehab center on Monday, and Rebecca had had to concede that the in-law apartment was the natural place for her to come. Phoebe was moving around on a walker now, and progressing day by day in the vast new labor of life's simplest tasks, learning to eat left-handed, to dress herself in clothes with Velcro fasteners instead of buttons, to "toilet," as the occupational therapist put it delicately. Her speech had improved, and she had begun to work on her reading; often she and Mary Martha would spend their afternoons with one of Mary Martha's Dick-and-Jane books, worrying out laborious sentences of three words or less, sounding out the words together. At the moment, Mary Martha was slightly ahead, but Phoebe was coming on fast.

Rebecca had been quietly dreading this day since she had received the wedding invitation. She had not said a word to Mike about his marriage proposal in the weeks since the afternoon at Phoebe's cottage, and she was afraid that he would take advantage of Bonnie and Bob's nuptials to make his case anew. She'd felt terrible, cruel even, leaving him dangling in such uncertainty, but she'd simply been unable to address the issue. It was hard to say why, even to herself. She knew that he was sincere; she didn't believe for a moment that he'd proposed just so he wouldn't have to lose his cleaning deposit. This was a guy who had arrived without a penny in his pocket, carrying all his possessions in a satchel the size of a gym bag.

Nor was it that she didn't love him. She did feel some concern that the prosaic reality of Phoebe's need to move into the in-law had forced Mike into a premature commitment, but commitments were where you found them, and if Phoebe's situation had forced them to go straight from courtship to crisis, it had also deepened their intimacy. In many ways, they were like war veterans together now; they had the cryptic understandings, the dark humor, and the easy camaraderie forged in shared combat. She trusted him, more than she had ever expected to trust anyone; she relied on him, so much that it was a little scary. She knew that she could never have been so magnanimous with Rory if she hadn't known she was going to be able to come home and relate the whole court scene to Mike in all its irony and incongruity, as a funny story, as a strange, now-shared slice of life. And she could remember thinking, watching him with her mother when it seemed that Phoebe wouldn't make it, that she wanted him there with her when Phoebe died. She'd thought then that she wanted him with her always.

That feeling had only gotten stronger as the crisis passed and the realities of daily life began to come into focus again. Every day of relative normality seemed to bring an endearing new revelation. Mike sang old Eagles' hits in the shower, and he'd shown an unsuspected passion for Mexican food. He'd discovered Sue Grafton's mystery novels, but he was only up to *B Is for Burglar,* which she'd told him laughingly was real evidence of having been in a monastery for twenty years. He was truly bad with money, to be sure; he spent it like a man who believed that God would provide, with no thought for the morrow, but she could live with that. She could live with everything she'd learned about him and, she honestly felt, with everything she was going to learn. That wasn't the issue.

What *was* the issue, then? Maybe it was just too much, too fast. This was a man who had spent twenty years in resolute opposition to what most people thought of as normal life. She didn't want Mike to wake up one day five or ten years down the line thinking he had thrown away his chance for God— whatever that meant—for the secular mediocrity of marriage to her. But Rebecca didn't really believe this. Mike knew what he was doing; he'd made it abundantly clear to her that he thought this was the right move even for his soul.

It was that notion—the idea of rightness for the soul—that came closest to the heart of her resistance. Maybe that was why it was so hard for her to admit it even to herself. Mike believed wholeheartedly that this marriage would be good for his soul; but Rebecca was not so sure it would be good for her own. To put it that bluntly unnerved her. These were not terms in which she was accustomed to thinking; the language of matters of the soul had seemed like so much bad hocus-pocus to her for so long that she was hesitant, even embarrassed, to use it now. But there it was. Mike had thrown himself into the challenges and dilemmas of the everyday with a kind of passion and found a spiritual significance in grappling with the machinery of regular life; for him it was a giant step forward. But it was precisely the machinery of regular life that gave Rebecca pause now. She kept going back to those days and nights at her mother's bedside, remembering the hush that had finally come upon her there, the beauty of the silence beneath the sea of grief. Something extraordinary had happened, something had opened in her then, and she didn't want to just write it off as an interesting aberration and get back to the heedless grind.

She'd found herself unwilling to go back to work at Utopian Images as well. She had tried, as things had calmed down and it became impossible to plead Phoebe's condition as an excuse. She'd stood at the N-Judah stop with her sketch case, in her new code-compliant outfit, and the train had pulled up and the doors had opened and the rest of the commuters had boarded. The driver had looked at her and she had just stood there; she simply hadn't been able to make herself get on. The doors closed and the train pulled away and still she just stood there on the sidewalk, until another train came along. The doors had opened, the fresh group of commuters duly boarded, and again she hadn't been able to make herself move and the train had rumbled off downtown. And the next train too, until she finally just went home, where she had sat quietly in the backyard, marveling at the delicate orange blossoms on the pumpkin plants and thinking that she must be nuts, that she'd lost it completely, that she'd degenerated into an irresponsible freak.

It seemed too ironic—ridiculous, even. She'd fought so long and hard to make her tiny life work, and her tiny life had been blown open in spite of everything. Now Mike was offering her a chance to put that tiny life back together in an immeasurably more appealing way. How could she tell this ex-monk, who had come so far to make his peace with the world and offered his own life so generously to the constraining realities of her own, that she was afraid to marry him and succumb to the demands of the ordinary? But it was close to the truth. She didn't want to lose sight of the still, calm place she'd glimpsed from Phoebe's bedside. She wanted to give this weird, deep pause a chance.

Despite her concerns, Mike played it cool throughout the morning, keeping to the work at hand so resolutely that Rebecca suspected, as she often did, that he had read her mind. He was surprisingly deft, handling the drill with a jaunty air, frankly showing off. They had fun at the hardware store, picking out a long-handled shower brush and a cute washing mitt with a pocket for soap. They laughed over how few possessions Mike had to move upstairs. And still he didn't say a word on the spectacular obviousness of the subject of marriage. It was almost maddening.

They broke off at noon to dress for the wedding. Bonnie had gone all out, and Rebecca's bridesmaid's dress was an extravagant concoction in lavender that made her feel like a big carnation with a floppy purple hat. But there was no help for that. Mike had bought himself a stiff new navy blue jacket much like the one Rory had worn in court, not necessarily well fitted, with matching new slacks that bunched at the ankles. The knot in his tie was uneven, but his hair was carefully combed. He looked awkward and earnest, like a high school basketball player complying with a road game dress code.

"I hope you didn't blow your life savings on this outfit," Rebecca said.

Mike shrugged. "My life savings were only three weeks old."

"It's just Bonnie and Bob."

"It's us in public. I can't believe how nervous I am. I feel like I'm taking you to the prom or something."

"So where's my corsage?"

He hesitated, then sheepishly brought his hand out from behind his back to reveal a boxed gardenia on a pin. Rebecca laughed.

Just then Mary Martha poked her head around Rebecca's hip. She was already dressed for the event in a blue dress with a white lace collar and a brocaded bodice, a lavish little outfit that Phoebe had bought for her last birthday.

"Hey, we're color coordinated," Mike exclaimed, and Mary Martha laughed.

"What's in the box?" she asked.

"It's a flower."

"For who?"

"For you, of course," Mike told her without missing a beat.

Mary Martha gave a gratifying coo. As Mike knelt to pin the gardenia to her dress, he gave Rebecca a half-apologetic glance over Mary Martha's shoulder. But Rebecca just smiled back at him reassuringly. Flowers were easy; it was family life that was tough. She'd been looking for years for a man who could handle the fact that his prom date had a daughter.

The wedding was at Grace Cathedral, on Nob Hill in downtown San Francisco. Bonnie and Bob had spared no expense. As Rebecca, Mike, and Mary Martha came up from the parking garage into the dilute light of an overcast sky, they were greeted by a tuxedoed usher, who gravely directed them into the cathedral's cool interior. The nave was lined with flowers, and the front pews were already full; Rebecca spotted a sizable crew from Utopian Images, most of whom she hadn't seen since Phoebe's stroke. The three of them skirted the labyrinth tapestry on the entrance floor, and Mike and Mary Martha seated themselves in an empty row, while Rebecca hurried off to join Bonnie in the dressing room next to the vestry.

She found her friend in front of a floor-length mirror with her mother, fretting over her cleavage. The princess gown was beautiful, with sleeves of alençon lace and a full satin skirt overlaid with billowing crinoline, but the neckline seemed a little racy.

"I think Bob will love it," Rebecca offered.

Mrs. Carlisle looked dubious. She was a solid, kindly woman with a big laugh much like her daughter's and the same slightly mournful blue eyes. Bonnie gave the gown a little hitch around her breasts and peered at herself critically in the mirror.

"Oh, what the hell," she said at last. "If you've got it, flaunt it."

The great organ boomed Mendelssohn's "Wedding March." Rebecca gave Mike and Mary Martha a wink as she paraded in with Bob's best man and took her place to the left of the high altar with its blocks of Sierra Nevada granite and redwood top. Bob was waiting with the priest, a tanned, buoyant woman who seemed capable of shedding her black robes at a moment's notice and doing some serious rock climbing. The swallowtail lines of Bob's cutaway black tux made him look taller, Rebecca noted with some relief; Bonnie had been concerned that she would tower over him in her heels. He gave Rebecca a proud smile, a little impersonal; he seemed almost dazed with happiness.

Bonnie came up the aisle on her father's arm, kissed him, and took her place beside Bob. From Rebecca's vantage point, the imposing east window shone above the couple, *Il Cantico di Frate Sole,* luminous in rose and blue and gold. Bonnie was radiant, her face shining beneath the tulle blusher veil. Even Bob seemed to have acquired some dignity in his devotion. The cathedral fell quiet as the priest launched into the ceremony in simple, ringing tones, the classic vows: for better and for worse, for richer and for poorer, in sickness and in health. Bonnie's mother was weeping quietly in the front row, and Rebecca's eyes filled and spilled over too, because it was so beautiful and so right. She had expected more irony, somehow.

The newlyweds embraced and made their recessional promenade to Widor's "Toccata." Outside, they were pelted with birdseed instead of rice, to spare the digestive tracts of the local pigeons. As the forty-four bells of the cathedral carillon chimed from the Singing Tower, the sun broke through the clouds, to the wedding photographer's delight. It really was as perfect as it could be.

At the reception afterward, in the spacious banquet room of the Diocesan House, Bob got a little tipsy after the toasts and began regaling the guests with the story of how he had proposed to Bonnie. He had taken her to a wonderful little Italian restaurant in North Beach and had the waitress bring an enormous bouquet of lilies to the table; he'd gotten down on one knee, right in front of the whole restaurant, and when Bonnie had accepted, a violinist had appeared, playing one of Brahms's Hungarian dances.

Everyone oohed and aahed over how romantic it was. Bonnie's eyes met Rebecca's, begging her to be kind. Rebecca just gave her a wry little smile. It seemed easier to be kind lately.

Jeff Burgess was dancing with his wife. He had recently moved back into his house on Potrero Hill and was already speaking of the interval with Moira as a "midlife fling." He actually seemed happy, in a chastened way, and certainly his time with Moira had improved his wardrobe. Rebecca had told him the week before that she wouldn't be coming back to Utopian Images, but he didn't seem to have a problem with that. The lightbulb man campaign for PG&E, its final touches applied by Bonnie, had recently hit the airwaves and was a big success. The commercials seemed to be everywhere: the lightbulb man in Rebecca's final, pure Gene Kelly version, whirling around lampposts and singing in the rain, interspersed with gritty, moving shots of PG&E workers repairing downed lines in bad weather. There were lightbulb man posters at bus stops and on the sides of the MUNI trains. There was a lightbulb man action toy. It made Rebecca wish she had asked for a percentage of the proceeds.

"He looks a little sad," Mike had noted when he saw the commercial on TV. Rebecca had loved him for that. No one else had mentioned the lightbulb man's obvious ambivalence, the poignancy of his plight as a misshapen artist.

"He's just dancing as fast as he can," she had told him.

At a table in the far corner, Moira Donnell was crying quietly over her champagne. Rebecca crossed the room and sat down beside her.

"Chin up, sweetie," she said.

"That bastard," Moira said. "He told me twice a week he was going to divorce her, the whole time we were together."

"These big commitments have a life of their own. But it's better in a way, isn't it? That marriage is so stubborn. You'll find yours."

"I don't know if I can ever believe in love again."

"You didn't love Jeff, honey," Rebecca insisted gently.

Moira snagged a champagne from the tray of a passing waiter.

"He cleans up well, doesn't he?" she said morosely, her eyes on Jeff and his wife. "I mean, I *gave* him that haircut. I bought him that *tie*."

There was a stir near the door. Bonnie had apparently decided that Bob had had enough to drink, and the happy couple were making their grand exit. A crowd of giddy young women hastily gathered in anticipation of the bridal bouquet. Bonnie surveyed the scene serenely; her eyes met Rebecca's in a knowing glance. Rebecca shook her head slightly, but Bonnie just laughed and flung the bouquet like a football across the room. There was nothing to do but catch it.

A cheer went up. Bonnie and Bob waved gaily and headed for their limousine. The band swung into "You Are the Sunshine of My Life," and Jeff took his wife out for another spin. Across the room, Mike was dancing with Mary Martha, which was so adorable that Rebecca thought her heart might burst.

Moira was eyeing the bouquet with undisguised drunken sentiment: purple and pink anemones, hydrangea, roses, and sweet pea, with a sprig of fuchsia, more evidence of her sad plight. Rebecca hesitated, then handed her the flowers, and Moira smiled self-consciously at her readiness to accept them.

"Christ, I'm pathetic," she said. "Did you notice the shoulders on the best man?"

On the way to the car, Mary Martha discovered the white and gray terrazzo labyrinth in the courtyard and plunged in. Rebecca and Mike sat down on a bench to the side, under some plum trees. A few massive calla lilies were still blooming, their velvety white heads drooping, and the air smelled faintly of jasmine. At home, she knew, there were pumpkins on the vine: unlikely greenish-orange things the size of Mary Martha's fist. It seemed like a sort of miracle to Rebecca. They were going to have pumpkins for Christmas.

"I can't wait to get out of this dress," Rebecca said.

"What a production," Mike agreed, loosening his tie and unbuttoning his jacket. "I'm thinking that if we ever do this, we'll go to a justice of the peace, with Mary Martha and the building's janitor as witnesses. I'm thinking a Wednesday afternoon."

"I'm thinking Lake Tahoe," Rebecca said. "One of those little instant wedding chapels on the Nevada side. I'm thinking we have Mexican food and margaritas in some dive afterward and are in bed by nine o'clock."

"Is that a yes?"

Rebecca laughed. "I knew you were going to do this."

Mike smiled smugly. "I knew you knew."

Mary Martha had reached the center of the labyrinth and started the outward spiral again, hopscotching now, singing to herself. Mike's eyes met Rebecca's and they smiled quietly. It was fun, playing parent.

"She's not always this cute," Rebecca said.

"Don't I know it."

They watched in silence for a moment. Beyond the cathedral spires, the early winter sunset had flecked the high clouds with rose. Behind them, the traffic on Taylor and California seemed distant, baffled by the plum trees to a dull roar like the ocean's. A sparrow sang in the branches above them, two sharp notes and a lilting treble.

"This is what it felt like in the hospital sometimes," Rebecca said. "Like a secret. Like love is the only thing that was ever real." She glanced at Mike. "Is that how it was for you in the monastery?"

"Sometimes."

"This . . . *peace.* This hush. I would sit there by Phoebe's bed and promise myself I wouldn't forget it. That I wouldn't let myself just fall back into the same old busy sleepwalking."

"Mommy, come walk the maze with me!" Mary Martha called.

"In a minute, sweetheart." She met Mike's eyes again. "I know that you know what I'm talking about."

Mike was silent for a moment. Then he said, almost reluctantly, "There was a print in the monastery library, a copy of Filippo Lippi's painting of St. Augustine beholding the Trinity, from the Uffizi museum in Florence. Augustine is sitting there with a scroll on his knee and a pen and ink pot in his hands, gazing up at this three-faced sun shining down on him from above his desk. And he's got three arrows sticking out of his heart."

"Ouch."

"Exactly. I used to look at that picture all the time. I thought that was *it,* you see: the vision, the light, the ecstasy and the rapture. I thought that after a moment like that there was nothing left to do on earth. All I wanted was to be that guy gazing raptly at the sun, and I figured that the arrows were just part of the price of vision—an occupational hazard, if you will."

"And now?"

He shrugged. "And now I know that the moments of vision come and go—'no man shall see My face and live.' We're not equipped to live in that light all the time. The vision fades and life goes on and all we're left with is the arrows."

"A cheerful thought," Rebecca murmured glumly.

"In a way, I think it is," Mike said. "I think the arrows are so that we don't forget."

Mary Martha, her patience exhausted, walked over and seized Rebecca's hand. "*Mom!* Come *on*—"

"Okay, okay," Rebecca laughed, surrendering and allowing her daughter to haul her to her feet. She gave Mike a mock-rueful glance. "You coming?"

"I think I'll sit this one out," he said.

She could appreciate the subtle point of parental negotiation: he'd been dancing with Mary Martha all afternoon. She blew him a kiss and let Mary Martha lead her to the labyrinth's entrance. Her daughter ran on ahead immediately, but Rebecca took it slowly. The terrazzo path was comforting somehow, simple and finite, one step after another.

The first curve looped disconcertingly close to the labyrinth's center and she wondered briefly whether she had somehow done something wrong, but then the path turned outward again. Mary Martha whizzed by, a full spiral ahead of her already; at her next turn Rebecca caught a glimpse of Mike sitting contentedly on the bench. He had lit a cigarette and looked wonderfully placid. Rebecca gave him a smile and made her next turn, and her next, and for a moment she was filled with a sudden quiet joy. There was nothing ahead of her but the cathedral, its upper reaches drenched in sunset gold, and the plum trees in the evening hush, waiting for spring. There was nothing ahead of her but all the steps to be taken.

Acknowledgments

Gratitude first and foremost to Renée Sedliar, my beautiful and brilliant editor at Harper San Francisco, for her poetic touch and Dante tattoos, and for her savvy and unerring taste. Thanks also to Calla "The Devlinator" Devlin, for her Midas touch and Frank's last name; and to Margery Buchanan, Miki Terasawa, Chris Hafner, Priscilla Stuckey, and the rest of the awesome team at HarperSF. An ancient debt of thanks to Elizabeth Pomada for a sympathetic reading and encouraging response to the first draft of this book in 1988; and more recent gratitude to Judith Ehrlich for a timely and insightful perusal of the evolving text, and to Carolyn Brown for a genuinely synchronistic and fruitful edit. Thanks too to Sybil MacBeth for the poetic meditations on prayer as manicure, which I ripped off shamelessly; to my Aunt Mary Ann, SNJM, the only person I know whose copy of *John of the Cross* is more beat-up than mine; and to Anne Poole for her title suggestions, her watercolors, and for our many shared gin and tonics.

Less alcoholic gratitude to Fr. Bill Sheehan for ongoing lessons in centering prayer and "hanging out with God;" and to April Swofford and the sacred crew at the Monte Maria Monastery in Richmond, Virginia, for making and sustaining such a precious place of prayer. I'll do your dishes anytime, April.

Fir Emmanuel's early reading of the story was most heartening, as was Lynn Mason's. Laurie Horowitz, the funniest woman in the world, is as always a mainstay. Kathleen Barratt taught me how to breathe during the course of this book; and Angela Phillips schooled me in the mysteries of yogic surrender. Mirabai Starr's radically contemporary grappling with the spirituality of John of the Cross has been an inspiration, and her fresh version of *The Dark Night of the Soul* is a treasure. Thanks too to Laurie Chittenden for heroic efforts in a lost cause, and for the heads-up on the Gloucester Daffodil Festival. And I am ever grateful to Kate "Just a Novelist" Johnson for her ideal readership and for quoting me to good effect.

As ever, heartfelt thanks to the lovely Linda Chester, of Linda Chester and Associates, for elegance, grit, and unwavering support. I owe an unpayable, ever-accumulating debt of gratitude to Laurie Fox, my agent, editor, beloved friend, fellow novelist, and brave companion of the literary road: for joy, wisdom, laughter, and good meals out, and for all the gifts of her extraordinary spirit. And to Claire, my graceful partner through fiasco and fandango and the patient sufferer of all my missteps, the whole of my awed and grateful love.

Reader's Guide to *The Monk Downstairs*

by Tim Farrington

PLOT SUMMARY:

"Let us face the fact that the monastic vocation tends to present itself to the modern world as a problem and as a scandal."

THOMAS MERTON

Rebecca Martin is a single mother with an apartment to rent and a sense that she has used up her illusions. "I had the romantic thing with my first husband, thank you very much," she tells a hapless suitor. "I'm thirty-eight years old, and I've got a daughter learning to read and a job I don't quite like. I've got a mortgage. I'm making my middle-aged peace with network television and tomorrow is just another day I've got to get through. I don't need the violin music." But when the new tenant in her in-law apartment turns out to be Michael Christopher, a warm, funny, sneakily attractive man on the lam after twenty years in a monastery and smack dab in the middle of a dark night of the soul, Rebecca begins to suspect that she is not as thoroughly disillusioned as she had thought.

Her six-year-old daughter, Mary Martha, is unambiguously delighted with the new arrival, as is Rebecca's mother, Phoebe, a rollicking widow making a new life for herself among the spiritual eccentrics of Bolinas. Even Rebecca's best friend, Bonnie, once a confirmed cynic in matters of the heart, seems to have lost her sensible imperviousness to romance, and urges Rebecca on. But none of them, Rebecca feels, understand how complicated and dangerous love actually *is*.

As her unlikely friendship with the ex-monk downstairs grows by fits and starts toward something deeper, and Christopher wrestles with his despair while adjusting to a second career flipping hamburgers at McDonald's, Rebecca struggles with her own temptation to hope. But it is not until her mother suffers an unanticipated crisis and Rebecca is brought up short by the realities of life and death, that she begins to glimpse the real mystery of love, and the unfathomable depths of faith.

At once a romantic comedy and a tale of spiritual renewal, *The Monk Downstairs* is a love story in every sense of the word, a tender exploration of the unforeseeable ways in which individual journeys interweave, and of the ways we are changed by the opening of the heart.

TIM FARRINGTON ON *The Monk Downstairs:*

"I suppose it was natural that I would eventually write a story about a slightly oversexed monk. I entered an ashram (an eastern monastery, in Oakland, no less) myself at the age of twenty-five, bent on shedding the world and finding God, and

spent two years absorbed in meditation, before eventually running off with the ashram cook, with subsequent complications. The two of us lived in a rickety shack in the mountains
of northern California, ostensibly in prayerful retreat from the
hectic world, but eventually it became all too clear that my
notion of prayerful retreat inclined toward sitting on a stump
contemplating the serene flow of the Eel River below and the
majestic sawtooth sweep of the mountains against the sky,
while hers seemed to involve a lot of uprooting blackberries
and clearing old trails of poison oak. She thought I was lazy
and I thought she was driven. Eventually she went to India to
work with Mother Theresa and I got a job in a lumber mill in
Willits, which seemed like a prayerful retreat itself by then. So
the theme of what Thomas Merton called 'contemplation in a
world of action,' the difficulty of reconciling a vigorous life of
service in the world, the *vita activa,* with the *vita contemplativa,*
the life of quiet prayer, is one that has absorbed me throughout
my own spiritual journey.

"For many years, the working title for *The Monk Downstairs*
was *That Good Part,* a phrase from the New Testament story of
Martha and Mary, in Luke 10, which serves as the novel's epigraph: 'But Mary hath chosen that good part, which shall not
be taken away from her.' The two sisters in the Bible story, one
busy to the verge of distraction serving her Lord, the other sitting at His feet, languidly devotional, are classic examples of the
contrasting spiritual types I experienced so vividly in the
mountains of Mendocino County, with Martha representing
the *vita activa* and Mary representing the contemplative approach to God. In the novel, it was my intention to bring an
overloaded single mother, a de facto Martha-type with a fre-
netic modern life, together with a disheartened monk, a sort of
wounded Mary, fresh from twenty years of apparently fruitless
prayer. I wanted to explore in the relationship between the two

the complex dynamics of worldly activity and contemplative perspective, and hopefully to find some balance of the apparently conflicting approaches in the reconciling depths of a love story. Through the novel's unfolding action, Michael Christopher, the lifelong Mary, moves by often-unwilling degrees toward a transforming involvement with the realities of life and love in the world, while the Martha-type Rebecca is brought inexorably to an unanticipated immersion in the peace at the root of all action, and a revelatory taste of the silence of God."

Topics For Discussion:

1. Michael Christopher initially tells Rebecca that he left the monastery because he "had a fight with his abbot." Why do you feel he really left the monastery? What was he looking for? What did he find?

2. When the story opens, Rebecca has reached a point in her relationship with Bob Schofield where he feels emboldened to propose marriage. In refusing him, she realizes that she has been tempted to "settle," to compromise her longing for deep love and intimacy, for the sake of security and simple companionship. Her friend Bonnie suggests that she might be holding out for "the fairy tale thing," while her mother, who has known a fulfilling marriage, tells her briskly that "there's no need to settle for mediocrity." What do you think? What is the balance between realistic compromise in intimacy and the longing for "a marriage of true minds"?

3. In his first letter to Brother James, Michael Christopher says, "There is a prayer that is simply seeing through yourself, see-

ing your own nothingness, the emptiness impervious to self-assertion. A prayer that is the end of the rope. A helplessness, fathomless and terrifying." Is this an aspect of spirituality you can relate to? What is the difference, if any, between a dark night of the soul and mere depression or despair?

4. What is Rebecca's view of God at the beginning of the novel? What is her view of love? How do these evolve through the course of the story?

5. Mother-daughter relationships are central to the novel. Compare and contrast Rebecca's relationship with Phoebe, her mother, and with her own daughter Mary Martha. What sides of her does each relationship bring out? What kinds of love does each bring into play? What kinds of frustration?

6. What are the crucial points at which Rebecca and Michael Christopher are able to move closer? At what points do they fail to move toward intimacy, and instead move away? Why?

7. Michael Christopher's troubled relationship to his former abbot, Fr. Hackley, has obviously been central to his religious life, and his struggle to come to terms with it continues to be so even after he leaves the monastery. What is your sense of what the real issues were between the two men? How does the evolution of Christopher's understanding of his former abbot reflect his own spiritual development throughout the book?

8. Similar to Michael Christopher's need to make some peace with Abbot Hackley and what he represents, is

Rebecca's challenge in coming to terms with her ex-husband, Rory. What is your understanding of the history between the two? How has the relationship affected Rebecca's view of love? How do the changes in Rebecca's attitude toward ex-husband reflect her own development throughout the book?

9. Rebecca is ambivalent about her job throughout much of the novel. Like her longing for true intimacy, her craving for a fulfilling career is in delicate and conflicted balance with her sense of what is realistic. In what ways does her work at Utopian Images fulfill her and exercise her real gifts? In what ways does it stifle her? How realistic *is* it to hope for a career that is more than a tedious way to pay the rent?

10. St. Augustine defined a sacrament as "an outward and visible sign of an inward and spiritual grace." There are at least two examples in the novel of unorthodox "sacraments:" the baptism of Sherilous's baby at Stinson Beach, and Michael Christopher's administration of last rites to Phoebe in the hospital. What is your sense of the spiritual "validity" of these impromptu rituals? What is a true sacrament?

11. Michael Christopher says, "We don't hear much of the danger of prayer, but it is the deepest sea and I believe there are many who are lost en route." What is your sense of the sea of prayer and its hazards? Is it really possible to be lost?

12. In their conversation in the kitchen in Chapter Five, Michael Christopher tells Rebecca the story of the failed

love that propelled him into the monastery. How much of his commitment to the religious life do you think was a positive longing for God, and how much was simple flight from the challenges of intimacy and work in the real world? Is a true monastic vocation possible?

13. On the morning after their first night together, Rebecca and Michael Christopher run aground on his reluctance to let their relationship pass into a more public knowledge. What is your reading of the situation, and of Christopher's conflictedness? Do you think Rebecca over-reacts?

14. In one of his letters to brother James, Michael Christopher describes God as "an unfathomable darkness," and the peace of God's presence as a perfect silence and "a kind of nowhere." How does a radical unknowing like this differ from atheism? In theological terms, Christopher's spirituality could be characterized as a *via negativa* or "apophatic" approach to God, a focus on God's ultimate unknowability, in contrast to the more familiar kataphatic path in which God is known and loved through an emphasis on divine attributes such as love, mercy, and justice. What is the place of a dark night spirituality such as Christopher's? Is it compatible with life in "the world"? Wouldn't it be better if he just, like, lightened *up* a little?

15. How does her mother's crisis affect Rebecca? How does it affect Mike? How does it change their relationship?

16. Do you think Rory is really ready to change, after the judge lets him off the hook? Does his relationship with Chelsea have a chance to succeed?

17. How about Bob Schofield and Bonnie? Will their marriage work out? And what about Rebecca and Mike?

18. One of the book's central themes is stated in the contrast between the active Martha and the devotional Mary in the book epigraph from Luke 10. Discuss your own sense of the balance between the life of busy service and the contemplative life, and how the theme plays out in the novel.